The Shadow of Doctor Syn

'Serve God; honour the King; but, first maintain the Wall.' Slogan of ROMNEY MARSH.

To Emma Treckman with grateful thanks for her collaboration.

Black Curtain Press
PO Box 632
Floyd, VA 24091

ISBN 13: 978-1627554442

First Edition
10 9 8 7 6 5 4 3 2 1

The Shadow of Doctor Syn
Russell Thorndyke

Chapter 1. Two Topics of the Town

In the year 1793, not only in the isolated taverns of the remote district of Romney Marsh, but in the fashionable clubs of London, two subjects of news were passed from mouth to mouth, and were discussed in leading columns of the papers. The first of these was the Reign of Terror, raging across the Channel—terrible and bloody. The second, and perhaps more popular, because of its humour, the latest exploits of the mysterious Scarecrow, who, in spite of the danger in France and the unpopularity of the British with the French, managed to keep successful his mighty organisation of contraband running, backwards and forwards across the Channel.

Even the most literary of the political periodicals found space enough to exploit the adventures of the Romney Marsh smugglers, in the same editions that screamed out execrations against the murderous Paris mob. Indeed they used the Scarecrow and his men as an excuse to howl against the Government, which seemed quite powerless to put the audacious scandal down. True, they had offered a thousand-guinea reward to any person who should hand over, or cause to be handed over, this notorious malefactor, alive or dead, but although this sounded a large sum in proclamation, it was nothing when compared to the many thousands which were slipping through the fingers of the Revenue.

'In the devil's name, who is this Scarecrow?' was the question on everybody's lips. The general opinion was that he must be a man of education, since it was known that he spoke French fluently and was as powerful in the coastal districts of France as he was in his own territory of the Marsh. But on both sides of the Channel his real identity was unknown. He was the Scarecrow—L'pouvantail. Well, whoever he was, he was certainly a public benefactor. To the vast majority his adventures were a joy. His audacity made the world chuckle, while locally he was keeping his followers' necks out of the Government's noose, and by risking his own he made the poor rich, so long as they obeyed his orders, and played the dangerous game against the Revenue men, according to his rules.

There were other adventurers who played a dangerous game without adhering to any code of fairness, and one of these was Captain Foulkes, a successful gambler and soldier of Fortune. Oh yes, 'Bully' Foulkes, not without reason given this nickname, played for the highest stakes in the most exclusive London clubs. He cheated so cleverly that his fashionable victims innocently paid their losses and called them debts of honour when trying to balance their accounts. Whenever Bully Foulkes was accused of not playing fair, by gentlemen who were not quite so innocent in the ways of roguery, the noble Captain was so insulted that he sent his second immediately to arrange a meeting. This was not a very risky thing for the Captain to do since he happened to be brilliant with sword or pistol. He had to his record twelve gentlemen whom he had spitted in St. Martin's Fields, and seven he had shot dead at Chalk Farm Tavern, where such matters were dealt with conveniently to all parties. Yes—a brave man might well think twice before meeting Captain Foulkes in an affair of so-called 'honour'.

Yet he was not without disciples—young men of rank and fashion who admired his dash and tried to emulate his success. Such a youngster was Lord Cullingford, who, having recently come into his family title, found that he had mortgaged the next three years of his income.

He had raised the money from the City Jews in order to satisfy his creditors. But since it was utterly impossible for a young lord of the realm to live in the lap of luxury without a penny piece for three years, these same kind financiers advanced him a further sum, which, banked, would bring him in sufficient for his needs. Unfortunately the noble lord did not bank the money.

Instead he cut a great dash with it, and for a few glorious and hilarious weeks managed to make himself the envy of his rivals, the other young dandies who roistered in the company of Captain Foulkes. Indeed, while the money circulated, he was raised to the rank of the Captain's boon companion, and was privileged to swagger arm-in-arm with him when taken the air in St.

James's. The Captain permitted young Cullingford to imitate him, knowing that this was a form of flattery, and being well aware that, while the money lasted, the vain and stupid fop could never eclipse him when they were seen together.

Captain Foulkes cut a fine figure, tall, broad shouldered, athletic.

Cullingford was not so tall, thin shouldered and effeminate. But the tailors managed to pad out his shoulders, and the bootmakers elevated his feet, while the Captain's personal barber attended on him. In fact, the general opinion was that Cullingford's friendship with Captain Foulkes had improved his looks and bearing considerably.

One miserable night in late autumn Lord Cullingford left the gamingtable at Crockford's and strolled over to the fire. All day he had played cautiously, which is often an ill thing for a gambler to do. On this occasion it was certainly an ill thing for his young lordship. As he gazed into the flames, his mental arithmetic told him he was down to his last three hundred pounds, and was owing to various tradesmen. His credit was good enough, since none of the tradesmen in question were aware of the precarious state of his purse, but having tasted the dubious honour of being the chosen companion of so envied a man as Bully Foulkes, he had no desire to be given his conge.

Foulkes had no use for anyone who could not stay the course. An ignominious position to be in, and one thing was certain to his lordship—he must play no more tonight. In fact, Lord Cullingford was very sorry for himself. His nerves, none too good, from a succession of routs and late parties, were strained to the highest tension, when a burst of noisy laughter from the table behind him aggravated them beyond bearing, which decided his lordship to go home to bed, thinking that a stroll up St. James's in the fresh air would dispel the fumes of wine from his head and his financial worries with them.

As he turned to put his resolution into practice, Bully Foulkes pushed back his chair, swept a pile of guineas from his place at the table, and swaggered over to him.

'Come on, Cullingford,' he said; 'my luck is in, but I'm quitting for an hour as I have an appointment at Bucks. Take my place.' 'Oh, the devil damn the rascal that first thought of cards and dice!' snapped his lordship. 'I've lost all day and will play no more.' 'Then take my place and perhaps your luck will change all night,' replied Foulkes. 'And damme, I hope it may. You've been an ill enough companion for the past week, and if there is one thing I can't abide 'tis a poor loser.' 'I tell you, man, I have no wish to play and am going home.' 'I vow you're as sulky as the bear in Southwark pit,' laughed the Captain, taking his arm. 'Come, a glass of brandy will cure your spleen and a rattle of dice will take that sour expression from your face. My place is reserved for you. I beg you to take it and try one throw. A hundred guineas round the table and the highest takes the lot. 'Tis a quick way to earn a thousand, and I warrant a thousand guineas will soon cure you of the sulks.' 'I'm bored and tired—not sulky,' replied his lordship, trying to free himself from the persuasive arm that was leading him towards the empty chair.

'Take the throw yourself as your luck's so good.' The grip on his arm tightened as the Captain's voice took on a bantering tone. 'Never change my mind. 'Tis a good rule which helps a man never to break his word. Don't be a fool, Cullingford. Play.' There was something dominating about Foulkes which Cullingford, to his cost, had always found difficult to resist.

'All right. One throw—and damn you, Foulkes, if I lose.'

He went to the table. He threw. So did nine other gentlemen. Foulkes's place had served him well that evening, but it did no miracle for Cullingford.

He lost.

'Try again,' cried Foulkes, who now seemed in no hurry to leave. His unfortunate victim, already flushed with excitement and subject to the gambler's delusion that this one throw will bring a run of luck and retrieve all, called his opponents to cast again.

Again he lost, but stung by what Foulkes had said he challenged the gentlemen to double the stakes.

The loud rattling of the dice-boxes answered his lordship's wager, and the enthusiastic cries of acceptance to a sporting bet in no way disturbed the flow of polished conversation being carried on by three gentlemen in a remote corner of the room. Seated at their ease, near a glowing log fire, they smoked, sipped a fine old brandy, talked and listened, as cultured men are wont to do who admire and respect each other, knowing that each, in his own way, is master of his calling.

Indeed, it was a remarkable trio, and had the interest not been so high at the gaming-table, the more curious might have wondered why a dignitary of the Church should be in the company of two notables of the Theatre, but he was listening with the greatest attention and obvious enjoyment. Here was no ordinary parson. Although dressed in the sombre black of his calling, the cut of his clothes and the way he wore them might have put to shame any of the well-known dandies present. Relieving the severity of the clerical garb was the exquisite white linen at neck and wrists, and the slim hand holding the brandy glass denoted a man of taste and refinement. The fire-light played on the silver buckles of his elegant shoes as, legs crossed, one elegant foot slowly swung to and fro. His free hand swept back a stray lock of hair which he wore long and loose to his shoulders and unhampered by the ribbon of the day.

Indeed he was setting a new fashion for the clergy, who still wore the formal white wigs. But for his glasses and the slight scholarly stoop of his shoulders the casual onlooker might have taken him for a younger man, since his hair was still raven black, making an unusual contrast as it framed a face pale and classical. In repose it might be the face of a man who had lived and experienced much, but at the moment his features were full of charm as he expressed contentment with the luxurious surroundings and gay companions.

In fact—Doctor Syn, D.D., Vicar of Dymchurch-under-the-Wall and Dean of the Peculiars of Romney Marsh, was enjoying himself. Proffering a snuff-box to his companions, he remarked: 'Yes, indeed, Mr. Sheridan, the loss of Garrick dealt a sorry blow to the Theatre, but it has ever been a puzzle to me why you of all people should have forsaken Old Drury for Westminster.'

'Pray, Doctor Syn, do not encourage Richard on that subject,' laughed the youngest of the party, 'or we shall have an eloquent lecture lasting all night.' 'Indeed, Mr. Kemble—and begging your pardon, sir, you being manager of Drury Lane,' replied the parson, 'but I vow I have not seen a play to my liking since Mr. Sheridan's School for Scandal. So I trust you will prevent the Theatre from going to the devil, for that indeed would be a further bar to the fulfillment of my ambition.' 'Yes, you would have made a good Hamlet, Doctor Syn,' said Mr. Sheridan, 'for apart from your natural qualifications, they say that the Church is closely akin to the Theatre, and were I still manager of the Lane, I'd engage you here and now, but I vow no one will get a chance with Shakespeare now the Kembles are come to Town. Your brother's first appearance has been a great success, I'm told.'

Philip Kemble smiled his acknowledgment to Mr. Sheridan's tribute and, turning to Doctor Syn, said laughingly: 'My brother Charles promises to make a fine comedian, sir, so that you and I, of sterner stuff, need have no fear of a rival there. But plague take it, Sheridan is almost right about the state of the Theatre, since the one topic the public wish to hear about is the latest play-acting of this confounded Scarecrow. Now there's a great actor and a comedian too, eh, Sheridan? And he is one of your parishioners, Doctor Syn, is he not?' 'Come, Kemble,' cried Mr. Sheridan. 'I may now turn the tables on you; for should you encourage Doctor Syn to pursue that subject we shall have an eloquent sermon lasting all night. Do you not know that his orations against this rogue are highly thought of in all circles?' Doctor Syn laughed, and addressed the young manager of Drury Lane.

'I had a mind to rehearse my next Sunday's sermon to you and Mr. Sheridan, so that you might gauge the quality of my acting, but after such a neat example of table-turning, I will refrain; and indeed, he is right; it would take all night, for I have planned a most vehement one, and 'tis time a poor old parson in his dotage were a-bed.' So saying he rose from his chair and stood awhile by the fire.

Mr. Sheridan watched him, noting the easy grace and dignity of his bearing. Then smiled and said: 'Your claim to senility is ill-founded, sir, and carries no conviction. Indeed, I fail to see why you should wish to add to your years. For my part, I'll warrant, you are as youthful and virile as any of those foppish fire-eaters yonder'—indicating with his brandy-glass the crowd round the gaming-table.

'I thank you for the compliment, my dear Sheridan,' said Doctor Syn.

'But pray, in truth now, would you not prefer a comfortable dotage to that strident-voiced braggart yonder?'

'Egad, you're right, 'tis Bully Foulkes. The most insolent and tiresome dog in Town, though 'tis not the policy to say so to his face. I have no wish to be called out. St. Martin's Fields are too damned chilly in the early hours of the morning. So have a care, Doctor Syn, when you refer to the stridency of his voice, though of course your calling protects you from the rogue.' As they were talking the noise round the table grew louder and a heated argument took place, in which this said gentleman seemed to be the central figure. Loud oaths and proffered bets reached the far corner of the room, and the Captain's voice took on a bantering tone. 'The Scarecrow. I am heartily sick at the very sound of his name.' 'Because his adventures are fast eclipsing your own, eh, Foulkes?' cried a voice from the far end of the table.

'Have a care, Sir Harry,' warned Foulkes, with an unpleasant edge on his voice, 'when coupling my name with that of an ill-bred smuggler from some outlandish place in Kent. Confound it, why can't the Government rid us of this rogue? Easiest thing in the world if you've the brains and ingenuity, and for two pins I'll do it myself.' 'The Government will give you more than two pins should you succeed,' replied Harry Lambton. 'A thousand guineas is their latest offer, and I vow I am as bored as you are with the subject. 'Twould be a relief to get back to normal and lay our wagers on the colours of Mrs. Fitzherbert's latest gown. I'll gladly add another thousand to the Government's, should you succeed in ridding the Marshes of the Scourge and the Town of this plaguey topic.' The offer was greeted with loud applause, and in the excitement and speculation that followed no one noticed the dejection of young Lord Cullingford and the look of blank despair on his face. He cursed himself for having listened to Foulkes, not daring to think how much the evening's rash play had let him in for and knowing that his fair-weather friend took occasion to quarrel with anyone who kept him waiting for the payment of a debt. As in a dream he heard the voices round him. 'The Government offer a thousand guineas and Harry Lambton doubles it.' He was desperate and must clutch at any straw. In a flash he made up his mind. Whether Foulkes went or no, he determined to try himself. One thing was certain, he must get on his way before Foulkes. Thank heaven there was one remaining horse in his

London stables and that a good one. He determined to start at daybreak, and with the possibility of earning so large a sum his courage returned and he made a rapid calculation of his night's losses. If he should succeed he reckoned he should have funds enough to keep him till he was on his feet again, and so with glowing prospect in mind he was able to face the Captain with his usual gaiety.

'Why, Foulkes,' he cried, "tis the first time I have known you to hang back on a bet. Or is it that you daren't leave Town in case I cut you out with La Belle Harriet? Should it relieve your mind suppose we all promise not to call upon her till you return victorious?' Stung by the youngster's banter into a quick decision, Foulkes replied hotly: 'I have yet to meet the rival that I fear will oust me in the affections of any woman, just as I have yet to meet the man whose bet I will not take. I accept your wager, Sir Harry, and if I fail I'll double the stakes.' An even louder cheer greeted the acceptance.

Then Sir Harry spoke. 'You're a brave man, Foulkes, and 'tis a sporting thing to do, but have a care. You may not get as far as Charing Cross. Then poor Harriet will have a long wait, since we all pledge we will not visit her till your return. I take it there should be some sort of time-limit?'

'Ten days should be all I need,' replied the Captain. 'And I'll set off tomorrow on the morning Mail, so you meet me here today fortnight to settle accounts. I'll now go and convey to Harriet the reason why her salon will be deserted, though I warrant she will not mind waiting for me. Come, drinks all round, and I'll give you a toast.' Glasses were filled and Captain Foulkes being once more the centre of interest became his ostentatious self. He strolled over to Cullingford and put a patronising hand on his shoulder. 'Poor Cully,' he said. 'You've had damnable luck tonight, but I'll take your I O U and will not call upon you till tomorrow week.' It was while the glasses were being charged that Doctor Syn took his leave of Sheridan and Kemble and was strolling past the gaming-table on his way to the door. For the first time the Captain became aware of the parson's presence and in his growing mood of arrogance put himself in the way.

'Zounds,' he cried, looking Doctor Syn up and down in an insolent fashion.

'A parson—in Crockford's? Are you seeking the devil in cards and dice?' 'No, sir, I have known both cards and dice all my life and I have learned that they are innocent enough. Unfortunately the devil is sometimes in those who handle them. Your pardon, sir,' and Doctor Syn would have passed on but the Bully did not intend to lose this chance of amusement.

'A neatly turned phrase, sir,' he said. 'Come, give the parson a glass and he shall drink my toast. Are you ready, gentlemen?' Glasses were raised in assent and the Captain proposed: 'Damnation to the Scarecrow, and may he not escape Bully Foulkes.' The gentlemen drank, but when Foulkes lowered his glass he perceived that that parson's wine was still untouched. 'You did not drink, Parson. Did you not understand the toast? Being at Crockford's I thought you had a London living. But perhaps your parish is so remote that you have never heard of the Scarecrow.' 'I did not drink, sir,' replied Doctor Syn, 'because I thought it unseemly to drink damnation to one of my own parishioners.' The atmosphere was tense and the gentlemen present listened in delighted silence. A parson was getting the better of Bully Foulkes, who at the moment appeared to be at a loss for words. The next move came from Doctor Syn, who continued politely: 'I could not fail to overhear your bet, sir.

Drink damnation to the rascal by all means and you will be in good company, for he has been damned by Army, Navy and Revenue alike. But all the King's horses and all the King's men have never succeeded in catching him. A thousand guineas. Oh, I beg your pardon. Two thousand guineas, for you doubled the stakes, is a lot of money to lose, though nothing to losing one's life. I feel 'tis my duty to warn you—knowing something of this rascal's methods, indeed, having been one of his victims—that although he may permit you to reach the Marshes safely, it is very doubtful whether he will see fit to let your return to London alive.' Doctor Syn glanced round with an almost apologetic air, and then handing the glass still untasted to the Captain, he added regretfully: 'I do hope I have not depressed you, sir. Good night—Good night,' and before the astonished company had well recovered, the parson had left the room.

None of the gentlemen dared speak, fearing that the Bully thwarted might be in an evil mood. He broke the silence himself. 'Who in the devil's name was that? And what does he mean by claiming to be one of the Scarecrow's victims?' Sir Harry Lambton supplied the information. 'Why, did you not know? I thought Doctor Syn was as famous as the Scarecrow. He is the Vicar of Dymchurch, and his courage in preaching against this rogue is highly spoke of. Threats do not stop him, though he has had many warnings, and on one occasion he was actually lashed to the gibbet post in company with a Bow Street Runner. A learned man—well travelled—indeed, no ordinary parson.' 'And how have you managed to glean so much information about him?' growled the Captain.

'Oh, my informant is a great friend of his and one whose word you must believe in unless you are seeking lodging in the Town. 'Twas none other than the Prince of Wales himself.' 'Yes, indeed,' said another gentleman, emboldened by Sir Harry's attitude and the mention of the Royal name. ''Tis all over the Town that the handsome snuff-box Doctor Syn carries was given him by the Prinny himself, who maintains that Syn is the only parson who can make him laugh.'

'Devil take it,' replied the disgruntled Captain. 'I don't know what he finds to laugh about, for I never saw a more sombre figure in my life.' Standing at the Captain's side, Lord Cullingford had missed nothing and he vowed that upon reaching Dymchurch he would present himself at the Vicarage and seek assistance from such a learned gentleman.

This same learned gentleman was at the moment seeking assistance elsewhere, for having made his way to the writing room he sat penning in fine scholarly handwriting a lengthy list of instructions. An enigmatical smile changed the gravity of his face to an expression of impish humour as he wrote the address and planned how it should be delivered to:

Mr. James Bone, at the Mitre Inn, Ely Place, Holborn.

Chapter 2. Two Beaux in Search of One Topic

Mr. James Bone was in an excellent humour, in spite of the fact that he had not been to bed all night. He was warm and comfortable:

sprawled at his ease in a well-padded armchair, feet on the mantel, the logs still glowing in the fireplace of one of the many back parlours of the Mitre Inn. Beside him was a tankard of ale heavily laced with spirits. On the same table as the tankard a branched candle-stick gave sufficient light for him to read once more the letter which had put him in such a pleasant frame of mind. With a final chuckle he rose, took a long draught from the tankard, and with a yawn of satisfaction, raised a well-booted leg and kicked the logs into a blaze. He then dropped the letter into the heart of the flames and watched it burn. Gentleman James left no traces, and had memorised the instructions he had received, word for word. A glance at his handsome fob watch told him that he had plenty of time before starting to carry them out. Stooping his great frame to enable him to see into the mirror that hung over the fire, he straightened his cravat and retied his hair-ribbon. The picture that he saw did not displease him. A weather-beaten face, maybe, but attractive enough, especially when he allowed an engaging smile to wrinkle the corners of his eyes, blue and merry, as many a serving-wench knew to her cost; though 'twas not only these buxom lasses in the inns on the Dover Road who fell for his attractions; many a fine lady or London beauty going visiting by coach wished to see more of Gentleman James in spite of the fact that he may have taken their diamonds. A likeable fellow, who had learned early in his career that to have ladies on one's side was half the battle. His easy grace and polished manners had earned him the name of 'Gentleman James'. Indeed there was not a lady between London and the Kent coast who would give information to the Bow Street Runners against so charming a rogue. But politely relieving the fashionable travellers of their valuable gewgaws was not Mr. Bone's only occupation. He it was who superintended the vast organisation required on the road for moving the Scarecrow's contraband to its various destinations. There was not a 'hide' in cottage or castle in Kent with which he was not familiar. No wonder that the Bow Street Runners were hard put to lay him by the heels. At the moment, when we first meet him he was just emerging from an enforced vacation after a rather tricky affair on the Chatham and Maidstone Road.

Feeling in need of breakfast, he went to the door and called for the serving-girl. Her prompt appearance suggested that she also had been up all night, and her rosy face told him that she wished he had called for her earlier, through her speech belied this.

'What a time to get a poor serving-wench out of her bed,' she teased. 'I vow I would not do the same for the Prince himself.' 'Then I vow I would rather be Gentleman James than all the crowned heads in Europe,' he said, giving her a resounding kiss. 'You're a good lass, Dolly, and prettier than many a fine lady I know. I only wish I could stay here longer, but in half an hour I take to the road to gain the top of Shooter's Hill by dawn, so do you bring me some breakfast now, and make it a hearty one for the Bow Street Runners are apt to interfere with the regularity of my mealtimes.' 'So long as it's only the Bow Street Runners and not them Kentish Jezebels, then Dolly will do your bidding.' She laughed and hurried off to the kitchen, adding: ''Tis all prepared. I have only to bring it in.'

Mr. Bone went to the further corner of the room, where carelessly flung over a chair was his great caped riding-coat, beneath which were his pistols in their holsters. These must be in perfect working order, and indeed were his pride and joy, having lifted them a few years earlier from a Colonel of Dragoons who had evidently known how to purchase fine weapons. Mr. Bone took them to the table, and, sitting down, cleaned, primed and polished. He was engaged upon this vital task and was nearly finished when Dolly came bustling back, tray piled high with pewter covers and a flagon of mulled ale.

Gentleman James set to, while Dolly hovered to anticipate his every want, for which she was rewarded with another kiss and a bracelet which Gentleman James had kept back from the receivers.

Ten minutes later Gentleman James was thundering across London Bridge and in less than an hour he saw the dawn breaking from the summit of Shooter's Hill.

* * * * *

The weather had cleared. There was still a high wind blowing, but the direction of the blown clouds and the clarity of the morning star gave promise for a fine, crisp, autumn day. It was yet the small hours but my Lord Cullingford was already wide awake, having had a poor night, sleeping fitfully and haunted by dreams of the Scarecrow who, at Crockford's, had seemed such an easy solution to his problems. Surrounded by laughing companions without a care in the world and exhilarated by good wine, the horror had seemed remote enough; but now alone, and in the coldly calculating hours of early morning, Lord Cullingford felt extremely frightened, rather small, and of no account. Alone in his great Town house, unable by his penury to retain his servants, he had conjured up terrifying visions of the creature he had sworn to himself to seek. In fact, to poor Lord Cullingford, the Scarecrow had assumed gigantic proportions; every shadow made him shudder and every night noise in that vast old house made him jump. In fact, Lord Cullingford, in Marsh language, had a bad attack of 'the dawthers'.

Although he did not know it, he was not as cowardly as he thought, for many a braver man than he, trained to danger and employed by the Realm, had worse than 'the dawthers' when ordered to confront the Scarecrow or his gang. Cursing the fact that he had no servant to help him dress nor to bring him a cup of chocolate, at least, before setting out, he struggled by the flickering light of one solitary candle with breeches, hose and riding-boots. Another thought too was worrying him and an equally unpleasant one at that—the presence in the Captain's pocket of his I O U for Trembles.

'The devil rot Bully Foulkes,' he said aloud, and his voice went echoing to the lofty painted ceiling. 'Bully Foulkes.' 'Had it not been for him,' he thought, 'I should not be in this confounded predicament. I vow, if I get out of this alive, I'll see him in hell before I consort with him or his kind again.' Feeling more the man as he got into his handsome riding-coat, he permitted himself one ray of hope in the dark uncertainty before him—the Vicar of Dymchurch. A kindly, learned man this Doctor Syn had seemed last night. Had Cullingford felt better he would have chuckled at the remembered scene, of the parson getting the better of the Bully. As he pondered on this, it struck him that from the moment Foulkes had been so truculent and illmannered towards the dignity of the Church, he had gone down in his estimation, and was no longer an idol in the eyes of his disciple. Cheered by the thought of visiting Doctor Syn, and the possibility of having his assistance, he made his way along the gallery and down the sweeping stairs.

Holding the candle before him, he was just able to see his way. Egad, the house looked miserable enough. Great dusty marks were on the wall where pictures of his ancestors should have hung, and dust-sheets covering such furniture as was left. 'Property,' he thought, "tis but a millstone round a fellow's neck.' Then, filled with shame as the accusing spaces on the walls above him seemed to answer back, 'Yes, but in our day this house was well run, well loved, and filled with beautiful people,' he crossed the hall and went into the library.

'If I am to carry this thing through, then I must be well armed,' he thought. He selected a fine pair of duelling-pistols and the holsters, which he must fix to his saddle. He buckled on his sword and, feeling braver under the weight of so much metal, he made his way to the stables, thanking heaven that at least the family groom had remained faithful and that his last and favourite mount would be well groomed and ready for him. He was right. The old man was there, hissing through his teeth and rubbing his hands together in the brisk morning air, but on seeing his lordship he quickly led the mare into the yard. A beautiful animal, in fine condition. 'She has had a good feed, milord,' said old Peters as Cullingford mounted.

'Which is more than I have,' thought his young lordship, and in a fit of sad generosity he handed the faithful old groom a couple of golden guineas; and so, looking a finer figure than he felt, he rode into the London streets, joining the early cavalcade of carts as they wended their way towards Covent Garden. This annoyed him, for he wished to be quit of London before any of his acquaintances should be about and recognise him, and he did not want his slightly suspicious departure to get to the ears of his one-time patron. So, somewhat delayed, and more than a little hungry, Lord Cullingford crossed London Bridge a mile or so behind Gentleman James.

Captain Foulkes was not in a good humour when he awoke. He had a damnable headache, and his servants were late in calling him, so that he had to hasten with his breakfast and even his meticulous barber cut him most abominably. This, added to the rush and bustle in the Captain's chambers, made his throbbing head the worse, for there is nothing more irritating to any gentleman who has wined unwisely the night before than to be precipitated into an enforced activity, and indeed the necessity to hasten. In fact, the Captain had a thick head and, in Marsh language, was in a 'pretty dobbin'.

Cravats were flung about as he attempted to get one to set to his liking, and as each attempt meant a fresh cravat, his valets came in for a deal of abuse. And then, to make matters worse, the shaking hand of one of them spilt the boiling chocolate down the Captain's best white buck-skins. Yet all this commotion in the Captain's dressing-room was as nothing to the turmoil in the Captain's head. The events of the previous night had not alleviated the irritation which he realised had started during his unsatisfactory passage of words with that confounded parson at Crockford's, for the Captain was more than aware that he had come off worse in that encounter, and there was nothing he hated more than being made to look foolish in the eyes of his fashionable followers. There had been no man living as yet who had got the better of him. It was, therefore, most galling to have been so verbally pricked by a clergyman against whom there was no retaliation. Bad enough to have been soundly slapped in the face, not only morally but actually, by the beautiful Harriet, who had proved not so docile, in spite of his boastings.

'Confound all women and parsons too. They should not be permitted to trade on social protection,' for the Captain had to admit to himself that his visit to the lady in question had not been a success. Having left Crockford's and made his way to her apartments on the farther side of the Park, it was most irritating, therefore, to be kept waiting on his arrival, and then, when she did deign to appear, instead of a creature all smiles and caresses, eager to please and charm him, which might have somewhat cured his irritability, he was met, in truth, by a virago, demanding already to know why her salon had not been visited that night, and he had the greatest difficulty in explaining to her the reason of his wager. The scene was stormy, and instead of applauding him as a brave man, and the hero he wished to appear, she soundly rated him upon the fact that for the next few days her life was to be so dull. Then in the way of all women, being thoroughly inconsistent, she vowed that his proposed journey had nothing whatever to do with the Scarecrow, but that, tiring of her, he had elected to go chasing some Kentish trollop, 'who', she had said, being quite confident of her own charms, 'probably looks like a Scarecrow anyway. I swear I will not wait for any man, and shall put to the greatest advantage your very convenient absence. I shall enjoy myself vastly and be seen everywhere about the Town, so that the gossips will say that Harriet is not the one to sit at home and twiddle her fingers while Bully Foulkes goes adallying elsewhere. Indeed, sir, you may depend upon it that the whole Town shall know that I have given you your conge.' Which in truth dated from that very moment, for with a strength that surprised him she smacked his face and flounced out of the room, so that he had gone home in high dudgeon, promising himself at least the satisfaction of having his revenge on her by calling out any gentleman she might happen to favour. Not that his heart was affected in any way, for he prided himself on the fact that there were many other beautiful women who would be delighted to be seen in the company so splendid a fellow as Bully Foulkes. Yet these two rebuffs, vexing though they might be, were entirely swept aside by a curious feeling which the Captain had never experienced before. Certain words of the parson's kept ringing in his ears. What was it the miserable fellow had said? 'All the King's horses and all the King's men had never succeeded in catching him yet. Although he may permit you to reach the Marshes safely, it is very doubtful whether he will see fit to let you to return to London alive.' These words in themselves would never have worried a man of the Captain's stamp in the ordinary way, but upon reflection, he had to admit to himself that there was something about the way in which the parson had said them, and a curious sense of foreboding gave him an uncomfortable feeling in the pit of his stomach as he pondered that he might not return to London alive; and having permitted himself the luxury of an extravagant wager, he had, as yet, not the slightest idea of how he was going to carry it through. And so, cursing himself for not only jeopardising his reputation but also his life, and cursing his servants for their incompetent behaviours that morning, it was indeed the last straw when an unfortunate lackey was unable to secure a cabriolet to carry him to the coaching yard, which entailed making a spectacle of himself by running the length of St. James's, and along Pall Mall to Charing Cross, sword flapping and wig awry, a breathless servant at his heels hampered by the weight of the valise, and derisive cries of errand boys ringing in his ears. In this unenviable state of mind and body, Captain Foulkes only just succeeded in reaching the 'Golden Keys' in time. The final indignity was being bundled in headlong by the infuriated guard, and the coach was moving off up the Strand.

* * * * *

Doctor Syn spent a very comfortable night at Haxell's, in the Strand. It was a quiet and comfortable house, with good plain cooking and an excellent cellar, if you were popular with the landlord. Doctor Syn was popular with the landlord, who respected a country parson who seemed to be quite a connoisseur in French wines. Consequently Doctor Syn was ever a welcome guest at this family tavern, which was famed as a respectable country home in the hub of London life. Yes—the very place for a learned scholar who preferred the noise of the capital to be outside the windows, with quiet, wellmannered guests within. Haxell's was also very handy to travellers who wished to catch the Kent-bound coach from Charing Cross, for you had only to inform the Coaching Counting House situated at the 'Golden Keys', which faced Duncannon Street, and the guard would reserve your seats and pick you up at Haxell's on the way to London Bridge. Having on this occasion taken the precaution, Doctor Syn was under no anxiety about missing the mail, which pulled out at ten o'clock for the coast. He was called at half past seven with a dish of tea into which he poured a strong measure of brandy. Having ordered his breakfast for fifteen minutes past eight, and being dressed before it was ready, he strolled as far as St. Martin's Church to encourage his appetite. The storm of the night before had cleared the skies, and he was welcomed by a pleasant sun, and cold, crisp air. His steps took him past the church and into Hedge Lane, famed for its book market. Many a poor scholar he found there before him, reading greedily from old volumes piled on stalls before the shops. To some of these Doctor Syn addressed a cheery good morning as he passed—with some of them he discussed the merits of a volume which the reader seemed tempted to purchase. Indeed, for one poor man he bought a book outright when he ascertained that the old fellow had not the money to indulge his taste, but called each morning just for the pleasure of holding it in his hand. Imagine the student's gratitude for this generosity. It was indeed a gift from the gods, and had Syn been Jupiter himself he could not have received more adoration. Passers-by noted the elegant parson with the charming smile and stopped in pretence of viewing the bookstalls in order to watch him the more closely. Certainly he seemed to have done a great favour to the old student who, clutching his prized volume to his heart, kept bowing low before his benefactor while tears of gratitude ran shamelessly down his cheeks. Indeed it seemed that the parson was becoming embarrassed with such loud laudations, such hymns of praise, for he was overheard to say, 'My dear sir, there is nothing more to be said. If that book is to be somebody's property, that somebody must be you, since nobody could have shown me better than you what love a man may bestow upon a work of art. Besides, your taste is good. In all this great jangle street of literature you have found a gem. You appreciate its worth, and the regard you give to it but adds to its value. And pray do not thank me. It is for me to thank you for permitting me to spend a few coins in order that a great work shall be truly cared for. If that will not bring me a blessing—then blessedness is dead in our age. No more, dear sir, no more.' Doctor Syn seemed to be attempting to pass on, but the grateful receiver of the book begged to know his name in order that he might remember it in his prayers. 'You carry a pencil-case, sir, no doubt? Will you not writer your name for me in the fly-leaf of the book?' With a smile Doctor Syn took a silver pencil-case from his pocket and wrote his name and address, which the old man, blinking through his spectacles, repeated aloud. The name brought the shopkeeper out on to the pavement, where, catching sight of Doctor Syn, he greeted him profusely. 'So it was you, Doctor, who has proved to be this ardent bookworm's benefactor. 'Tis like you, sir. And now I trust you will find that your goodness to a stranger brings you a reward. In short, I have a book for you within the shop. An agent from Paris left it for you. A French translation of the |niad—a fine first edition, too, which I know you have long sought for. If you step in, reverend sir, I shall be glad to give it to you.' Taking leave of the happy old student, Doctor Syn entered the shop and in a few minutes was handling tenderly the fine copy of Virgil referred to.

'As I received it, I deliver it,' explained the bookseller, 'though I should like to remove these untidy slips of paper which some reader has cluttered it up with. Book-marks, no doubt. But they spoil the appearance of such a beautiful piece of printing. The fellow has undoubtedly torn up an old letter for the purpose. I cannot read the French myself. Used to regret it, having so many fine volumes in my shop that I could not understand. But since they started losing their manners as well as their heads, I have no mind to lose any sleep studying the language of such barbarians.' Doctor Syn had already examined one of the slips in question, and with a twinkle of satisfaction in his eyes he answered: 'This reader was at least not barbaric enough to mark the book with his own notes. Do not trouble to remove the markers. I will take them with the book. 'Twill be interesting to see if he has penned any erudite ideas.' A quarter of an hour later the volume lay on the table beside Doctor Syn as he breakfasted in Haxell's Coffee Room whose windows looked out upon the busy Strand. His walk had put him in good appetite and he thoroughly enjoyed a generous helping of grilled ham and eggs. But while waiting for the second cover, he picked up the book, and a close observer might well have been surprised to see him paying far more attention to what was written on the book-markers than upon the exquisite volume itself. He would have been more surprised still had he known what was written on those same book-markers. But why should anyone pay the slightest attention to such a normal sight as a scholarly cleric engrossed upon the French translation of a classic while enjoying a typical English breakfast?

And so, at five minutes past ten the warning notes of a coach-horn cleared the traffic in front of Haxell's, as with a flourish and jingling of harness the Dover coach pulled up, and Doctor Syn stepped inside.

* * * * *

Yet another traveller had been awakened that morning in time to make preparation for the same journey. In the large bedroom of the best suite that the 'Golden Keys' could offer, propped up by pillows in a gigantic fourposter, sat a little old lady. From beneath the frills of a modish night-cap twinkled a pair of intelligent bird-like eyes, while over the rim of a tankard of small ale her aristocratic nose made her look like the proverbial early bird in search of the worm. The small, shapely hands holding the tankard seemed to be weighed down by the vast collection of rings that she wore on almost every finger, while at her wrists innumerable bracelets jingled and flashed, as she gave orders to a French lady's-maid. Beside the bed was perched an enormous white wig in the style that had been favoured by the ladies of the French Court, and which at the moment the maid was dressing. Upon the bed, curled up on the old lady's feet, brushed and beribboned, looking like another wig, lay a white poodle, sleepily regarding his mistress out of one eye and paying not the slightest attention to the open jewel-case under his nose, for indeed he knew he was wearing his own jewellery—golden bracelets hung with little bells that tinkled merrily when he moved his two front paws.

Finishing her small ale with a gusto slightly incongruous for so frail a lady she put down the tankard and gave the tapestry bell-pull a vigorous jerk, which brought scurrying feet along the corridor, and an answering tap upon the door. The old lady raised herself and prodded the white dog with a playful bejewelled finger. 'Come now, Mister Pitt. 'Tis time for your morning perambulation.' Then, speaking to the maid: 'Lisette, open the door for Mister Pitt, and tell the chambermaid to take him downstairs and see that he amuses himself in the yard. And see that he really amuses himself, for the poor gentleman will be cooped up in a stuffy old coach all day, and you know what happened on the journey to Aberdeen on my best tartan travelling-rug.' With a disapproving sniff, Lisette swept the dog from the bed and handed him over to the chambermaid, returning to her work at the wig-stand and punctuating the rolling of each curl with a fresh sniff.

'Whatever is the matter, woman?' snapped the old lady. 'Have you caught a cold? Can you not use your pocket handkerchief?' To which Lisette—a solid, angular woman with the nimblest fingers and the slowest brain—replied with spirit: 'Oh, madame, 'tis this 'orrid journey. Already we travel the week and no sooner do we arrive in a nice city like London than we must on again to this terrible place called Marsh. I talk 'ere with a serving-wench who say she will not visit Marsh for all the tea in China. Do you know, madame, that there they 'as terrible 'appenings. There are apparitions on horse-backs and they do say the sea is higher than the land, and I cannot see how that can be. Oh, madame, we shall drown!' 'Fiddlesticks, woman!' cried the old lady. 'Serve you right if you did drown for listening to postboys' tales. There's a perfectly good sea wall that will keep you from paddling. Get on with my packing and give me my handmirror and the patch-box.' Lisette did as she was told but continued protesting. 'Madame is not of the nervous disposition, but after these tales I have the horrible nightmares. I do not want to go to this Marsh where the peoples are made crazy by living Scarecrows.'

'Stuff and nonsense!' retorted the old lady, snapping the lid of the patch-box, and sticking the latest fashion in patches on her powdered cheek, which, curiously enough, happened to be a tiny figure of a Scarecrow. 'You know as well as I do that Romney Marsh is ruled by my own niece's husband, Sir Antony Cobtree, whose house is within sight of your French coast. So if you don't like the Marsh, you can paddle to Calais, where I warrant you'd have worse nightmares, if they were good enough to leave you a head to dream with.' So saying, the old lady got out of bed, her frills and flounces quivering angrily as, no higher than the mattress she had just slid from, she announced, 'For my part, I should rather like to meet this Scarecrow. I'd scare him.' Which remark appeared to scare Lisette, who began to think that the horrors of her native France might be worse than the outlandish place she was about to visit. So she stopped grumbling, and knowing the old lady was ready for her breakfast did her best to hasten her mistress's toilet, which was successfully accomplished by the time Mister Pitt returned from his amusement.

For so small a lady she partook of the largest breakfast served in the coffee room, criticising the abominable method of cooking porridge south of the Border, and praising the quality of the grilled steak, and the excellence of the cold game pie.

Allowing herself a glass of Madeira, she was, therefore, in the best of humours when the proprietor, anxious to please so distinguished a guest, personally escorted her to the coach. So despite her seventy-odd years, which she defied in a gay velvet travelling-dress, her face more bird-like than ever beneath the enormous white wig, and resembling from behind a miniature snowman wrapped in a white ermine cloak, Miss Agatha Gordon, of Beldorney and Kildrummy, stepped into the Dover coach, followed by Lisette and the barking Mister Pitt.

She settled herself in a comfortable corner facing the horses, and was tucked up snug in her tartan travelling-rug, Mister Pitt on the seat beside her, his two front paws on her lap, Lisette, still looking somewhat resentful at being swept up from the gay city so soon, took her place opposite, and the coach was about to start when there was a deal of noise and shouting above the sound of the horn, as the door opened and a gentleman was precipitated into the moving vehicle. He landed head first, almost in Miss Gordon's lap, causing a shriek from Lisette, who dropped the jewel-case and surprising Mister Pitt so much that he continued to bark and bob about excitedly, while the gentleman, who seemed to be in the worst of humour, made curt apologies and tried to straighten himself out. Indeed this hullabaloo had only just died when the coach stopped again outside Haxell's in the Strand. The door was opened and in stopped a clerical gentleman for whom it appeared the other corner seat facing the horses had been reserved.

And so, ten minutes later, with passengers and mails complete, yet several hours behind Gentleman James and Lord Cullingford, the Dover coach rumbled its way across London Bridge.

Chapter 3. The Little Affair of the Dover Coach

A mile or so beyond Canterbury at the beginning of the long stretch of Roman road, known as Stone Street, Gentleman James reined up, and allowed his tired horse to nibble the fresh grass that fringed the footpath. He turned in his saddle and listened. All the morning he had been aware of a horseman not far behind him, having heard at every turnpike the sound of hooves thundering in his wake. Thinking it might be a Bow Street Runner, he had spurred his own horse on and kept well ahead, but now deep in his own territory and knowing that but a few miles farther on he had a safe 'hide' where he could be freshly mounted on his favourite horse, he thought it advisable to ascertain exactly who it was that rode so furiously. So he turned his horse off the road and took cover in a convenient coppice, where, unseen, he commanded a clear view of the straight road. Sitting comfortably in his saddle, he waited. It was noon and the promise of the early morning had been fulfilled. The racing clouds had been swept seawards, the sky was high and clear, and a generous sun warmed his back. An exhilarating morning, and Mr.

Bone was extremely glad to be back at work again. As all master craftsmen, he was in love with his job, and this one promised to be both amusing and profitable. He had not long to wait, for in a few minutes the figure of a horseman topped the distant slope and was silhouetted against the white road.

He could now see the rider distinctly. Here was no Bow Street Runner—Mr.

Bone knew them all only too well. Nor was it a riding officer of the Revenue, for he knew them too. At a hundred yards distant Mr. Bone summed up the stranger in his mind, having decided already not to waste time upon small fry that morning, and this, though obviously a gentleman of fashion, was small fry. He rode well, and Mr. Bone admired a good rider, yet he must be in a devil of a hurry, for the fine animal beneath him, flecked white with foam, showed signs of hard going. 'The manner of his riding and his extreme youth,' thought Mr. Bone, 'suggest one of two thing. He rides either to visit a pair of sparkling eyes and get them before a rival, or on some business which may fill his purse with guineas. In which latter case,' chuckled Mr. Bone, always an opportunist, 'the luck of the road may deliver him into my hands on his return journey.' With this cheering thought in mind, Mr. Bone graciously allowed the traveller to go unmolested, and Lord Cullingford, unaware of the danger to the last few guineas in his pocket, spurred the tired mare on towards the coast.

At a leisurely trot Mr. Bone, now satisfied that at least there was no immediate concern that the Revenue were on his tail, proceeded along Stone Street, turning off down a narrow lane to the right and making his way to a farm-house that lay in a hollow unseen from the road.

Here he was greeted by his old friend who gloried in the nickname of Slippery Sam—a name well earned by his ingenious method of escaping the long arm of the Law, for on the occasion of his being surprised one night by a party of King's men, who were about to batter down his bedroom door, he smeared his naked body with oil, flung open the door and challenging his pursuers to get a grip on him, thus slipped through their fingers. A tall middle-aged man with a bald head and a squint, he had a great liking for the carefree highwayman. In fact, he and Missus Slippery treated him as the son they never had. So Jimmie Bone was given great welcome; his horse was led to be rubbed down and fed, the saddle removed and put on his own favourite black horse. The three of them then repaired to the farm kitchen where Missus Slippery fussed and mothered him, the while he received news from Sam of the latest activities of the Scarecrow's men, in exchange for Mr. Bone's information concerning the London Receivers.

Knowing that he had an hour or so to his credit, Mr. Bone allowed himself the luxury of complete relaxation. With the wing of a chicken in one hand and a foaming tankard in the other he exchanged confidences and he felt, as indeed he was, prince of the road.

It was while Mr. Bone was in this enviable position that the coach came down Strood Hill and then with horn blowing gaily, rattled across Rochester Bridge. The four occupants by this time had become more or less acquainted through such close proximity, though for some time after leaving London the Captain had appeared aloof and ill-mannered. It had by no means improved his temper that he had to sit with his back to the horses, and, having been so rudely bundled into the coach, it was annoying enough when the coach stopped again so soon after Haxell's to pick up, as he thought, such an insignificant passenger, who had bespoken the only other comfortable seat. A parson was the last person he had wished to travel with, for his mind still rankled when he thought of his encounter with one at Crockford's.

Imagine then his rage upon closer examination when the coach had left the City and the daylight streamed through the windows to discover that here he was cooped up with none other than that confounded cleric who had so quietly scored off him the night before. Coupled with the warning he had received, the uncomfortable feeling he had hoped to forget was increased a thousandfold by the presence in the coach of its instigator. So he had turned up his collar and glared in sulky silence out of the window, purposely ignoring the fact that they had met before, at the same time somewhat mystified that the parson did not seem to recognise him. To feign sleep was out of the question owing to the continual barking of that confounded dog and the perpetual chatter of the little old lady who, damme, appeared to have another poodle on her had. And so he continued to sulk and stare.

Miss Gordon, on the other hand, had found a fellow traveller to her liking, for Mister Pitt, contrary to his habit of being thoroughly rude to strangers, had swept aside all social barriers, and with much jingling of bracelets, he had attempted to lick the parson's nose. Miss Gordon, though secretly delighted, had pretended to be horrified, as she exclaimed, 'Fie, Mister Pitt, manners, please. What a rude gentleman we are. Lisette, lift the Minster of War off the minister's lap.' Whereupon Mister Pitt showed his warlike tendencies by worrying with obvious enjoyment one of the Captain's silver coat-buttons. The old lady had then produced a miniature handkerchief edged with the finest lace and handing it to the parson requested him to use it.

Doctor Syn, declining, was amused and charmed and settled down to enjoy her lively wit, while Miss Gordon, making a mental note that she must remember to reward Mister Pitt for introducing to her such a delightful travelling companion, prattled gaily.

'I am indeed felicitated that we are bound for the same part of the coast and quite overwhelmed that I should be talking to the famous Doctor Syn whose ecclesiastical books are widely read by our ministers in Scotland. So you see, Mister Pitt, what a clever dog you are to have recognised such a wellknown figure. Is he not like his namesake, sir,' she said, 'in bestowing honours where honours are most due'—and she laughed so infectiously that Doctor Syn quite looked forward to the remainder of the journey, and was delighted to discover that she was a relation of his old friend, Sir Antony Cobtree, to whom she was paying a visit.

'Then I vow, madame, you are no stranger to me, for I knew your niece, Lady Cobtree, before she married Tony, and your name has ever been a household word in the family. Indeed, on more occasions than I can remember I have heard Tony refer to 'me wife's Aunt Agatha'.' Here Doctor Syn gave such a graphic imitation of the Squire of Dymchurch that Miss Gordon was quite paralyzed with giggles. "Tis Tony to the life. You have caught his excellent pomposity. But he's a good boy. I have ever been fond of him, though I think he regards 'me wife's Aunt Agatha' as a most eccentric old body, and what he will think of me now I hardly dare think, since it is many a year since I have visited them. Indeed, sir, the last time I was in Dymchurch was when you must have been away in the Americas. They often spoke of you. I was deeply distressed to learn of my favourite niece's death. Poor Charlotte. She was so young.' Engrossed in her family reminiscences, she failed to note the look of pain that for a moment clouded the Doctor's face on her mentioning the name of Charlotte. 'But tell me,' she went on, 'what of Cicely? I hear she is a fine girl. Good rider too. That's to my liking. Indeed, she is my god-child. And thank heaven for that, since I never could abide her elder sister Maria. 'Twas a great blow to Caroline and Tony, as you must well know, when Maria went off and married that French nincompoop, though naturally now they are in a great state about her, and no wonder. To have a daughter of Maria's disposition in the midst of these Paris horrors must be more than worrying. Indeed, I had a long letter from Cicely upon that subject before I left Kildrummy. It seems that the poor girl is worrying herself to a fiddle-string about her sister, though goodness knows Maria never cared a fig for anyone except herself. But tell me, Doctor Syn,' she continued, 'is not the position serious?—especially as we are now at war with France. Tony, with his English insularity, is often apt to deceive himself. I can almost hear him saying, 'Damme, they'd never dare to touch a Cobtree. She may have married a Frenchman, but she's still my daughter, sir." Which rendering was as perfect an imitation of the Squire as Doctor Syn's had been, which amused them both considerably, but returning almost at once to the seriousness of the situation, she added: 'But I have a notion that that French husband of hers is not worth his salt and would be far too concerned for his own safety than to worry over Maria's. For I am not sharing Tony's convictions, and am quite certain after what they have done to their own Royal Family, one Cobtree more or less wouldn't worry 'em.' And so the conversation rolled on from one topic to another. Doctor Syn had by this time politely insisted upon Lisette taking his more comfortable seat, which though it infuriated the Captain, placed him in a better position for conversing with the old lady.

By the time the coach had reached Canterbury, their talk had brought them to the most popular topic of the day—occasioned by Doctor Syn remarking the little grotesque black patch upon Miss Gordon's cheek—the topic which was inevitable at any fashionable gathering—namely, the Scarecrow, whose exploits amused the old lady vastly, though Lisette, frightened out of her well-trained servility, showed signs of apprehension at every mention of the name, till the old lady rated her for being a superstitious fool, and told her not to listen.

The Captain, on the other hand, appeared to come to life for the first time on the journey and listened to every word with avid attention, though neither he nor the old lady noticed the gleam of amusement that lurked behind the parson's spectacles, as he spoke to the Captain.

'I trust, sir, you will forgive a comparative stranger for addressing you, but you will understand from our conversation that our Marshes are not considered healthy at the moment.

Indeed, Dymchurch-under-the-Wall is not as fashionable as Brighton.' Then with an admirable piece of play-acting he pretended to recognise the Captain for the first time, exclaiming: 'Dear me—your face is familiar. Have we not met before?' To which the Captain was forced to reply: 'Yes, sir. Last night—in Crockford's.' 'Yes, indeed, of course—the wager. Had you but spoken sooner, I would have recognised your voice. Pray forgive me. My eyesight, you know.

At Crockford's, yes. Foolish of me to think you were coming to Dymchurch for your health.' Although to the ladies the words conveyed precisely what they meant, the Captain had that same uncomfortable feeling at the pit of his stomach that he had experienced earlier in the day.

Doctor Syn, turning to Miss Gordon, added: 'May I present, ma'am, a very famous English gentleman, and indeed a brave one, for he has wagered two thousand guineas that he will catch our Scarecrow within the week.

Captain Foulkes—Miss Gordon.' Miss Gordon gave the Captain a curt nod and did not seem very impressed, though Lisette was obviously gratified that she was riding in the same coach with a fine gentleman who was about to destroy the chief cause of her worries.

And so, on through the busy narrow streets of Canterbury, with the coach-horn playing a merry tune which caused Miss Gordon to exclaim:

'Sakes alive, is that the only tune he can blow? Have you noticed he has played nothing else the whole journey?' To which Doctor Syn replied with a smile: 'You have a musical ear, madame. 'Tis the 'British Grenadiers' is it not? In honour, no doubt, of our noble Captain here.'

'Oh, I know the tune,' replied Miss Gordon. But what she did not know was that the honour was due to the Scarecrow, who by this ingenious method told his followers throughout the countryside of his activities, each tune played meaning a different order. Had the guard been of a communicative disposition he could have told the occupants that in Scarecrow's music, the 'British Grenadiers' meant 'A false run tonight to lead the Revenue astray.' Pulling up at the 'George and Dragon' for a final change of horses and half an hour's rest, they started off again to the strains of the same enlightening tune, past the

Cathedral and shops and on into Stone Street with its long stretch of straightforward road, lying open and innocent save for the lurking farm-house, and the coppice which had served its purpose earlier that morning. A good run until the southern end—the dread of every driver—Quarry Hill. Here the coach had to be stopped for skids, and then slowly down the winding gorge, which was overhung so heavily with giant foliage that even in the strongest sunlight it was like passing through an endless tunnel.

So went our coach—the horses straining back, the coachman leading them and the occupants forced to cling to their straps, as the vehicle lurched on its tortuous way down the hill.

'Might be in the Highlands,' exclaimed Miss Gordon.

'Yes indeed,' replied Doctor Syn. "Tis precipitous as the stretch which we have just left is straight. You must blame the Romans if there is any blame for such a lasting road. The hill takes its name from the quarry which they used to work, transporting the stone for the building of Canterbury. Though we may not like to admit having been conquered, we must yet thank the Romans for much. Indeed there cannot be a man o' Kent on our coast who does not sing their praises for the ingenious construction of Dymchurch sea- wall—a magnificent piece of engineering. Otherwise the seas would still be lapping against the hills behind the Marsh.' 'There, Lisette, what did I tell you?' cried the delighted old lady.

'Though the sea is higher than the land, you will not get your feet wet.' The maid, at last understanding the significance of the wall at Marsh, was loud in her praise of those ancient builders. And so on down the hill, their voices echoing against the steep wooded sides of the gorge, the Captain uncomfortably tilted back, and being exceedingly bored at this archaeological lecture, cried, 'Confound the Romans, say I. I would they had made this road straighter, and I fail to see why we should overpraise them. For my part, I have no wish to render unto Caesar praise or anything else—' 'No, my fine gentleman, but you'll have to render a lot more than praise to Gentleman James,' rang out a strong voice.

Our friend, the highwayman, had timed his attack to a nicety. The coach had stopped at the bottom of the hill, and both coachman and guard were busy removing the skid chains, the latter having most carelessly left his loaded blunderbuss upon the roof of the coach. Both men, taken by surprise, and powerless to assist, took cover behind the huge wheels, while a gay masked face and two horse-pistols menaced the confused passengers. The terrified Lisette, thinking the apparition none other than the Scarecrow, broke into her native tongue and mingled with the Captain's oaths and Mister Pitt's excitement; the voices of the little old lady and Doctor Syn were hardly heard at all.

'Come now,' cried Mr. Bone, enjoying the joke hugely, 'who will be the first to render unto Jimmie Bone? Oh no, Captain, I shouldn't try and touch your sword. This is my territory—not your St. Martin's Fields.' And that angry gentleman, whose fingers indeed had been twitching at his hilt, was flummoxed into silence. 'Ladies first, sir, I'll relieve you of that later,' continued Mr. Bone. 'Come, miss, the guard will assist you to descend.' The trembling maid, clutching the jewel-case, was helped out of the coach while Mr. Bone emptied the jewel-case into his saddle-bag. Lisette, having no personal effects, was allowed back into the coach, and Miss Gordon was the next to descend, which she did, all outward indignation, though secretly enjoying the adventure. Taking the rings from her plump little fingers, she advanced fearlessly to Mr. Bone and handed them to him. He had to stoop low in the saddle to take them from her and he said, ''Tis a crying shame to take the rings from such a pretty hand.' 'I have no wish to cry, and no compliments, please,' she snapped. 'I am too old for jewellery, as anyone can see, but 'tis most annoying of you, sir, or rather 'twill annoy my niece Cicely Cobtree, for I had planned to leave them to her. And shall have something to say to her father if he can't keep order on his own land better than this.' So saying, the old lady handed over the rest of her baubles, and called to the poodle, 'Come, Mister Pitt, give the gentleman your bracelets.' Thus summoned as he thought for another perambulation, the white poodle took a happy flying leap through the open door and pranced, jingling, round the hooves of Mr. Bone's horse, which said gentleman was so amused and having taken a liking to the courageous old lady, swept off his hat and laughed. 'Though I have robbed many a dirty dog, ma'am, I have no wish to rob a clean one, and with such a famous name to boot.' So Mister Pitt, with property intact, followed his mistress back into the coach, and Jimmie Bone peered inside to select his next victim.

Upon seeing Doctor Syn he seemed to be most annoyed. 'Devil take it!' he cried. 'A parson, and I must live up to my old slogan and respect the cloth.

I never robbed a cleric yet, though I once had the Archbishop himself in my power, and I don't doubt that the old Agger-bagger hadn't more in his bags than you, eh, Mr. Clergyman?' And had anyone been able to see beneath Mr.

Bone's mask they might have been surprised to see him give Doctor Syn a gigantic wink.

So there was nothing else for the Captain to do than to scramble ignominiously out on to the road, while Jimmie Bone surveyed him critically, and said: 'Well, here's a fine gentleman, and with a fine reputation too if I'm not mistaken. I warrant you'll be visiting the coast for the good of your health.' Again, the warning note. 'Then you'll not be needing the sword that's hanging by your side. Come, sir, hand it over. Oh no, sir, sheath and all. You might be tempted else to pick one of your customary quarrels with some poor Kentish lad.' And the glowering Captain could do nought else hand over his infamous duelling-sword. After which he was made to turn out his pockets while the guard was ordered to go through the mail bags and luggage. So it was that when the Captain was finally prodded back into the coach by the tip of his own sword, he had very little left other than what he stood up in, his stock-in-trade, guineas for gambling, and weapons for killing gone, as were his beautiful Hessian boots.

And so it was with bulging saddle-bags and full pockets that Mr. Bone bade them a cheery farewell, and putting his horse to the bank, rode up it and vanished in the dark seclusion of the woods.

The person who seemed least affected by this untoward adventure was Miss Gordon, who, although she had lost a considerable amount of valuables, could hardly retain her laughter at the Captain's discomfiture, as he sat, a sorry sight, in his stockinged feet. Indeed she had to hold her muff to her face to hide her uncharitable amusement. Doctor Syn may have noticed this, for hie was the first to break the silence, by addressing the Captain. 'My dear sir,' he said, 'this rascal has left you in a deplorable state. Indeed you must be regretting already your resolve to visit our part of the country. For my part, I cannot apologise enough, for I should have included highwaymen in my list of dangers that you might encounter on the Marsh. Now, we must see what can be done. It is my duty to assist you. Your feet. Dear me. Now—I have a pair of carpet-slippers in my bag—perhaps you would—you couldn't? No? Oh well, perhaps you're right. A village cobbler, perhaps. Then please let me lend you a guinea or so, until you find yourself in funds? Oh, in insist,' and the Captain had the mortification of having to accept Doctor Syn's offer. He also had a nasty feeling that the parson was laughing at him, so that he was further piqued when this ambiguous gentleman continued solicitously, 'And your sword, sir. Your favourite weapon. Dear me, what a loss. Now, if you will permit me? I have a very fine collection of Toledo blades. I used to fancy myself somewhat as a swordsman—in my younger days, of course. You have only to call at the Vicarage and make your choice of weapons. Can I advise you further?' 'I can,' laughingly broke in Miss Agatha Gordon. 'My further advice would be—when next you go a-coaching, you should disguise yourself either as a parson or a poodle.' At the 'Red Lion' in Hythe, the Dymchurch passengers left the coach, where Miss Gordon was met by a smart turn-out with postilions, the Cobtree arms upon the panelling, so that Doctor Syn, who had intended to take a local coach, was prevailed upon to join her. Luggage piled in, they caught a final glimpse of Captain Foulkes surrounded by laughing postboys and a crowd of gaping yokels, who, having heard from the guard that the robbery had been so neatly done by the popular Jimmie Bone, laughed the louder as the Captain's stockings picked their way gingerly and painfully across the cobbles to the doubtful seclusion of the bar parlour. With no weapons with which to force his will, he looked as he felt, a bedraggled shadow of his former self. Indeed, the Captain's courage had vanished with his boots.

Chapter 4. The British Grenadiers

Midway between Hythe and Dymchurch the marsh road joins the seawall and then for three miles runs parallel but beneath it, thus sheltering the traveller from the full force of the sea breeze, for indeed in rough weather it was well night impossible for pedestrians to walk upright upon the footpath that ran along the top of this great stone and grassy bank, though on this autumn evening the weather was calm enough. Dust was falling and the postilions spurred hard to reach home before lantern light, so the smart little chaise sped along the dyke-bound road in fine style.

The comfort of the well-sprung vehicle and the absence of their illmannered companion put them in a merry mood, and Miss Gordon, her face no longer hidden by her muff, was able to join Doctor Syn in a hearty laugh when they discussed Captain Foulkes's misfortune.

'I vow I would not have cared a fig for his feelings had that roguish highwayman deprived him of his breeches too, for I have seldom met with such a boorish oaf,' she chuckled.

Which latter thought had already occurred to Doctor Syn with satisfaction, for he had other matters to see to before being able to give his undivided attention to the Captain. This notion, however, he did not convey to Miss Agatha Gordon.

The journey, though short, was also not without interruption, for at a lonely farm-house the postilions, having already apprised Miss Gordon of the fact, stopped to deliver a package that had come down with the mail. This being done, the old tenant came out to pay his respects to the Cobtree chaise, and was delighted to find that the Vicar of Dymchurch was in it. With much bobbings and pullings of forelock, he was presented to Miss Gordon as one of Sir Antony's worthy tenants. It was during the ensuing catechism put to him by the old lady that Doctor Syn, absent-mindedly, no doubt, fell to humming a gay little tune, which the old farmer, strangely enough, for he was rather deaf, seemed to have caught, for after is respectful leavetaking he went singing lustily through the farmyard, 'some

talks of Hal-ex-ha-han-der, hof the British Gren-ha-ha-ha-
dears.' Though he may have taken some liberties with the
original text, he most certainly conveyed the meaning of the song
itself, for the catchy tune was caught up by half a dozen
labourers working round the farm, and even a fat milkmaid
some three fields ahead of the chaise was singing it and marking
time in rhythm as she pulled. Indeed, fast as the chaise sped on
towards the village, the tune preceded it all the way, till Miss
Gordon exclaimed, 'That teasing tune again. And this time the
fault is yours, Doctor Syn, for being quit of the guard we had
escaped it, till you started up the plaguey thing again.' To which
Doctor Syn, pleading ignorance that he had hummed the tune,
apologised profusely and offered to make amends with a little
Handel on the harpsichord at the Cobtrees' next musical. But
upon entering Dymchurch, he could not deny but that the
village was ringing with it. Workers returning from the fields,
dyke-cleaners swinging their trugs, the blacksmith at his forge,
housewives closing shutters, fishermen mending their net and
a host of small children running this way and that, all singing,
whistling, moving to the self-same tune; while Mr. Mipps, the
sexton, was executing on the churchyard wall as neat a
hornpipe as Miss Gordon had ever seen in her native Highlands,
and in a voice that seemed to have been tuned and broken at
the capstan bar, sang loud enough to let the Frenchies know on
t'other side of the Channel the full glories of the British
Grenadiers.

At the corner of the churchyard wall upon which Mr. Mipps
was thus disporting himself, the postilion, on Doctor Syn's
request, pulled up, and the Sexton, recognising with obvious
pleasure his beloved master, finished his dance with an intricate
twiddle and with surprising agility leapt down to the road before
Doctor Syn had stepped on to it. Shouldering the valise, he
stood waiting while the Vicar was taking his leave. He hovered
happily, his impertinent ferrety face wreathed in seraphic
smiles, and his strained black hair, twisted and bound into a
tarred queue, resembled a jigger-gaff, though at this moment it
quivered with expectancy reminiscent of a pleased puppy about
to wag its tail. His wiry little body suggested more the sailor
than the Sexton, and his clothes certainly had something of a
nautical air. The villagers regarded Mr. Mipps as a person of

importance with whom one could not take a liberty, for it was rumoured that being press-ganged into the Navy he had been captured by the famous pirate Clegg and had had to serve him as ship's carpenter. Maybe there were some who had their own opinions on the subject, but they would not have dared to voice them, least of all to Mr. Mipps, who, as Parish Clerk, Sexton and Undertaker, was admired and respected. He was the Vicar's general factotum, though some had their suspicions regarding his other activities. In fact, many a Revenue man worsted by the Scarecrow and his gang was ready to swear that when Mr. Mipps wore that look of injured innocence he had in all probability been up to a bit of no good, and indeed knew more about this plaguey smuggling than he cared to admit. But they never seemed able to put their finger on it, and Mr. Mipps, conscious of his own importance, continued to bask in the reflected glory of his well-loved master.

Before taking farewell of Miss Gordon, Doctor Syn begged her to convey his felicitations to the Cobtrees and excusing himself for not accompanying her on the grounds of their family reunion, promised to visit them on the morrow. With a pat on Mister Pitt's head, and counselling Lisette not to lose sleep over the Scarecrow, he irrevocably won the old lady's heart by kissing her hand. Then with a bow he joined the waiting Mipps, and the chaise went on to the Court House.

Mr. Mipps, trotting to keep up with the Vicar's long, easy strides, became as voluble as he had previously been silent, and embarked upon a long series of questions, answers, happenings, and more questions till Doctor Syn advised him to postpone verbosity as they had the evening before them, adding with an enthusiasm that might have seemed strange to an outsider, that for his part his immediate ambitions centred around a long, strong drink.

'Well, we know where the best brandy is in Dymchurch, sir,' suggested Mr. Mipps, as they entered the Vicarage. Panelled in ivory white, the room was of exquisite proportions. Indeed it had been specially designed and personally supervised by Doctor Syn's friend, the great Robert Adam himself.

The fireplace had a dignified mantel with bookcases in pillared alcoves on either side. A log fire burned brightly in the hearth, and the Vicar warmed himself in front of it while Mipps got bottle and glasses. Doctor Syn was glad to be home. He loved his parish and he loved his house, and he stood, glass in hand, appreciating his own taste both for fine old brandy and good furnishings. He watched Mr. Mipps lighting the huge candelabras that stood on the refectory table, and as each candle came to life some aspect of the room pleased him more. The great staircase with its sweep of fluted banisters curving into the room. The deep bow windows with diamond panes, through which twinkled innumerable lights from fishing-boats already putting out to sea, while a great painted globe of the world stood, shining and inviting, in its brass stand as if enticing him to leave home waters and once again put out for distant seas.

For one exhilarating moment he allowed his mind to cover those vast oceans which he knew so well, smiling at some remembered escapade.

Strange that this Mipps, his close companion and lieutenant in those tempestuous days, should now be with him in this haven of rest, decorously lighting the candles. It was not often that he permitted himself the luxury of allowing his mind to cram on canvas and to carry him back to the enchantment of spiced islands in the tropic seas, or the heady dangers of blustering broadsides in some open fight.

But Doctor Syn was in a reflective mood—the outcome of his activities during the past week, with which he was fully satisfied. Yet when he pondered over the accomplishment of his latest enterprise he was fully aware that this had but started the overture to a new drama in his life. While his seafaring instinct had always told him, 'No petticoats aboard', yet, at this very moment, having stifled the sailor in him to become the parson once more, he realised upon looking round his pleasant home that it did, in very truth, lack that one thing. So it was with an almost imperceptible sigh that he dismissed the future with the past, and brought back his vagabond thoughts to the present.

'Well, Mipps, is all according to plan tonight?' 'Yessir,' replied the Sexton, blowing out the taper. 'Three cries of the curlew it is, and the 'British Grenadiers'. No, I'm not anticipatin' any trouble tonight—though since you've been away, sir, we've been sent a bran' new box of soldiers, as pretty a troop of

Dragoons as you ever did see, and who do you think is in command?' 'I haven't the faintest idea, Mipps.'

'No, thought you wouldn't, sir, so I'll save time by telling you,' said Mipps. 'Major Faunce.' Doctor Syn received this intelligence with a raised eyebrow of surprise.

'Never the charming fellow who served with Colonel Troubridge here?' 'No, not the charming fellow who served with Colonel Troubridge here,' echoed Mipps. 'His younger brother, and as like him all them years ago as two peas in a pod.' 'Well, well, that's very interesting,' nodded the Vicar. 'We must endeavour to entertain Major Secundus, as we did Major Primus.' 'No, no, sir,' protested Mipps. 'Faunce is the name, sir.' 'Yes, Mr. Mipps, I stand corrected,' smiled the Vicar. 'My mind seems to be playing truant tonight and at that moment I was back in the Lower Third at Canterbury School.'

To which Mipps, slightly mystified, replied, 'Oh well, of course if you're going back to your second childhood, p'raps you'd like me to fetch you a nice hot glass of milk before tellin' you the rest of the news!' 'Well then,' continued Mipps, 'item number two. There's a new Revenue Officer come to Sandgate, and he's been nosin' round here too, though I ain't expectin' much trouble from him neither, for all they say he's smart as paint. We'll soon blister it, eh, Captain?' 'Mr. Mipps'—warned the Vicar.

'Oh, sorry, sir. Quite forgot—eh, Vicar. Wants to see you alone. I don't do. Leastways I didn't, so he said. Still, he'll soon know who does and who doesn't round 'ere. But knock me up solid, I'd forgotten all about that there Kitty-run-the-street.'

'I beg your pardon, Mr. Mipps. And what might that mean?' 'Well, sir,' explained the Sexton, 'someone else come nosin' round 'ere today and wants to see you most particular. I shushed him off but back he come. Wouldn't go away. Said he'd wait. Sat there. Missus 'Oneyballs had to dust round him. Ever such a ernful young gentleman he was. Look like WillJill to me.' 'Mr. Mipps, would you do me the favour of speaking in plain English?'

Marsh term for the common heartsease or pansy.

'Sorry, sir. Forgot I was talking to the Lower Third. Well, since you're so judgmatical, 'alf past two, it was, to be exact. As fine a young dandy as ever you did see comes prancin' up the path. I 'appen to be puttin' a nice bit of manure into the rose-beds at the time, and not wantin' to be disturbed, I nips into the tool'ouse, and lets Missus 'Oneyballs deal with 'im, but, blow me down, if she don't come and find me. I give her a talkin' to, but she says I'd better come and keep a weather eye on him, 'cos she wasn't goin' to be left alone with him, not with 'Oneyballs workin' two miles away. So in I goes, and there he be. And that's what I told you, see?'

'Yes, Mr. Mipps,' nodded the Vicar, 'you have done full justice to your powers of observation. I gather from your graphic tale that someone has been here who wished to see me.' 'Right, sir. You've got it, sir. First shot, sir.' Mr. Mipps was delighted as he added, 'And what a one you was for layin' a gun, sir.' 'Mr. Mipps,' warned the Vicar again, then asked: 'And what did you do with the young dandy?' 'Do with him? Nothin' I could do with him till he get so 'ungry that he stopped titherin' about and went back to the 'Ship' to get somethin' to take the sad look off his face. Leastways I 'opes it do, if he's goin' to come 'ere again, which he said he would, first thing tomorrow mornin'. Oh, blow me down, give me his card he did. Now where did I put it? Oh yes—'ere.' And out of the depths of his capacious pocket he produced an assortment of queer objects. Spigots for barrels, bits of tarred string, measurements for coffins, a twist of tobacco, and amongst all these slightly bedaubed with fish manure, was a card that he triumphantly handed to Doctor Syn. Which said gentleman was not at all surprised when holding the delicate piece of paste-board that had lost its elegance since morning, to find that the name engraved on it was Clarence, Viscount Cullingford.

'Clarence,' snorted Mr. Mipps as the Vicar read the name aloud. 'Silly sort o' name for a silly sort o'—' Mr. Mipps did not finish the sentence, but added, 'Don't bother your 'ead about who he is or what he wants. I'll flip round to the 'Ship' and soon get charted up on him.' But he took care not to mention that he had already slipped there and gained several drinks from the gentleman in question.

'You need not trouble, Mr. Mipps. I have him spotted. Well, what else? Nothing to report from the Court House?' 'Coo—I should say there be and well you knows it. The 'ullabelaybaloo started as soon as you'd gone. I 'ave 'ad Sir Antony round 'ere every day with his face as long as a yardarm askin' for you. Got tired o' sayin' you'd gone preachin' in London. He finally writes a note which he says I'm to give you the first minute you gets back.' 'Well, I've been here more than a minute, Mr. Mipps.' 'That's right. So you 'as and 'ere it is.' And from the desk, Mipps handed Doctor Syn a letter which read as follows:

Nov. 12th, 1794 The Court House, Dymchurch-under-the-Wall, Kent.

My Dear Christopher, Not knowing your whereabouts in London I have been pestering the good Mipps for knowledge of your return. Will you send word of your arrival, for I find myself in need of your counsel. In fact, my dear Christopher, I am confoundedly worried, the reason being that Cicely, ever wayward, has vanished into thin air. She rode off saying that she had a mind to visit the Pemburys at Lympne, but we now find that she never went there, and not a sign have we had from the naughty miss since. Caroline is in a pretty pet as her Aunt Agatha is due here for a visit, and she wanted our girl to make a good impression. I know you cannot fully appreciate the trials and tribulations of a family man, nor understand my mortification when Caroline looks at me as though it were my fault. So do be a good fellow and come and help me out.

Yours affect, Tony.

Which appeal from an obviously harassed paterfamilias caused the Vicar no astonishment. He almost appeared to have been expecting it. Nor did he show the least surprise on hearing outside the window footsteps crunching the shingle and someone whistling quietly the opening bars of 'The British Grenadiers'.

Chapter 5. Mr. Bone Whistles the Same Tune

Mr. Bone stepped into the Vicarage and greeted Doctor Syn with the easy familiarity of an old friend. He was invited to divest himself of his riding-coat and partake of the best brandy in Dymchurch, which he did with obvious appreciation, standing with his back to the fire while the Vicar sat comfortably in the corner of the settle. The brightly burning logs and the candles in their sconces over the mantelpiece reflected upon the lofty moulded ceiling the shadow of the highwayman, whose giant frame dwarfed the hovering Mipps as he tithered about the room, filling churchwardens from the generous pot of Virginian tobacco, and keeping the glasses, his own included, up to the brim. His inquisitive nose and the quivering tarred queue behind that balanced it made him look more foxy than ever as he chuckled with delight at Doctor Syn's account of the journey by coach, of Foulkes's discomfiture, and the bravery of the little old lady with quaint manner and an even quainter dog; which same old lady in the Cobtrees' best spare bedroom was now, with the help of Lisette, changing into evening finery. If the gentlemen at the Vicarage considered her manner quaint, they might have considered her language to be more so when she was reminded by her empty jewel-case that Gentleman James had not left her a single bauble. In fact she rated him so fiercely that had Gentleman James but heard her he might have considered her no lady. The old lady was well-nigh forced to borrow her dog's bracelets. How surprised she would have been then had she known that at that very moment the fate of her missing jewelry was being discussed by none other than the learned pleasant gentleman with whom she had travelled and the robber himself, and this but a stone's-throw away at the Vicarage.

'I am extremely sorry, my dear Jimmie,' Doctor Syn was saying, 'but I had no idea that the old lady would be travelling by that coach. May I suggest, since the Cobtrees are such friends of ours' (at which Mr. Bone grimaced appreciatively, thinking of the many broadsheets Sir Antony had put out against him), 'that we have a little private transaction. You being as good a valuer as any of the Receivers, what do you estimate they are worth to you?' Mr. Bone threw back his head and pulled at his ear as he made rapid mental calculations, but upon realising the full significance of what the Vicar had in mind, brought it sharply back again with a quick retort. 'Oh no, you don't,' he cried. 'If you're thinking of buying back the old Scotch lassie's jewellery and are a-thinking that I'd let you do it, then my name's not Gentleman James. I liked her so well that I came here tonight with the lot in my pocket, so will you kindly do me the honour of getting them back to her with my compliments? I should like to have done it myself, but my presence at the Court House might have embarrassed the Squire.' At which statement Mr.

Bone smiled somewhat ruefully, thinking that perhaps after all the life of a gentleman of the road was rather a lonely one. Doctor Syn thanked him warmly, knowing it was hopeless to argue further against his friend's generosity. 'Besides,' went on Jimmie Bone, 'I shall have made a tidy profit on the effects I lifted from that swaggering Bully.' 'Upon which,' put in Doctor Syn quickly, 'I shall refuse to take my tithes.' And they both laughed heartily.

But the Highwayman's voice took on a more serious note as he asked, 'What do you intend to do with the blackguard, since you told me of his wager to catch the Scarecrow? The blustering fool. As if he had a hope in hell. Would you like me to deal with him?'

'Time enough to think of that, my dear James,' replied the Vicar, 'but there is something I would like. A glace through the papers in his wallet.' 'Easy enough,' said Gentleman Jim. "Tis intact save for the paper money which I changed into gold before it could be traced.' 'A wise precaution,' laughed the Vicar. "You're incorrigible, Jimmie.

For here I find myself aiding and abetting when I should be showing you the errors of your ways.' Saying this as he went through the wallet quickly, and finding the paper he required, handed it to Mr. Bone for his enlightenment.

'An I O U for a thousand pounds, eh? From my Lord Cullingford. Is your reverence about to aid and abet some other arrogant fool?' Doctor Syn shook his head. 'No, I intend to show that misguided fool the error of his ways and make him mend them.' 'And I have no doubts but you will do it good and proper, and by the time you've finished with him he'll be glad to follow the straight and narrow path.' Mr. Bone, glancing at the wallet which the Vicar had returned, remarked: "Tis so full of other I O Us that he'll not miss a paltry thousand.

And since you're about to help this wayward youngster, I'll follow your example and relieve the others,' and he threw a fistful of scribbled slips into the fire.

Thus dismissing the subject of the coach and its occupants they fell to discussing more serious matters, plotting the manner of the 'runs' for the following week, and the false 'runs' that should precede them, to throw Major Faunce and his Dragoons on a false scent.

Mr. Mipps, having cleared the refectory table, unrolled a large survey map of Romney Marsh, pinning it flat for easy perusal. Over this they stood, while Syn's long, pointed finger moved this way and that, as he unfolded his plan of campaign and fully explained his tactics. Indeed they looked for all the world like generals setting their plan of action before a major battle, while Mr. Mipps, as fussy over details as any aide-de-camp, followed the series of actions, making copious notes and rough diagrams in his undertaker's notebook. Thus they worked for an hour or so poring over maps, listing movements of the ships and cargoes, settling the number of pack-ponies required, and discussing the merits of local horses necessary for the nightriders. Not that the Scarecrow depended upon the contents of his followers' stables. Far from it. He had imposed a custom that had become almost a law, for by the ingenious method of various chalk-marks upon stable doors, the ostlers, who for the most part were in the game, saw to it that the doors were left ajar. Indeed, many a fine gentleman, even the Squire himself, spoiling for a good day's sport following hounds, had, much to his chagrin, found himself mounted upon a tired and jaded animal, who, by reason of its equine inability to gossip, was unable to inform its spurring master of the questionable activities it had been forced into all night. Their plans completed and the maps put away they had a hasty meal, washing down an excellent cold collation with fine red wine from Burgundy.

'And will you be needin' Buttercups tonight?' asked Mr. Mipps.

'Yes, indeed, Mr. Mipps,' returned Dr. Syn. 'And the panniers packed.

You know I go a-visiting.' 'Visitin' my—'Ave some more cheese, sir? Old Mother 'Andaway, o' course. Worst of these false runs, which I owns is necessary for the foxification of authorities, is that you has the same dangers but hasn't the happlause what goes with the openin' of a cask. Oh well, we'll stow away now. By the way, sir, what about them you-know-whats? When are you goin' to fetch 'em from you-know-where?'

'That's all settled Bristol fashion, Mr. Mipps,' replied the Vicar as the Sexton refilled the glasses. 'I found occasion to visit our old friend Captain Pedro whose vessel lay in London Pool. He will by this time have already sailed and is expected across Channel.' 'Why, blow me down! That takes you back. Pedro, me old amigo.

Remember what he done up in Tremadoc Bay?' And Mipps plunged back to reminiscences of this old and trusted member of the Brotherhood. Indeed they became so engrossed that it needed three cries of the curlew to bring them to their feet. Mipps to the stables to saddle the Vicar's fat white pony, Buttercups, while Jimmie Bone handed back the old Scotch lassie's jewels and took his leave, after settling his rendezvous for the following day. Doctor Syn went up the first flight of stairs where on the landing stood his old seachest. From this he took a selection of queer garments, strange comforts for the sick old body he was about to visit, anyone might have thought who could have seen him later filling the baskets that hung on either side of his pony's saddle. Thus it was that the Vicar of Dymchurch on his fat white pony, followed by his Sexton astride the churchyard donkey, Lightning, ambled along the Marsh road, bidding a cheery good night to a picket of Dragoons, who marvelled at the old gentleman's fortitude when they themselves were feeling none too courageous as they watched for any signs of the Scarecrow's ghostly riders through the shifting curtain of sea-cloud. Indeed, such courage as they had completely left them when but a few minutes after the fearless old gentleman and his whimsical follower had disappeared, there came upon them suddenly, out of the encircling mist, a wild apparition-hideous face gleaming with a phosphorescent glow—it seemed to be one with the fiendish black fury it rode. In a panic, the terrified Dragoons leapt into the nearest dyke, while thundering hooves skimmed their submerged heads, and unearthly cries screamed away into the night.

Chapter 6. In which Lord Cullingford Gains More Than He Loses

Upon leaving the Vicarage where he had been not a little irritated by the feigned stupidity of that odd-looking servant with the ridiculous name, who, he felt, knew more than he cared to impart concerning the Vicar's return, Lord Cullingford, forced by hunger, betook himself back to the Ship Inn. Indeed, he had eaten nothing all day, having spurred his horse to its extreme limit to reach Dymchurch before Captain Foulkes. So feeling low not only in body but in spirits, he walked the short distance through the village and was conscious that all eyes were upon him. It was extremely disconcerting as he passed by cottage windows to know that the curtains were being furtively peeped through, and that his presence was being discussed by the invisible inmates. His feeling of discomfiture increased, however, when upon gaining the fastness of the 'Ship' and getting no attention in the coffee room, he had, perforce, to go into the bar parlour which up to the moment of his entrance had sounded like a veritable Tower of Babel. On his appearance this noise suddenly stopped, as again every eye was upon him, and our fine gentleman, wishing that he could vanish through the floor, had to shoulder his way through closely knotted groups of yokels who watched him with stolid amusement, whilst those who had any liquor left in their tankards emptied them quickly, hoping by this to convey their meaning to this finely dressed gentleman who, they felt, should buy his intrusion with a free round of drinks.

Scanty as his purse was, the same idea had occurred to Lord Cullingford, who by this time was feeling the dire necessity not only for a drink himself but for a few words of cheer, so with an authority he did not feel, he called loudly to the stout lady on the other side of the counter.

Whereupon the crowd seemed to surge round him the closer, tankards were thumped on the bar and many voices cried out, 'Missus Waggetts. Wanted.

Gentleman's orders.' 'Comin'! Comin'! 'Ere I be,' and the enormous proprietress bustled to that end of the bar and began filling innumerable tankards, which operation, taking considerable time, it was not for ten minutes that Mrs. Waggetts, almost as an afterthought, asked if there was anything he required for himself.

So, not wishing to be thought superior, he ordered a tankard of the same, and upon tasting it found that it was heavily laced with brandy, which though not displeasing on his own account, being the very thing that he needed, was, he thought, taking his generosity a trifle for granted. However, putting a good face on it, he flung a guinea on the counter, and making sure that this time he would not be misunderstood, he ordered himself another glass of brandy with a request that the food should be served to him as soon as possible in the coffee room. But half an hour later Mr. Mipps, overcome by his insatiable curiosity regarding the Vicar's unusual visitor, walked into the bar parlour himself and found Lord Cullingford still indulging his newly acquired taste for beer and brandy.

'Why, blow me down and knock me up solid!' exclaimed Mipps, 'who would have thought we'd meet again so soon?' But he did not mention that he had come there expressly for the purpose, having been told that the young dandy was in the bar parlour at the 'Ship' and was pushing out the boat, which indeed Lord Cullingford, must to his surprise, found that he had been doing steadily since his first order. By this time, however, having grown somewhat reckless, he had thrown caution to the wind, several other guineas on the counter, and again to his surprise discovered he was enjoying himself.

So greeting Mr. Mipps almost as a long-lost friend he called to Mrs. Waggetts to supply him with a good measure. Mr. Mipps winked at Mrs. Waggetts.

Mrs. Waggetts winked back and served him with a double noggin of brandy neat, which the Sexton tossed down in one, and pushed the glass forward for another, apologizing for his undue haste and remarking that he seemed to be a bit behind the others.

As soon as he had caught up to his satisfaction Mipps paused, and, after surveying Lord Cullingford attentively, remarked: 'Well, well, now whatever should bring a fine young gentleman like yourself down to the seaside at this time o' year? If you're thinkin' of indulgin' in that there newfangled bathin', you'll find it 'orrible cold. Or was it fishin' you was thinkin' of? Our Dover soles is famous.'

'If it's fishin' he's thinkin' of,' chortled an old crony, 'he'll be after something bigger than them Dover tiddlers, I'll be bound. I do 'ear tell that several London gentlemen 'ave a mind to go a-fishin' for our Scarecrow. 'Tis a tidy reward they'd get, and p'raps London ain't so full of guineas as they wouldn't want to earn it.' Which remark being exceedingly pertinent to his lordship, warned him to keep his own counsel, so he did not rise to the bait, and fortunately enough, before the inquisitive yokels could question him further, the conversation was interrupted by the arrival of a Sergeant of Dragoons with half a dozen troopers, who came in for the probing badinage and facetious heckling which otherwise might have been directed towards him.

"Evenin', Sergeant,' said Mr. Mipps. 'Found what you've been lookin' for, or ain't you been lookin' today?' The red-faced sergeant swung across the bar parlour, spurs jingling and banged a gauntleted fist upon the counter, as he called for drinks. His attitude was that of a pugnacious game-cock, which, though it did not intimidate Mr. Mipps, had the power of paralysing his enormous troopers.

'We don't want none of your quips and quirks, Mister Sexton,' he snorted. 'We've been out today and well you knows it. Though we didn't find what we was lookin' for, we finds out quite enough to help us to go on lookin', and if I knows anything about the look in Major Faunce's eye, we'll be out again lookin' tonight.' 'Well, they do say,' croaked the old crony in the corner, 'that there's none so blind as them as looks and can't see.' And so it went on, the yokels baiting the red-coats who generally came off worst. Indeed, had not Mrs.

Waggetts' beer been of such excellent brew, some pretty quarrels might have ensued; but its soothing qualities acted quickly on the tired Dragoons, and, putting them in good humour, the sallies were taken and returned in good part.

Lord Cullingford, used to the polished wit of the London exquisites, was bored with the crude clowning of these bumpkins, and welcomed the news that his dinner was ready in the coffee room, where he was delighted to find that the fare, though simple, was yet well cooked while the cellar list might have put most London taverns to shame.

The only other occupant of the coffee room was an officer of Dragoons who for some time was engrossed over military papers at the far end of the long table, but upon the serving-wench bringing in his dinner, he moved nearer to Lord Cullingford and the two were soon engaged in conversation.

Major Faunce, although an older man and a typical soldier, possessed a manner both frank and engaging, and Lord Cullingford was relieved to find someone of his own class who seemed eager to converse upon the one thing which his lordship most wished to hear—namely, the Scarecrow.

'Though I have been over here but a week,' Major Faunce explained, 'I have learned to appreciate the difficulties before me. The ways of the Scarecrow and his gang are devilish tricky, as my own brother knew to his cost. Many years ago that was, too, and since then the organization has been so built up that I don't believe anyone will stop it. Still, orders, you know.

Though as far as I'm concerned I shall be glad when I'm ordered to France, for I'd rather fight the Frenchies than have to deal with this hole-and-corner business.' Which statement served to plunge Lord Cullingford back into his former despondency. And it was not until the Major said that he had received information that there was to be a run tonight and that he hoped for some action, that he saw again some ray of hope, and indeed his spirits soared when the Major laughingly suggested that if he wanted a good ride and had no objection to jumping a dyke or two, he might care to come along and see something of the Scarecrow's work.

'Though, understand me, sir,' concluded the Major, 'I cannot promise that we shall see a thing.' This offer Lord Cullingford accepted eagerly, though protesting that having ridden from London that day, his acceptance must depend upon the condition of his mare. And warming to the subject, having for some time been in sore need of a confidant, he found himself blurting out the full extent of his difficulties and the reason of his visit to Dymchurch.

The kindly soldier treated him as he might have done a somewhat foolish younger brother, and though he may have been secretly amused at the thought of this stripling confronting the Scarecrow and succeeding where so many accomplished men had failed, he did not show it.

'Let the youngster ride out with us tonight,' he thought, 'and he'll soon see the impossibility of succeeding, and go squealing back to London with his tail between his legs.' So he treated the boy's confidences in a sensible way, proffering the loan of one of his own chargers if the mare was spent.

And so it was that some hours later Lord Cullingford, freshly mounted, rode with the Dragoons. Trotting at Major Faunce's side he felt an exhilaration he had not experienced before. This was a different type of horsemanship to the foppish caracoles he was accustomed to in London, and a fresh loathing of his squandered opportunities and meaningless life seized him. He looked back at the troop, and the moon, appearing from behind the driven clouds, flashed on breastplates and trappings and lit up the crested helmets, under which the faces of the men held firm by tightened chin-straps were set into lines of determination and became to Cullingford symbols of purpose.

Although for some time they encountered nothing tangible, yet there was an air of expectancy on the Marsh that night, as if behind the shifting spirals of low-lying mist strange activities were about to be set in motion.

Even the cries of the night-birds sounded ominous, and seemed to be woven into some furtive pattern, as if all were awaiting a master signal. The cry of a curlew surprisingly near was echoed at intervals into the far distance, each mocking note being answered back by the satirical hootings of an owl, so that the soldiers felt as if they were being made the target of some vast jest.

As indeed they were; for though the purpose of the night's mobility was but a practice for the smugglers, and a valuable one at that, since it enabled them to test, without the risk of losing contraband, the best way to tackle the 'run proper', yet they saw to it that the Dragoons were fooled into thinking that this exercise was the real thing. So following false trails the soldiers were led on by a tantalizing will-o'-the-wisp, in and out the shining patchwork of the moonlit dykes.

And then from lofty Aldington that towered above them there shot to the skies a mighty flame. The beacon had been lit. Signal received—the whole Marsh came to life. Luggers off-shore put in, and empty barrels were swung into place. Strings of pack-ponies appeared, and, quickly loaded, were herded off in various directions, whilst circling the whole manœuvre were the Nightriders, hooded and masked, and mounted on the swiftest horses and uttering wild cries, and looking like a host of demon riders, enough to quell the stoutest heart.

Major Faunce, swinging his sabre as signal for attack, called to his men, and the whole troop charged; yet as hard as they rode, the Nightriders, led by the Scarecrow on his plunging black horse, Gehenna, outpaced and outwitted them. Across flat fields and over dykes went this mad cavalcade, till the bewildered Dragoons, breaking formation and riding each man for himself, were scattered, and the whole Marsh was in confusion. Shots were fired, and terrified sheep stampeded under the whistling bullets, hampering the cursing horsemen.

It was during this wild skirmish that Lord Cullingford, riding a horse he did not know, misjudged a jump and was heavily thrown.

Upon regaining consciousness, his first impression was that this must be Death, and worse, it must be Hell. He was in the Infernal Regions, surrounded by demons and ghouls, and confronted by the Archfiend himself.

His lordship closed his eyes, hoping the nightmare would vanish, but on hearing a harsh voice cry out 'Next,' he opened them again, thinking that indeed his time had come. The place in which he found himself seemed to be a huge brick oven, whose circular wall tapered high above him into a narrow chimney and around him some sort of trial seemed to be taking place by torchlight. He was lying propped up by huge bolsters of sackcloth, which smelt most strongly of hops. Indeed, had he but known it, Lord Cullingford was in an oast-house and watching, what many a man would have given his eyes to see, a trial of miscreants conducted by the Scarecrow. Upon two of the prisoners sentence was being passed, and when his lordship recovered his senses the voice of the Archfiend was delivering the verdict and pronouncing punishment.

'Having found you both guilty of systematically defrauding the fellowship of Romney Marsh by false figures in your account, thereby cheating your comrades, we sentence you to be deported as the Scarecrow shall think fit, the length of time depending upon your future behaviour.

Remove them.' The next offence was of a more serious nature, and the Judge's voice took on a tone of cold contempt as he described to the full circle of hooded figures a crime of treachery and asked for their verdict, of which there was no doubt, for the ghostly jury, though silent, stretched out their right hands, thumbs pointing down.

The awesome figure of the Judge inclined his masked head as he uttered the dread word. 'Death, and the manner of it will be ignominious. By promising to betray our whereabouts to the Revenue, thereby hoping by your treachery to gain the Government reward, your body will be found tomorrow morning hanging from the public gibbet, where you hoped by your vile deed to place us. Remove him.' And the terrified prisoner, screaming for mercy, was gagged and dragged away.

By this time Lord Cullingford was well aware that he was not in Hell, but in the power of the notorious Scarecrow, whom he had so gaily set out to track. Indeed, upon realizing how closely his crime tallied with the last prisoner's, he had to admit to himself that he was extremely frightened, and when upon receiving orders to take his stand before the Judge, and being helped to his feet by two Nightriders, he found that his legs would hardly support him. Was this to be the end of his wasted life? And upon that moment he wished he could have had a chance to redeem himself, a he had planned to do when riding with the Dragoons. Perhaps this was his chance. He could at least die bravely; and it was thus when Lord Cullingford was steeling himself to hear the fatal verdict that the figures of the Nightriders filed down the stairway of the oast-house and melted away into the night. Only two remained, and these, supporting him, as sick from his fall, and exceedingly weary, though feeling more the man than he had ever done before, he faced the Scarecrow, who demanded, in somewhat softer tones, 'And what fate are you expecting, my Lord Cullingford?'

Surprised at the use of his name by this uncanny creature, his lordship replied bravely: 'If it is to be the same as the unfortunate creature that I saw removed, then I ask but one thing—that it shall be swift.' Which remark appeared to please the implacable figure before him, though it answered sternly enough: 'That creature was unfortunate indeed. He had committed the crime for which there is no pardon. What then should be the punishment for one who has not played the traitor to us, but to himself?' Lord Cullingford was silent. Who then was this judge who not only knew his name but also his inmost thoughts? The voice went on: 'You have seen justice done tonight to traitors of our cause. Your punishment shall be to see that you do justice to yourself. And this may help you to it,' and he handed to the mystified young man his I O U to Foulkes. 'This may remove the necessity of your trying to remove me and claim the Government reward of a thousand guineas. I see the sum tallies. As to this Bully—Foulkes. He is our common enemy, for I do not allow wagers of his kind to be pardoned as I am pardoning you. Destroy that paper as I shall destroy the man to whom it's due.' The young man thought he must be dreaming, and indeed, before he had time to stammer out his thanks, the strange figure seemed to vanish before his tired eyes. Faint with fatigue and emotion, he knew no more until he woke with the dawn breaking, to find himself outside the Ship Inn. And yet it was not a dream, for there, clutched in his hand, was the I O U. And so as the rim of the sun came over the sea, Lord Cullingford, seated upon the sea-wall, pondered that though he had lost a good night's sleep he had gained his selfrespect.

Chapter 7. Concerning Various Happenings and in which
Aunt Agatha Hears a

Different Tune Fashionable London would have been exceedingly surprised had it been able to see what was going on in the kitchen of the Ship Inn at Dymchurch at half past seven in the morning of November the thirteenth; for my Lord Cullingford was breakfasting in a style unheard of in polite society. Seated at the far end of the long, scrubbed table, he was doing full justice to an enormous plate of sizzling bacon and crisp fried eggs, while a thick chunk of farm-house bread, lavishly spread with creamy butter, rested against a foaming tankard. His immediate neighbours were a boot-boy and a comely chambermaid, while grouped round the table were various members of the Ship Inn Staff—some serving-wenches, an ostler, two milkmaids and a cowman, all presided over by an apple-faced cook. The reason for this unorthodox behaviour being that his lordship, having sat for some time on the sea-wall and watched to his great satisfaction the tiny pieces of paper that had comprised the I O U vanish with the receding tide, had become a trifle chilled. He was also not a little tired and very hungry, so finding the front door of the inn still on the chain, he had wandered round through the coach yard in the hopes of seeing someone who might let him in. A most appetizing smell of frying breakfast emboldened him to look through an open window, which caused the aforesaid gathering to rise from their places and stand awkwardly gaping at the peevish coxcomb they had served the night before.

This morning, however, he might have been a different gentleman, so changed he was, for in a most natural, unaffected manner he asked if he might join them, and suiting the request to the action, he stepped through the window without further ado.

It was about the time when Lord Cullingford was attacking his sixth hunk of bread and butter that Mrs. Honeyballs was walking through the village on the way to her morning work at the Vicarage. Although she had never been out of Dymchurch in her life she had a habit of conveying to any passer-by that she was a complete stranger, greeting each building as though she had never seen it before. And in order that there should be no mistake she would enumerate aloud in great surprise the names of all the shops she passed, and the people that she saw. So if you followed Mrs. Honeyballs along the street you might hear this curious little sing-song catechism. 'Ah, lovely morning—isn't it a nice place—there's the Church, just see the steeple. Quested, the pastry-cook. 'Morning, Mrs. Hargreaves. There's Missus Phipps. Oh—sweeping out the Bonnet Shop; doesn't look so well again.

Hope it's not the megrims. Searly, the butcher—see he's selling oxtails. Mr.

Mipps' Coffin Shop. Wonder who the next'll be. Mrs. Wooley's bad again.

Now what's around the corner?' She knew perfectly well what was round the corner for she had asked and answered that question for the past twenty years, and she was just about to say, 'Ah, there's the dear Vicarage. Privilege to work there,' when the words stuck in her throat, for on rounding the corner she saw something that was not in her itinerary—in fact, this time Mrs.

Honeyballs was really surprised—in truth she was terrified—and flinging her apron over her head and hitching up her voluminous petticoats, she ran screaming at the top of her voice for the Vicarage. What Mrs. Honeyballs saw would have surprised anyone—in fact it would have terrified most people, for hanging from the public gibbet, slowly revolving in the morning sun which glistened and on its protruding eyeballs, was the body of a man. A grizzly object indeed to meet on one's way to work, and a morbid group of horrified villagers were already in the Court House Square gaping from a safe distance, though one or two, bolder than the rest, were attempting to decipher the roughly scrawled warning stuck to the corpse's chest; while high above their heads, from the fastness of the rookery, the churchyard carrion in grim confabulation cawed out their greedy tocsin. The babblement below grew from spellbound whisperings to loud commotion as the message ran from mouth to mouth.

'A WARNING TO ALL TRAITORS ON THE MARSH.' No doubt who wrote it either, for underneath so all could understand, a crude but vivid drawing of a Scarecrow.

It was fortunate for Mrs. Honeyballs that her lifelong study of every nook and cranny in the village stood her in good stead, or hampered by her apron she would most certainly have come to grief. As it was, with the instinct of a homing pigeon she was able to travel thus blindfold at an incredible speed, finally coming to rest outside the Vicarage back door, where she was able to gasp, 'Thank goodness, here's the back door—never thought I'd get here,' as she took the protective covering from her head, and decorously straightened herself before entering the 'privilege to work there'.

Upon entering, however, she promptly bumped into Mr. Mipps, who was coming out, and this sent her into a paroxysm of the trembles.

'Oh, Mr. Mipps,' she cried, throwing her arms about him and well-nigh suffocating the bewildered little Sexton, 'never so pleased to see you. Oh, what a fright I had. Never thought I'd get here. Comin' round the corner, thought I'd see the usual—but hangin' in the Court Yard—glad it didn't chase me. Can I have a brandy?' From the hidden regions of her capacious bosom, the muffled voice of the Sexton plaintively appealed to be 'let go of', and extricating himself with difficulty, gasped out in his turn, 'Careful now, don't be so print.

Too early for canoodlin'. Can you 'ave a brandy? Phew! Need one myself after all that.

'Ere you are then. Take a nip and tell me why you've got the dawthers,' and producing a heavy flask from an inside pocket, he handed it to the grateful housekeeper.

Mrs. Honeyballs took a generous pull, sighed loudly, and sat down.

She then prepared to enjoy and freshly horrify herself with a description of what she had seen, but was disappointed when Mr. Mipps, dismissing the subject, remarked 'Oh, thought you'd seen something 'orrid. What's a corpse before breakfast? Undertakers 'as to live, don't they? He'll be buried in the parish, and them Lords of the Level allows me a god price. 'Ave to flip round there and measure him up after I've cleaned out the font for the christening.

Funny—I was only sayin' yesterday that while waitin' for old Mrs Wooley to make up her mind I could do with another corpse with brass 'andles.' At which Mrs. Honeyballs, somewhat disgruntled, seized mop and bucket and set to work, noisily relieving her frustrated feelings, until Mr. Mipps was forced to tell her to 'ush her bucket as the poor dear Vicar, after his long journey, didn't ought to be disturbed. Leaving her, certainly hushed though still resentful, he took himself off to the church, making mental notes while passing the cause of Mrs. Honeyballs' discomfiture as to the length and type of coffin it might need. Thus happily engaged upon his funereal but lucrative speculation, he started to clean out the font.

His enthusiasm, however, was not shared by the Squire of Dymchurch, who, irritated by 'a confounded babble goin' on beneath his bedroom window so early in the mornin', damme'—pulled back the curtains to see the cause of it. The sight of half the village 'gawpin'' at a corpse he hadn't convicted hanging from his official gibbet threw him into one of his before-breakfast rages, which, this morning, however, was perfectly justifiable.

Sir Antony Cobtree, though taking his position as Chief Magistrate and Leveller of Marsh Scotts very seriously, at heart preferred the more pleasant occupation of a country squire, to wit, his horses and his dogs; and indeed his favourite pastime was followin' hounds. So upon recollecting that he had promised himself a day's relaxation away from his extra duties as a family man, for 'them prattlin' women' were getting on his nerves 'in the most deuced fashion', he was deeply chagrined that an uncalled intrudin' corpse would necessitate his presence in that 'stinkin' Court Room' to preside over an Inquiry, thereby 'ruinin' a good day's sport, damme'.

Tugging at every bell-pull in his bed-chamber to no avail, almost crying with vexation, he trotted out upon the landing in search of another. He had just viewed one at the far end of the long gallery and was in full pursuit, when, tripping over his flapping nightshirt, he slid the whole length of the highly polished floor and reached it quicker than he had anticipated. His carpet slippers and a Persian rug flying from beneath him, bobbled night-cap obscuring his vision, he clutched despairingly at the bell-pull, which, unable to stand up to the full weight of the Squire, broke with snapping wires and clattered about his head, as he came down heavily upon that part of his person most pertinent to his saddle. There he sat for a considerable time before regaining sufficient breath to enable him to give vent to as many good round oaths as he could remember, and it was from this lowly position, where he had thoroughly damned beeswax and bell-pulls, that he espied upon the top of a tallboy a hunting-horn. Hope returned upon the sight of this familiar object, with which he knew he could give tongue. Having achieved possession of this he threw restraint to the winds and all his lung power into the blowing of a long series of 'View Holloas'. This unorthodox method of calling for attention had the desired effect. He immediately became the centre of interest.

Doors flew open all along the gallery. Housemaids peeped out and jumped back, thinking the Squire had run mad, while her ladyship came out in deshabille and high dudgeon and admonished him for drinking so early in the morning, and what would Aunt Agatha think.

As a matter of fact Aunt Agatha's thoughts were of the pleasantest nature, for this same noise had awakened in her happy memories of the hunting-field, and having told Lisette to open the door to enable her to hear the better, Mister Pitt, attracted by this rallying call, slipped unnoted from the room, and set out on a trail of investigation. Coming from the East Wing, he followed the dictation of his nose and ears till he reached the opposite end of the Long Gallery, where his dog's-eye view was of two curiously attired humans, the lady soundly rating the gentleman, who like a naughty boy was standing dumb before her. An inviting length of dressing-gown cord trailing on the floor behind him enticed Mister Pitt to creep nearer, and when the Squire, unable to tolerate this nagging further, put the hunting-horn to his lips and deliberately emitted one short crude noise in protest, the poodle's curiosity knew no bounds. As in answer to the Squire, he barked a highpitched 'Tally-ho' and charged, but met with the same difficulties, for with jingling paws and legs splayed out, he came skating towards the unsuspecting gentleman. Such uncontrollable velocity surprised Mister Pitt into biting the first thing that came into contact with his nose. This happened to be the Squire's big toe, and to make matters worse was the one that had been most damnably pinched by a 'tight huntin'-boot'. The scene that ensued was indescribable, since the Squire's language was so strong that it sent Lady Caroline, hands over ears, scurrying back to her room, where, after slamming the door, she succumbed to a fit of the flutters, while the irate gentleman, his tone at once persuasive and abusive, with such entreaties as 'Nice leetle doggie—let go—get away from me, you little brute,' at last succeeded in kicking loose and, making for cover, dashing towards his bedroom; while Mister Pitt, having, like a tiger, tasted blood, kept up lightning attacks upon the succulent retreating ankles. But surprisingly enough the Squire was too quick for him, and his nose came into violent contact with something that he could not bite—a slamming door, behind which the Squire had gone to ground.

Within his room Sir Antony's annoyance by no means abated, when he heard that the commotion outside the house had grown louder and he went straight to the window and flung it wide, intending to harangue the crowd.

Having lost his dignity with Mister Pitt, he quite forgot to assume it again for the villagers, and indeed upon seeing his own lackey, Thomas, in the front row of the corpse's audience, with his arm round a giggling housemaid, he so far forgot himself as to lean perilously far out over the sill, thus endangering not only his person, but his still precariously tilted night-cap.

Mixing hunting phrases with official language he soon succeeded in sending the villagers about their business, and the errant Thomas, crimson to the ears, was ordered to attend on his master immediately.

Having somewhat mollified his feelings, he was yet fully aware that he was certainly in for a 'damned dull, deucedly aggravatin' day, findin' out the identity of this impertinent corpse and probin' the pros and cons, to say nothing of Caroline's tantrums 'cos of what he'd done on the trumpet, while me wife's Aunt Agatha will be accusin' me of ill-treatin' that snappin', yappin', doormat of a dog'. Apart from these trifling but upsetting irritations, there was the sincere anxiety about his daughters: Maria, married to a Frenchman in Paris, with the Terror raging, and Cicely having disappeared without a word. Thanking God that Doctor Syn was back again from London, Sir

Antony Cobtree at least promised himself a pleasant evening. So, cheered by this prospect, he determined to make sure of it, and crossing to his escritoire he sat down and penned without any further ado the following—noting as he wrote the date that thirteen never had been his lucky number.

Nov. 13 th . The Court House, Dymchurch.

My Dear Christopher, I hear from me wife's Aunt Agatha that you are returned from London for which Heaven be praised. I shall be infernally busy all day, at the Court House. The reason of this you will know by now, and I'll wager it's the Scarecrow's work. Since morning and afternoon are like to prove irritating (and to say truth, I cannot abide them prattlin' women no longer), I intended dining with you tonight at the Vicarage where we shall be free of 'em. I will send over by hand of Thomas as much wine as I think we can conveniently consume, for I find myself in a mood to forget my troubles in the arms of Bacchus, and I have but recently opened a very special bin which I think will be to your taste, so have the goodness my dear fellow to postpone whatever else you might have thought to do, let the parish go hang for once and forgive me for thus inviting myself but I have the necessity to see you.

Affect. Yours, Tony.

Which somewhat unscholarly letter made Doctor Syn smile, when within the hour it was handed to him with his morning chocolate. He thought affectionately of this great warm-hearted overgrown schoolboy. Dear old Tony had not altered one iota since the far-off days when they had been fellow students together at Queen's College, Oxford. In fact Tony was unalterable, living out the same heritage as his ancestors before him. His world was bounded by London and Romney Marsh, for with typical insularity he had never asked for more, content to belong to that solid support of the country classed landed English gentry. Christopher knew himself to be entirely opposite—the type of Englishman who has to see the far, waste places of the world. And he fell to thinking what this simple old friend of his would think should he ever discover what manner of life his old College friend had lived or what he would do should he ever learn the truth.

His reverie was broken by Mr. Mipps coming in to his room for the socalled parochial orders of the day. 'There now,' he exclaimed upon seeing the Vicar's untasted chocolate, 'what did I say to Mrs. Honeyballs? 'Mrs.

Honeyballs,' I says, "ush your bucket and don't disturb the Vicar after his long tedious journey',' whereupon Mr. Mipps favoured the Vicar with a slow wink, whisked away the cold chocolate, moved two books from the shelf beside the bed, thus disclosing a neatly concealed bottle of brandy, remarking to the Vicar, 'Now 'ere is something that will do you good after a tirin' journey. What a ride it was! Oh, did you 'ave a good night? I do 'ope you weren't disturbed with all them goings on. Village is fair buzzin' with it all.

Oh, and of course, you don't know the latest news. There's a nice new corpse 'angin' on the gibbet. Scarecrow again, they says. Have to be careful, you know, sir—'preachin'' all them sermons against him. He's gettin' a bit above hisself. Shouldn't be surprised if he didn't try and get you and me next.

Wouldn't we look ernful on a broadsheet? Vicar and Sexton found dangling together.' Which last remark sent Mr. Mipps into uncontrollable giggles resulting in a fit of the hiccups, so that Doctor Syn had to pass the brandybottle for his relief. Which in truth was exactly what Mipps meant him to do.

'When you have recovered, Mr. Mipps, perhaps you will pass me back the bottle and discuss parochial affairs.' 'Yes, sir—hic—parochial affairs. Real parochial affairs—or er?' 'Yes, Mr. Mipps, we'll discuss that too.' 'Oh—that's what I wanted to know. First of all—it's them 'British Grenadiers' again today followed by 'The Girl I Left Behind Me'. The word is bein' passed as usual. Coaches playin' 'em both voyages, up and down.

Next, please? Oh, Jimmie Bone—messages from him this mornin'—says he forgot to ask you last night—if you'll be needing him to ride as the Scarecrow for you tonight.' 'Tell him to stand by till we know which way the cat's goin' to jump.' 'Oh, don't we know? Suppose we don't. Oh, talking of cats. That there Revenue man. Been seen prowlin' through Hythe. Ought to be here any minute now. Oh, talkin' of Hythe: 'ere's a bit o' news. Mrs. Waggetts' cousin twice removed has to go into Hythe on account of what she's expectin' grantiddlers.

She runs into her uncle, who has with him a relation of the bootboy at the 'Red Lion'.' Doctor Syn interrupted. 'I trust the news is not so involved as the relationships.' Mipps replied promptly: 'No, sir. Gets clearer. Well, I'll tell you. That there Foulkes. Now what worried the boot-boy was that he hadn't got no boots. Wasn't half in a dobbin about it too. Rantin' and roarin'. Foulkes I mean, not the boot-boy. Sends out for cobblers and shoemakers. 'Red Lion' in a uproar. But by the time he's measured the whole place knows what he's come for. But here's the best bit of news, sir. He's passin' the word and says he wants it passed that he'll challenge the Scarecrow in open duel. Quite positive he'll win, too. Says he'll wager a thousand with anyone.' 'That's very interesting, Mr. Mipps,' replied Doctor Syn. 'He's killed some dozen men already. I wonder what the Scarecrow will do about that?' 'Yes—that's just what I was wondering of, too.' 'I shouldn't let it worry you, Mr. Mipps. Yes, the Sluice Gates. Oh—let me see, high tide? Well, well. Now the christening; this afternoon, of course. Remember?' Mipps nodded. 'Just cleaned out the font. Ever looked down from the top of them Sluice Gates?' The Vicar nodded.

Mipps went on. 'A lot of lovely mud goes swirlin' round. Thin mud.

'Orrid mud.'

'Yes, Mr. Mipps, I have noticed that there is mud in the Sluice Gates.

And oh, by the way, Mr. Mipps, the Squire is dining with me tonight. Would you be so kind as to inform Mrs. Honeyballs to make an especial effort. I thought perhaps some few dozen oysters, that brace of pheasants, a little soufflT—.' But to this Mipps objected, 'Oh, shouldn't trust her with a soufflT. Not today. Got the dawthers, she's all of a shake. That corpse made her shake good and peart, and when Mrs. Honeyballs shakes—she shakes, and you don't want a shaky pudding. Better make it a trifle. Won't matter then if she is heavy-handed. By the way, sir, you was talkin' of Pedro—will he be comin' over tonight, sir?'

Doctor Syn nodded. 'Yes, Mr. Mipps, with the usual cargo, if all goes well. And I have instructed Pedro that all must go well this time. But he's a good man; I'd trust him where I'd trust few others. Now, Mr. Mipps, 'tis time for me to rise. I have a sermon to prepare and must balance up the Tithe Book.

And I must not forget to do that little errand for Jimmie Bone, though I think it would be well to wait for a day or so until the hue and cry for him dies down. I shall return the jewels to Miss Gordon personally. You know, Mipps, Gentleman James has got discernment, for the old lady certainly has character. I have a great liking for the Scots.' So saying, Doctor Syn got out of bed, went to the open window and stood for a while scrutinizing sea and sky as if reviewing the weather, while Mr. Mipps watched him in this familiar attitude, as though he were upon the aft-deck of his old ship Imogene, looking for dangers on the seas ahead. He wished they could both hoist canvas and sail the seas again. So, stifling a sigh of longing and regret, he went down to execute his master's orders.

An hour or so later Doctor Syn was busily engaged upon parochial accounts in the library, when Mr. Mipps disturbed him again with, 'Beg pardon, sir, he's 'ere again. That there Will-Jill. Looking a bit subdued like—not that I don't wonder—but he's ever so pleasant—and asked most polite to see you. The fright you give him must have done him good. Oh, beg your pardon, sir,' this upon noticing the Vicar's warning look. 'Shall I show him in, sir?' 'Yes, indeed, Mr. Mipps. I shall be delighted to make his acquaintance.

I somehow thought that he might pay me a visit.' And so Lord Cullingford, tired, yet with a new look of determination, entered the library and introduced himself to the Vicar.

'I must ask your pardon, sir,' he said, 'for thrusting myself upon you like this, uninvited, but I did not wish to return to London without fulfilling the idea with which I set out. The reason of my visit this morning, however, differs from my original intention. I came now, sir, simply to pay my respect.

Happening to be at Crockford's on the night when you confronted a certain gentleman of my acquaintance, I vowed that I would come to you for assistance, for I had set myself what I now know to be a herculean task—to catch or kill the Scarecrow. Oh, pray do not laugh at me, sir,' for Doctor Syn was regarding him with a kindly quizzical air, 'for I was in dire distress and most damnably in need of the Government reward.' He plunged into a full description of allthat had happened to him since he left the Ship Inn with the Dragoons, ending up with the strange appeal that Doctor Syn should not judge the Scarecrow too harshly, 'for, reverend sir, he must be a good man at heart. True, I saw him condemn a man to death as I told you, but it was justifiable according to the code—why, the Forces of the Crown would do the same. Yet what officer of the Crown would take the pains to show a foolish young man how best to prove himself, and become a tolerable good citizen?' He then explained in the simplest manner that he was going to take the Scarecrow's advice by avoiding his extravagant friends, and joining up with men who had to earn a living—in short, the Army. 'For though I have but a few guineas left in my pocket,' he said, 'I have at least gained something of great value—my self-respect, and I shall ever be grateful to this strange, incalculable being that people call the Scarecrow.' Doctor Syn had listened to this frank confession with mixed feelings—sympathy for the misguided but engaging lad who might indeed have been his own son, and admiration for the purpose he displayed, and was thankful that he had indeed been able to effect this transformation. Humbled a little by the knowledge of his own secret life, he determined to help this youngster further.

So with the greatest tact he persuaded Lord Cullingham to accept a loan of some few hundred guineas, laughingly telling him that there was life in the old Vicar yet, and as he was liable to be here for a number of years, would be delighted to see him whenever his lordship cared to call.

So half an hour later Aunt Agatha, having taken Lisette to see the wonders of the sea-wall of Marsh, passed a young man coming from the direction of the Vicarage, who raised his hat with a flourish and gave them a sweeping bow. She remarked to her maid that he must be in very good spirits for she never did see such a well-set-up young man, adding however that as men went, she still had a penchant for that naughty highwayman. She was further reminded of the said gentleman when, upon walking slowly back through the village, MisterPitt making almost as complete an investigation of it as Mrs. Honeyballs, the local coach went by in great style, horn blowing gaily. But Aunt Agatha's musical ear was slightly confused, for though the tune it played was undoubtedly 'those same dratted Grenadiers', it somehow merged into one of her own Scottish songs—a popular Jacobite air.

Descending the grand staircase on her way down to luncheon, she remarked to Lady Caroline that she was in good appetite, having thoroughly enjoyed her morning perambulation, but it amazed her to observe that, though having such bracing air, Dymchurch seemed a very sleepy place in the daytime, and she hoped that Sir Antony's tenants were not keeping late hours.

Then, strangely enough, as she passed into the dining-room, she found herself humming, quite loudly, that lively tune, 'The Girl I Left Behind Me'.

Chapter 8. The Squire Sums Up

Sir Antony's worst fears were justified. His day was 'decidedly aggravatin'

'To begin with, no sooner had he finished his breakfast when old Doctor Sennacherib Pepper was announced, and he was forced to go and watch the inquest. 'Most unhealthy, probin' about a corpse just after a meal—enough to make a feller's cold grouse freeze inside him'; which it did later, having eaten so quickly, thereby giving him a bad attack of his usuals. But on leaving the mortuary to be rid of the nauseating sight, he had bumped into a fat constable, and 'the great clumpin' creature' had trodden clumsily upon his throbbing toe, which so pained him for the rest of the morning that he was compelled to loosen the buckle of his shoe, surreptitiously easing it off beneath his robes, so that when the court rose for the luncheon recess, and he pompously led the procession down the stairs, it was not until he trod upon a coffin-nail that he realized he was without it; and so, in a most undignified manner, he had to scamper back up the stairs.

Retrieving the offending shoe with difficulty, he bumped his head against the reading-desk, which knocked his judge's wig askew, and since, by this time, things had gone too far and he had not bothered to put it straight, he knew, by the 'disapprovin'' look on her ladyship's face, that she thought he had been at it again. Stifling a desier to do naturally what he had done that morning with the aid of a hunting-horn, he tried to enjoy his food, but Sennacherib Pepper, whom he had purposely placed at the far end of the table, kept shouting details of his grisly trade, which 'me wife's Aunt Agatha', who sat beside him, kept 'hummin'' that maddenin' tune, that all the village seemed to have been at that mornin'. Indeed, upon whistling it himself that afternoon, he had not been able to understand why he was looked at by several in the Court in such a peculiar manner. The fact was that they did not understand why the Chief Magistrate was in truth passing the smugglers' signal for that very night. Blissfully innocent of this, however, he continued with the proceedings. After lengthy weighing of the pros and cons, during which he became painfully aware that his seat of jurisdiction had been badly bruised beneath that confounded bell-pull, the jury at last managed to agree upon one point, that the corpse in question was the remains of one Gabriel Creach which everyone had known in the beginning. Indeed, everyone having known him for years, the whole thing was, therefore, a shocking waste of time.

Well—there it was. He had been hanged by the neck until he was dead, by some person or persons unknown—to wit—the Scarecrow, which the jury found on one was able to do anything about, since the Army, the Navy, the Revernue and Bow Street Runners, to say nothing of private enterprise, had all been after him for years and failed to catch this notorious malefactor.

Sir Anthony Cobtree, in his summing-up, found there was so little to say upon the subject, that he had to try and spin things out, to make it sound better, and becoming thus gravelled for lack of matter, he discovered that in order to make some sort of impression, he had, after a lengthy, pompous oration, involved himself most damnably. In order to get out of this difficulty with what little dignity he had left, he had, therefore, quite without meaning it, pledged himself to a further thousand guineas, out of his own purse, over and above the Government's proclaimed reward, 'to any who shall rid us of this—er—this um—this thorn in our—um' (fumbling for the word that had escaped him, a twinge from his bruise gave him his cue) 'in our seat of um-er. Oh, well, anyway, in my seat of errum—of JUSTICE. I mean—this botherin' nuisance.' Finishing thus lamely, he sat down cautiously, perspiring freely and none too happy as to what Caroline would say to him for having so willfully mortgaged her pin-money. He was, therefore, agreeably surprised when the whole Court rose and cheered him for a 'jolly good fellow. Long live the Squire'. Villagers and jury alike, equally surprised that for once their Squire had done more than was expected of him, applauded him vigorously for thus turning what had been a thoroughly dismal and boring affair into a cause for jollification.

Gratified at the enthusiasm of his tenants, and pleasantly conscious that his personal success had put that 'dratted corpse in the shade', his departure from the Court House was like a triumphal progress, as amid loud cheerings, surrounded by bobbing villagers he followed the Sword of Justice borne by the Clerk of the Court out into the street. Here Sir Anthony, now thoroughly swollen-headed, was easily prevailed upon to repair to the Ship Inn for refreshment.

And so some two hours later, slightly dishevelled and smelling most strongly of the public bar, judicial wig over one ear and official robes looped high for convenience, he burst into the boudoir of his astonished lady wife, and, knowing that the best method of defence is attack pursed his lips, and loudly did what he had longed to do all day. Then he told her ladyship in no mean language that this time he had really been at it.

The Dymchurch beadle came in for a little of the Squire's reflected glory, for at the Ship Inn, Sir Antony, after several of Mrs. Waggets' specials, decided to have his Proclamation sent out there and then. So he and the Beadle had, between the rapid succession of rounds, written and solemnly rehearsed it together. This entailed a deal of serious thinking and was indeed thirsty work, so that before setting out on his rounds of the village the Beadle had had so many rounds with Sir Antony that his condition was pleasantly mellow.

Armed with bell, lantern and parchment he set off up the street to the Court House Square. Using the Squire's mounting-block for his pulpit, and much pomp and ceremony and many ringings of his large hand-bell, he commenced. His voice, well lubricated with good strong ale, intoned the familiar 'Oyez! Oyez! Oyez!' which caused Sir Antony, who was dressing for dinner, to open his bedroom window and wave to him in brotherly greeting while shouting encouraging remarks. The Beadle waved back, and after several false starts began.

'Sir Antony Cobtree, Chief Magistrate and Leveller of Marsh Scotts, deeming it meet and right, does out of his personal privy purse offer 1000 guineas over and above the Government reward already proclaimed, making in all 2000 guineas to be paid by His Majesty's Lords of the Level of Romney Marsh, to any person or persons who shall hand over, or cause to be handed over, the leader of certain evil-disposed persons who ship overseas shorn wool and gold in exchange for rum, brandy, sundry spirits and silks. This desperate character, trading under the name of the Scarecrow, is wanted for trial on a capital charge at the next convenient Assizes, to be held at the Royal Court House at Dymchurch-under-the-Wall in the County of Kent. God save the King.' Having delivered all this without a slip, he looked up at the window for approval, but Sir Antony, having heard the first bit in which his name was prominently featured, had lost interest and gone to the powder-closet, so the Beadle, somewhat disgruntled after this especial effort, went back to the 'Ship'. There, he had several more rounds before starting off again. This time, however, he met with greater success, for moving up the village street crying the Proclamation as he went, he became the centre of interest and hospitality.

All this only served as encouragement for a visit to the 'City of London'. This tavern, on the sea-wall, seemed to be filled with his friends, and the four-ale bar was crowded. After a considerable time spent in these congenial surroundings he, like Sir Antony, had very little interest left in the Proclamation, so thinking to settle the matter once and for all, he decided on a rendering then and there. But hoisted by his drinking companions to a position of vantage on the bar counter, he discovered that he had lost the parchment. He made, however, a valiant effort to remember Sir Antony's phraseology, but like a poorly rehearsed actor, he was lost without his script—and being an inebriated Beadle his voice was lost in the general ribaldry.

Early in the proceedings he decided not to try any more 'Oyezes', having been unanimously shouted down with a chorus of 'Oh nos'. So he plunged straight in. 'That Scrantony Frobtree—on the Level—marsquots—deeming it meet and drink—er—meet and right—oh, well, damning it right and left ù out of his person—into the Privy—no-no—oh, well, anyway—sundry spirits and sulks. Desperate character—God save the King.' And the Beadle, with a loyal gesture, overbalanced and disappeared behind the bar—where kind Mrs. Clouder left him to sleep it off.

Two hours later she woke him, and having cooled his fuddled head beneath the kitchen pump, he recollected to his horror that he had not read the Proclamation to the Vicarage, and knowing that the Squire would most certainly ask Doctor Syn if he had heard it, made up his mind that it was better late than never. The parlour cleared but for a few stragglers, the missing parchment was found on the floor, undamaged save for beer stains and sawdust. So clutching his errant muse he ran along the sea-wall, arriving outside the parson's house somewhat out of breath. He gave himself a couple of minutes in which to recover it before embarking upon this final test.

Mr. Mipps was filling a second churchwarden for the Vicar when the Beadle's bell sounded and the speech began. Doctor Syn went to the bow window, and pulling the curtains wide looked out over the moonlit Marsh. He stood listening to the Proclamation—Mipps followed him and handed him the full pipe.

'Hear that, Mr. Mipps? Two thousand guineas.' 'Our price goin' up, eh?' Mr. Mipps whispered.

'Two thousand guineas would be of great benefit to our Sick and Needy Fund. I suppose you have no idea as to the whereabouts of this deplorable ruffian?' 'Me!' echoed the Sexton. 'Why me? 'Aven't you got an idea?' At that moment there was a sharp knocking on the front door—which caused the Vicar to answer: 'No—but I have an idea that this may give us an idea. The door, Mr. Mipps.'

Giving the Vicar a quizzical look the Sexton went to open it.

Chapter 9. The Revenue Man Pays a Social Call

A curious feature of all the front doors in Dymchurch was that they possessed spy-hole grids. This enabled the person inside to identify a visitor before allowing admittance. It was wise to take this precaution if one's activities happened to be questionable. Who knows? It might be a Bow Street Runner or the Revenue. Mr. Mipps always took this precaution, and having done so, closed the grid, uttering in a coarse whisper, 'You know who it is, don't you?'

The Vicar nodded, and repeated, 'Open the door, Mr. Mipps,' which the Sexton did somewhat reluctantly. A tall man stepped into the room and quickly looked about him. Seeing Doctor Syn, who was standing by the fire, a look of courtly query on his face, the stranger bowed and advanced towards him, saying: 'Doctor Syn? Your pardon, sir. Revenue Officer from Sandgate.

Nicholas Hyde, at your service. I should like a few words with you, Reverend Sir—alone.' The last word directed at Mr. Mipps, who stood resentful and alert in the background. The Vicar bowed and said he was happy to make Mr.

Hyde's acquaintance, and then requested Mr. Mipps to leave them alone, which the Sexton did, throwing back a look of disgust at the Revenue man.

Doctor Syn invited his visitor to take a seat and asked him if he would care for a drink, and upon the other's, 'Thank you, sir,' poured him out a generous measure of brandy.

Mr. Hyde sat down in the chair to which his host had motioned him and took the proffered glass, while Doctor Syn watched him as he lit his long churchwarden from a taper at the fire.

He saw a broad-shouldered, determined-looking man, who, dressed in the dark drab uniform of the Revenue, had about him an air of pugnacious expectancy and the questioning look of suspicion which was the stamp of his trade.

The Revenue man, feeling it was his duty to watch people and not to be watched, shifted uneasily under the Vicar's penetrating glance. This was not at all what he had expected. His customary habit of generalizing both people and facts had failed. Here was no ordinary village parson in a humble Vicarage, but an elegant figure of fashion in a setting artistic and luxurious.

So, realizing that he could not use his bludgeoning manner here, decided on different tactics, and awkwardly opened the conversation with a compliment.

'This is an excellent brandy, Doctor Syn.' 'I am glad you find it to your taste, sir,' replied the Vicar, as he strolled completely at his ease to a chair at the refectory table. 'The Squire sent over some half a dozen bottles, as he was dining with me tonight.' Thereupon, seeing the other's quick glance at the bottle, he continued: 'Oh, you need have no professional qualms as to his credentials. He is our Chief Magistrate—Caesar's wife, you know.' Mr. Hyde, not being conversant with classical quotations, looked blank. So the Vicar added: 'Yes, well, perhaps I am mixing my metaphors; Sir Antony hardly resembles a frivolous Roman matron, eh?' Another blank look from the Revenue. 'But perhaps you have not met the Squire? Your visit to Dymchurch is not connected with lawbreaking? Gratifying indeed, Mr. Hyde? A personal matter? You come to ask me to publish the banns? You could not do better. Our Marsh girls are considered beauties, you know.'

Here at least was a statement that Mr. Hyde could understand and answer. 'I am sorry to disappoint you, Parson, but I am not a lady's man. Let me be frank with you, sir, my visit to Dymchurch is strictly in keeping with my profession.' Placing his elbows on the table, and leaning towards Doctor Syn, he added impressively: 'I am here to lay that rascally Scarecrow by the heels.' The Vicar, raising an eyebrow in surprise, asked him why he had not gone to the Squire, to which the Revenue man, begging his pardon, explained that he had been informed that Sir Antony Cobtree cared more for his foxhounds and his vintage port than he did for maintaining the Law, a Leveller of Marsh Scotts. The Vicar was about to expostulate, but Mr. Hyde cut him short with: 'And anyone wishing to do business with him after a certain hour is more like to find him under the table than in his chair of office.'

At this the Vicar protested: 'You do him an injustice, sir. The Squire of Dymchurch is moderate in all things; indeed, he is looked upon with great respect by his tenants.' Mr. Hyde capped this derisively: 'That's as may be, sir, seeing the Squire's known to wink the other eye.' Doctor Syn rose, and in a reproving tone told the Revenue man that he would not allow a guest to remain under his roof who questioned the integrity of his benefactor. His attitude conveyed dismissal. Mr. Hyde, cursing himself for a clumsy fool and having no mind to go before accomplishing his mission, apologized as far as his nature allowed, and explained that he had no wish to offend but that suspicion being his trade, he must, of necessity, suspect anyone who could tally with the Scarecrow's description, adding with conciliatory jocularity: 'Why, I might even suspect you were you as good a rider as Sir Antony and not known to be one of the Scarecrow's sworn enemies. Your sermons against this cunning rogue are highly spoken of, as is, indeed, your courage in delivering them; that is why I seek your assistance.' At which the Vicar, having reseated himself as a sign that he had accepted the other's apology, seemed amused, and enquired whether Mr.

Hyde was suggesting that he should ride out with the Dragoons on their manhunt.

Mr. Hyde snorted. 'Man-hunt?' he cried. 'Devil-hunt, more like, for I begin to think the creature's supernatural.' Then his tone became confidential.

'No, Parson, I am not asking you to do anything but give me such help as your calling allows. In a word, I want you to impart to me any information you may have heard, or any suspicions you may have, regarding the questionable activities of your parishioners.' At this the Vicar seemed deeply shocked, as he replied in severe reproof: 'Let us understand each other once and for all, Mr. Hyde. If I can be of any help to you be preaching more strongly against this evil, I most readily agree, but I should be a disgrace to the cloth were I to betray the sorry little secrets of my flock,' adding devoutly that he considered it his bounden duty to respect the confidence of all—black sheep or white. He smiled as he explained himself more fully: 'Revenue man and smuggler alike. A little more brandy, Mr. Hyde?' The Revenue man was completely baffled; he felt he had not made the progress he had anticipated, so to gain time he accepted the brandy before replying: 'You're spoken of as a good man, Doctor Syn, but I venture to think that you have not been so closely connected with crime all your life as I have.' With this the Vicar agreed. 'Possibly not, Mr. Hyde. Possibly not.

Possibly you could teach me a very great deal about crime.' Then seeming suddenly to change his mind, he suggested that perhaps they should work together after all, adding with timid eagerness: 'Do you really think we could catch this, er—rascally Scarecrow?' This was the attitude that Mr. Hyde understood, and he replied bluffly:

'All in good time, Parson, all in good time. Glad to see you've changed your mind, though if all goes well tonight, I may not need your help, for Major Faunce and his Dragoons are already combing the Marshes beyond Dungeness.' Doctor Syn seemed most interested, and the Revenue man, flattering himself that he had subdued the parson, and was on the way to getting what he wanted, continued aggressively: 'That infernal Scarecrow had the audacity to send me a note with details of tonight's man-hunt—but I'll fox the rascal. I have a special troop well hidden in Wraight's Building Yard.' The Vicar stared at him with astonished simplicity, and in a voice filled with admiration, said: 'Dear me, Mr. Hyde, dear me. I fail to see how this rogue can ever hope to pit his wits against yours—remarkable foresight on your part. The Building Yard? Now whoever would have thought of the Building Yard? Indeed, you have quite convinced me, I cannot go wrong if I listen to you.' Mr. Hyde was delighted and so full of self-satisfaction that he could hardly speak, and so Doctor Syn continued: 'But should you not succeed tonight, do not fail to tell me how you next intend to trap him, and let us see if my poor brain can add anything to that.' The Revenue man, seeing his object in sight, felt he could afford to be a little condescending, so he thanked the parson, adding: 'They say two heads are better than one.' Instantly the Vicar replied: 'Dear me, do they? I find mine quite satisfactory. I should not like to lose it. It is as valuable to me as I should imagine the Scarecrow's is to him.'

Mr. Hyde chuckled in confident anticipation. 'His won't be worth much by the time we've finished with him, eh, Master Parson?' His object achieved, and by now thoroughly convinced that his first impressions of this old clergyman were wrong, and that he was, after all, just as simple as the rest of his class, he rose and said that he had better be about his business, for although he would not get much rest this night, there was no reason why he should keep Doctor Syn from his.

Doctor Syn, on his part, remarking that he was loth to see such an entertaining visitor depart, escorted him personally to the door, where the Revenue man bowed, saying: 'Thank you for your hospitality, Reverend Sir, and good night.' Doctor Syn returned his bow with a cheery 'Good night, Mr. Hyde, and thank you. Your confidence is flattering—and most enlightening.' But had Mr. Hyde known just how enlightening his confidence had been he would not, upon leaving the Vicarage, have been quite so pleased with himself.

Chapter 10. With the Scarecrow's Compliments

Doctor Syn closed the front door and chuckled at the assurance of the Revenue man, and after reflecting how completely his play-acting had succeeded, the chuckle grew into a laugh, and when he thought that had Mr. Sheridan seen his performance he would certainly have recommended him as a comedian, his laughter grew the louder. Indeed, he was laughing so hilariously that he did not notice that Mipps had returned and was standing beside him.

The Sexton's tone was plaintive. 'You might, at least, tell me the joke. I don't see nothin' to laugh at. Least, not at a Revenue man. Funny—never liked 'em. Never saw nothin' funny in 'em, neither. And if he ain't goin' to get no rest, he ain't goin' to keep awake doin' nothin' funny under our windows.' And with this philosophical resolve Mr. Mipps went briskly to the curtains and pulled them close with an extra tug or two to show his indignation. By this time Doctor Syn's laughter had dwindled back into chuckles.

'Oh well, p'raps it was Wraight's Building Yard you was laughin' at,' pleaded Mipps, trying to get some sort of response from his master. This had the desired effect, for the Vicar raised a questioning eyebrow. Mr. Mipps knew what it asked and proceeded to explain. 'Oh, begging you pardon but anticipatin' nothin' humorous knowin' what Revenue men are, me ear didn't seem to want to get away from the key'ole. 'Mr. Mipps,' it said to me, quite jealous-like, 'you're always thinkin' of your weather eye, now pay a little attention to your weather ear.' I couldn't get it off, sir. Got paid itself out. It was burnin' fiery 'ot at the things he said about the Squire, and it positively blushed when you got on to them piebald sheep.' 'Then your sensitive ear has saved me the trouble of repeating it,' said the Vicar quietly, and then dropping his voice still lower, spoke quickly and urgently: 'You know the plans for tonight, but warn the men to keep clear of Wraight's Yard. Put sentries round to report any movement of the Dragoons.

Tell Vulture and Eagle to be in the Dry Dyke under the sea-wall in a quarter of an hour. And now we know which way the cat is likely to jump, tell Jimmie Bone when he returns as the Scarecrow from the false run to ride out again and see that the remaining Dragoons upon the Marsh are well and truly lost. I shall not need him as the Scarecrow tonight for the 'run proper'. I must do that myself. There will be too many decisions to be taken on the spur.

That's all, I think. The horses were all listed. Ah, yes. That reminds me. The Squire's stable. The horse called Stardust. See no one touches it.' It was now Mipps's turn to look quizzical. 'Oh! In case someone wants to ride it tomorrow?' 'Yes, Mr. Mipps,' replied the Vicar. 'In case someone wants to ride it tomorrow.' 'I see.' The only thing Mr. Mipps really did see at the moment was that he was thirsty, and knowing that their thirsts were usually simultaneous, he asked the Vicar hopefully if there was anything he wanted, adding as an extra hint that laughing was thirsty work. But this time, however, their thirsts did not coincide—for Mipps had certainly no taste for what the Vicar wanted.

'Water?' Mr. Mipps could hardly believe his ears.

'Yes, Mr. Mipps. Water. I asked you to fetch me a ewer of water.'

'Oh, water.' His tone conveyed that he had never heard of it, and although he went upstairs to find some, he continued to mutter question and answers during his search. "Water?' I says. 'Yes, Mr. Mipps. Water', he says. 'Water?' says I. 'I asked you to fetch me a ewer of water." Mr. Mipps shuddered. 'Ernful stuff.' He was extremely glad that he had had the foresight to refill his flask with brandy. He felt in his pocket for comfort, then remembered that he had left it in the kitchen, so with a fervent hope that Mrs.

Honeyballs hadn't been at it, he decided that the only thing to do in this emergency was to go and find out if she had. By this time he had forgotten what he was looking for, so having wandered aimlessly into the Vicar's bedroom—wondering why he was upstairs and not downstairs, he looked wildly about him for assistance. 'Come up for something,' he muttered.

'Come up for wot? I dunno—brandy?' No. No. Downstairs—hope she hasn't been at it—. Now what am I 'ere for?' He had asked himself this question several times before his weather eye decided to befriend him. It came to rest upon the Vicar's washstand, where, reposing innocently in its basin, was the object of his mutual stress. Water. So before it could elude him again he seized it and hurried downstairs, with a twofold prayer that it would not finish the Vicar, and that Mrs. Honeyballs hadn't finished his brandy.

The first part of his prayer was answered when, upon handing over the bedroom ewer, Doctor Syn did not drink it. Instead, after a polite, 'Thank you, Mr. Mipps, I began to fear that perhaps my well had run dry,' he did a stranger thing. Lifting a corner of the heavy cloth that covered the refectory table, he threw the ernful contents under it. Upon the instant, Mipps understood. With a long-drawn sigh of relief he said to the Vicar: 'You did give me a fright, sir. I thought you wanted water. Silly of me. I see. Better go.

Your well ain't dry, but mine is. Least, I 'ope it ain't.' And hurrying off, he discovered that Bacchus was on his side and that the second part of his prayer had been fulfilled. Mrs. Honeyballs's weather eye had let her down.

From beneath the refectory table came the protests of a disturbed sleeper. Oaths, yawns and splutterings, and in a short while there appeared the rubicund face of the Squire, his bald head bereft of wig and folds of the tablecloth draped about him like a toga. Doctor Syn regarded him with affectionate amusement. 'Not Caesar's wife, Tony. Egad, you're more like Nero himself.' Not having heard him mixing his metaphors to the Revenue man, Sir Antony did not appreciate the allusion. Instead, he expressed his customary surprise at finding himself in this position and began as usual to find the reason, before exerting himself to get up. With the assurance of one who has just discovered a great truth, he announced: 'D'you know, I have an idea. The second bin is stronger than the first.' The excuse found and not contradicted, he crawled back under the table, found his wig and reappeared again with:

'What's the time?' 'You've had your usual hour's nap, Tony,' said Doctor Syn.

Again this appeared to surprise Sir Tony. 'The devil I have. Did I snore? D'you know I had a most remarkable dream. Dreamt I was at one of her ladyship's putting parties—on the lawn. I was partnering the Bishop's wife and she kept fouling my ball. So I tu-quo-qued her and she turned into the Scarecrow, and I found I'd got no clothes on. Damned silly when you come to think of it.' 'Well, Tony,' replied the Vicar, still regarding him with amusement, 'while you were—er, partnering the Bishop's wife, the new Revenue man paid me a social call.' 'The devil he did,' said Sir Antony, putting on his wig and slowly getting to his feet. 'Thought I heard voices. Thought it was Lady Cobtree agitatin' me to put me breeches on.' Then the full truth of what Christopher had said dawned upon him.

'What?' he shouted. 'Revenue Officer at this time of night? What did he want? Why didn't he come to me? New man, eh? Doesn't know the ropes.

Should have come to me. Suppose he thinks I can't keep order. Suppose he was criticizing my jurisdiction. Damned unfair. Mean advantage. Me, standin' there shiverin' with nothin' on.' His dream had evidently been so vivid that he was still in it, and Doctor Syn, knowing of old that his friend was like to become quarrelsome if not placated, said in all sincerity: 'Now really, Tony; you should have heard the things he said about you.' The Squire was mollified, having taken this to mean that the Revenue man had paid him compliments, which was indeed Doctor Syn's intent; and so, after saying that no doubt the Revenue man was a damned decent fellow, he sat down comfortably in the chair from which he had so ignominiously fallen, and good-naturedly resumed the conversation with: 'What was I sayin' when I slid off?' Doctor Syn explained that his last words before disappearing under the table had been to ask for another drink. The Squire received this news with as much interest as though he had delivered a pearl of wisdom, adding that he might as well have it now. Then in an attempt to pick up the threads of their interrupted discussion, said that as far as he could recollect, he was being annoyed about something.

'Now what was I being annoyed about?' he asked himself. Again, the bruises of the morning reminded him of his misfortunes, and after a lengthy grumble, in which there figured prominently the faulty bell-pull, the remains of Gabriel Creach, her ladyship's bad temper, the waste of a good day's sport, that confounded doormat bitin' his toe; and then making that ridiculous offer of a thousand guineas for the Scarecrow who won't be caught, this gave him another hint and he remembered what he was being annoyed about, and said triumphantly: 'I know. Those fumblin' old Lords of the Level askin' the Dragoons to come and catch our Scarecrow. Read it in the papers. Lots of elephants tryin' to catch an eel. Damned silly. Know perfectly well, no smugglin' in this part of the country.' Even that did not satisfy him as being the real cause; so he started again: 'No, what was I bein' annoyed about?' Another ray of hope: 'Oh, I know. That confounded highwayman, stoppin' the Dover coach with me wife's Aunt Agatha. Must have been Gentleman James because of his good manners. Damned bad manners, I call it, takin' the diamonds old girl plannin' to leave Cicely.' Cicely. At last he had found the real cause of his annoyance, as is often the case, the chief worry having been obliterated by the trifling ones, and his voice now took on a sincerely worried tone. 'That's what I was annoyed about, Christopher—Cicely and Maria.

Bad enough to have a daughter in France; all those upstarts cuttin' people's heads off all over the place—then Cicely goin' off and not sayin' where she was goin'. Said she was goin' off to stay with the Pemburys, but she didn't go there. And just when I want you most you go off preachin' in London, and only return yesterday. No, I'm worried, Christopher.' Doctor Syn urged that there was really no cause for anxiety, pointing out that Cicely was well able to take care of herself; that she had probably changed her mind about the Pemburys and had gone to stay with other friends; that probably she had written, but that the mails were unreliable.

The Squire, always influenced by what Christopher said, was only too eager to be cheered up, and so saying that Christopher was probably right, he asked for a drink.

Thinking that his old friend had already drunk more than was good for him, Doctor Syn said he was extremely sorry but that he couldn't oblige, adding apologetically: 'We made rather a night of it, you know. Even my small cellar will need replenishing.' The Squire was most upset at this and asked him why the devil he had not said so before. 'Here we've been sittin' about, talkin' and shiverin'

'All his old grievances came back with a rush and he sneezed violently, announcing, as though it were a Christopher's fault: 'There, I knew I'd catch a cold on that lawn.' There was only one thing for it. They must go home and open another bin. And in order to carry out this excellent idea he went with all possible haste to the front door, and, flinging it open, found that his way was impeded, for there on the doorstep were two large casks. Annoyed at not being able to get out, but equally mystified as to why such things should be outside the door instead of in their proper place, he reminded Christopher that he had said there was nothing in his cellar.

Doctor Syn remarked that there was nothing in his cellar but there certainly seemed to be something on his doorstep, which gave the Squire a brilliant idea.

'I say, Christopher,' he whispered. 'P'raps they've left them. You know who I mean. They.' Then, not liking to admit to the possibility of their existence, he mouthed the word 'Smugglers'.

An even better thought then struck him. 'Come on, Christopher. Let's bring 'em in.' Doctor Syn, however, seemed doubtful, suggesting that this was a matter for the Revenue man, at which Sir Antony was highly indignant, saying that he didn't like the Revenue man anyway, and that he would handle this himself, and that it was a very good thing, since they could have a drink now, and wouldn't have to wait till they got home.

So, telling Doctor Syn in his best judicial manner to report this to him in the morning, he set to work pushing and pulling at one of the barrels, speculating the while as to its contents.

'Hope it's not rum,' he grunted; 'don't like rum. Her Ladyship can always tell.' After a deal of struggling, in which Mr. Mipps had been summoned to assist, both barrels were successfully man£uvred into the room, and at the Squire's orders the door was closed to prevent anyone 'pryin' in while he was investigatin'!' Heated from his exertions, he could hardly wait to tap the barrels, and Mr. Mipps having conveniently produced a spigot with the necessary implements, he was delightedly setting to work when he noticed some roughly chalked writing on the side of the casks.

'Hallo, who's been chalkin' on our barrels?' he cried.

'Looks as if they are your barrels, sir,' said Mr. Mipps, who was on his hands and knees peering at the writing. 'This one says 'For our Parson with C.O.M.P.S. from Scarecrow'. What does this one say?' Mr. Mipps crawled round to the other. "For our S.Q.U.I.R.T.' Squirt? 'Ope that don't mean you, sir.'

Preferring to receive the insult with the barrel rather than without it, the Squire replied indignantly that of course it meant him. 'Bad spellin'—that's all,' and added that it was a waste of time standing about spelling when they might be drinking, and that for his part he was going to open his right away.' At that moment there was a loud knocking on the door while from outside came what were obviously noises of the military. 'Confound it, Christopher,' grumbled the Squire, his thirst thwarted, 'why can't you have your callers at the proper time?'

Mr. Mipps, already at the spy-hole, whispered dramatically: 'It's the Dragoons, sir.' Sir Antony, fearing that the Law might cheat him of his drink, asked Mr. Mipps to tell them to go away. 'Never asked 'em here. Tell 'em to go home.' This seemed easy enough till the full horror of the situation dawned upon him. Here he was, the Chief Magistrate, receiving smuggled goods.

'Damned embarrasin'

'I think we had better find out what they want, Tony,' said Doctor Syn calmly. 'The door, Mr. Mipps.' Sir Antony, nearly crying with vexation, endeavoured to disguise his own barrel by draping himself round it, then finding that he was still holding the spigot, he endeavoured to hide such incriminating evidence, trying first one pocket, then another, and finally sticking it up his waistcoat, where it bulged most uncomfortably. By this time the door was open and Major Faunce and his Sergeant had come in.

'I beg your pardon, sir,' said the Major, addressing Doctor Syn, 'but I was told I should find Mr. Hyde at your house.' Doctor Syn greeted the soldier pleasantly and told him that Mr. Hyde had been gone for some little time. Then seeing that both the soldiers were caked in mud, he asked innocently if they had been fighting. To which the Major replied that 'paddling' would be a better description. He sounded and looked most aggrieved, explaining that they had been up to their necks in mud; in and out dykes halfway round Kent, and that he was positive monkey business had been going on with the signposts; that he had lost his men all but two, in this confounded mist, and hadn't seen a sign of any smuggling; and it was all the fault of that meddling fool of a Revenue man sending them off on a wild-goose chase. He then apologized for his outburst, adding that that was why he wanted a few words with Nicholas Hyde.

Doctor Syn was most sympathetic, and remarking that the Major certainly seemed to have had a trying evening, asked him if he would care for a drink, while the Squire, who had been endeavouring, behind the Major's back, to hide both himself and his barrel beneath the window curtain, and indeed had nearly succeeded, inwardly cursed Christopher for a forgetful fool, and made frantic signals in protest.

'Thank 'ee, Parson,' returned the Major, cheering up at the prospect of good drinking in pleasant company. 'Very civil of you.' 'You look as if you could do with something stronger than Marsh water, eh, Sergeant?' laughed the Vicar.

Major Faunce, thus relaxed, took a glance round the room, and perceiving the Squire in the shadow by the bow window, advanced to greet him, catching sight of the barrels as he went.

'Good evening, Squire,' he said, bowing formally, to which the Squire could not respond owing to the stiffness of his waistcoat. Perhaps it was the Squire's embarrassment which prompted Major Faunce to give closer inspection to the barrels, and upon reading the chalked inscriptions he became grave.

'So, gentlemen, I see that you have had other visitors here tonight besides Mr. Hyde and ourselves, and we sent off to the other side of the country—misled on purpose, I see. Nice little plot.' He warmed to the subject as he recollected the discomfort to which the Revenue man's stupidity had put them. But on second thought, was it stupidity? Duplicity might be the better word. Possibly Mr. Hyde was not averse to a noggin of smuggled brandy and a bag of guineas as a bribe, and he'd be in good company, too.

Perhaps they were all in it, against him. So he said aloud: 'I'm afraid this looks mighty suspicious, Parson.' The Squire seemed a trifle over-anxious to explain, and as always when he tried to use his best official tone, he became involved and ended up lamely that he was going out when the barrels bumped into him and he couldn't leave 'em there doin' nothin'.

This time, however, Doctor Syn helped him out and tried to straighten the matter, saying: 'I assure you, Major Faunce, we know nothing about it.

We have had a quiet evening here discussing parochial affairs, and as the Squire has just told you, we found them in the doorway. Naturally, as Lord of the Level, he wished to make an investigation at once, and ù' 'Much to your surprise you discover they are addressed to you!' interrupted the Major.

Doctor Syn replied that that was exactly what he was about to say, adding: 'So you see, Major, we are jsut as much in the dark about it as you are.' But the soldier, by now thoroughly suspicious, pursued the subject still further. 'But you didn't intend to remain in the dark as to what was in 'em, eh?' At this the Squire lost patience and exploded: 'Well, dammit, man, what did you expect us to do—stand and look at 'em? It's got my name on it.

Read it yourself. A gift's a gift. That's Law.' 'A bribe more like, and that's not Law,' parried the Major.

After so many years together in wild adventure, there had sprung up between Mipps and his master a system of signalling that had become almost thought-reading. During the above altercation this had been put into silent action, which resulted in the most innocent-seeming interruption from Mr.

Mipps: 'Beggin' your pardon, sirs, for interruptin', but the Vicar asked me to remind him about Mrs. Wooley's complaint.' The Vicar thanked Mr. Mipps warmly, as indeed he had forgotten all about it. He begged the gentlemen to excuse him, but he must ride out and give the old woman a few words of cheer and keep her in good spirits.

'Then,' said Major Faunce, intending not to lose sight of any possible clue, 'you'll not object to my sending a couple of my men with you, to see that her taste in spirits is not barrels of smuggled brandy?' Doctor Syn replied almost gratefully: 'Not at all, Major Faunce. On the contrary, I enjoy company on a long ride, and no doubt the poor old body will give them a glass of her parsnip wine for their trouble.' Mr. Mipps helped him on with his long coat, and the Vicar thanked him, adding an extra benediction on his good servant for reminding him of his duties. Then turning to the Major he requested: 'Pray, Major Faunce, do not fail to let me know what spirit those barrels contain. I must preach a very strong sermon against it next Sunday,' and with the pleasantest of smiles he went out to mount his fat white pony, whilst the Sergeant gave instructions to the two troopers that Doctor Syn was to be escorted across the Marsh and watched, adding that in his opinion the Major had gone a bit too far, being suspicious of a poor old gentleman what was only doing his duty.

Indeed, the Major was at that moment thinking the same thing himself and feeling a trifle ashamed for having entertained the slightest suspicions about such a good and kindly soul as the Vicar of Dymchurch. If, however, he too had been able to read thoughts, he might have taken even stronger measures.

Chapter 11. More Compliments from the Scarecrow

Sir Antony was peeved. It was deucedly embarrassin' bein' left alone with this Faunce. It wasn't like Christopher to let a fellow down, and he felt he had been left in the lurch. Indeed, the whole thing was Christopher's fault, and it wasn't like him to make mistakes. Why had he insisted on letting the fellows in? Easiest thing in the world to have sent them away. Could have told 'em the Revenue man wasn't there. Yes, he decided that he definitely did not like that Revenue man. And here he was alone with Faunce and didn't know what to say. The barrels were sittin' there lookin' at him. He'd got the devil of a thirst, and something was makin' Mipps grin. Righteous indignation made him breathe more heavily than usual, as he punctuated each thought with a snort. Thus it was that the spigot became loosened, and during a mighty intake of breath which of necessity moved the Squire's diaphragm, it fell with a clatter to the floor. Fortunately Major Faunce's back was turned so he was able to kick it beneath the settee. He was so pleased with this manœuvre that he did not even notice that he had done it with his bad toe, but upon the Major's turning round he decided that some explanation was due for the noise and the movement of his foot beneath the settee, and bethought himself of the Vicarage cat, knowing full well that it lived in the stables.

Making a series of jabbing movements with his foot as though inducing the playful animal to come out and chase his toe, he did some clicking noise with his tongue, and in the language usually employed when addressing cats he endeavoured to make his performance convincing. 'Nice Pussy, then. Turn along. Puss, puss, buss.' Once having embarked upon this course, he felt at a loss to know how to stop, and was about to go down on his hands and knees as further proof of its existence when Mipps came to his rescue by saying, in warning tones: 'I shouldn't, sir. She's ever so spiteful.' Straightening himself with a, 'P'raps you're right. N'other little family on the way?' he gave Mipps a look of deep gratitude. Mipps, from a position of vantage, returned this with a confidential wink and a, 'Yes. H'aint nature wonderful? D'you know, Squire, who I think it is this time? Mrs 'Oneyballs's black Tom. 'Orrid cat. Roguish.' The Squire, though grateful, felt that it really wasn't fair of Mipps to pin a family of kittens on to Mrs. Honeyballs's unsuspecting Tom.

Major Faunce wondered how he should next proceed, and, having discussed the matter in whispers with his Sergeant, had no mind to stay listening to kitten talk. He was extremely tired after two successive fruitless nights upon the Marsh, and in spite of the Squire's presence, he determined to take charge. So approaching the barrels he said: 'Well, Sir Antony, I suppose wwe had better get these over to the Court House and put in bond, and that will end my responsibility in the matter.' Mipps, however, had other ideas upon the subject, saying he didn't know how he was going to get 'em there, unless it were such good spirits as the barrels grew wings, and flew there. 'I'd give an 'and myself only what with my gravedigger's elbow I haven't got a lift left.' It was then that the Major realized that for once this odd little Sexton was talking sense, and he cursed himself for having sent his last two men with Doctor Syn, so he said to the Squire: 'Egad, sir, the fellow's right,' and not wishing to admit his mistake, tried to cover it up with: 'This is really the business of the Revenue man.' The Squire saw his chance and pounced. 'Well then, sir, let's dispense with the Revenue and open 'em here—out of hand. 'Twill not be agains the law. Magistrate. Witness.' He glowed with anticipation and thought it would serve Christopher right, too, for not being here to share. 'Test it together. I give us full authority.' Major Faunce agreed, saying that he didn't mind showing Mr. Hyde that he could do his job a deal better than Mr. Hyde could his, and ordered the Sergeant to assist Mr. Mipps in opening the barrels. But Mr. Mipps needed no assistance. Indeed, he was there already, attacking the Vicar's cask with the knowledge of an expert, when he suddenly stopped and said excitedly: 'Ere, where's the bung-'ole? 'Asn't go no bung-'ole. Something wrong with this barrel. Got a false top. 'Ope it ain't goin' to blow us sky 'igh.' Mr. Mipps was nearly blown sky-high, for as he spoke the top of the barrel flew off and a pistol was presented at his head, as over the rim of the cask the head and shoulders of a girl appeared, three-cornered hat slightly awry. Dazzled by the sudden light she commanded them in ringing tones to put up their hands.

'Haut les mains,' she cried. 'Vous-aussi. Les mains. Rendez vous tous.' The hands of all four men had shot up in bewilderment as they stared at this wild little figure, hair a mass of tumbled auburn curls, her lovely face alight with fierce excitement, which, in the next instant, and upon astonished cries from Squire and Sexton, changed to an expression of surprise and wonderment as, looking quickly round the room, she recognized it. 'Good Heavens!' she cried. ''Tis the Vicarage. And we are not in France. Oh, Mr.

Mipps, I thought you were a revolutionary rabble. Papa! Then we are safe. We are across the Channel. He did smuggle us, Papa. Don't look so scared. 'Tis Cicely.' The Squire, in his astonishment, had forgotten to drop his hands, and she continued, laughing gaily, 'Pray drop your hands, sir. 'Tis Cicely.' His fright and relief at seeing her turning to anger, he almost shouted, 'Dammit, girl, what does this mean? Lud, Cicely, what a fright you gave me. Thought you were going to stay with the Pemburys. What do you mean, miss, going off without a word? What do you mean, miss, causing such anxiety? Damme, I shall need an explanation—I'm your father. Popping out of a barrel like a jack-in-the-box. In the Devil's name where have you been, miss?' 'Pray don't be so cross, sir,' she answered. 'I can explain—I've been to France and I'm back.'

Sir Antony snorted. 'France—what do you mean, France? Have you seen Maria?' The girl's expression changed again to one of apologetic humour. 'Lud, Papa, I had almost forgotten Maria.' And then with a wave of her gauntleted hand to the other cask she said: 'She's in there—and when we let her out I warn you, sir, she'll start screaming again—but she's had a terrible time, poor lamb. Lud, I can't stand this barrel a minute longer. It smells like the Herring Hang. Dear Mr. Mipps, pray give me a hand.' Mipps, who had been gazing at her in admiration, leaped forward to help her, but seeing that the pistol was still unconsciously pointed in his direction suggested with a grin that he should hold the artillery. With riding-skirt held high she scrambled out, straightened the green velvet folds, and stretched luxuriously. 'Oh, it's wonderful to be home,' she cried. 'But I am as stiff as a dead starfish.'

Major Faunce was also gazing at her in admiration. His soldier's instinct told him that here was bravery. What manner of girl was this, who could talk so gaily of returning from an enemy country? He was curious to know what she had done and why. With approval he noted the determination in every line of her tall, almost boyish figure—her oval face was delicately cut, yet behind the large mischievous eyes there seemed to be a mysterious purpose. In spite of her youth, she had about her an air of authority. And with amusement he noticed how, impatient that the men were doing nothing except stare, she went swiftly, with easy graceful strides, to the other barrel and taking the command, ordered Mipps and the Sergeant to unfasten here and there, and to do this and that with: 'Come, sirs—make haste. She's been there long enough.'

Under her compelling personality, even the Sergeant came to life. Both he and Mr. Mipps acting as they would have done under a commanding officer, responded to her orders, and swiftly it was done.

The lid was off and as the Sergeant leaned over the rim to help the lady out, there came such piercing screams that he jumped back again, as a shrill little voice cried, 'Get away from me, you great French brute! Cicely! Cicely! Where are you, Cicely?' Sweeping the others aside, Cicely leant over the barrel and soothed:

'All right, Maria. I'm here. We're home. You can come out now.' But the screams continued, and indeed grew louder. 'Now, dearest Maria, don't be foolish,' calmed Cicely, and whispering to Mipps: 'You see, what did I tell you? She's been very vexing. Come out, my lamb,' she coaxed, leaning into the barrel. 'We're in the Vicarage and here's Papa.'

Up from the barrel leapt a distraught figure, a great travelling-cloak hiding the bedraggled finery of what had once been the height of Paris fashion. Her blonde hair, out of curl, hung limply round her tearstained face.

A woebegone little figure, who upon reaching the floor through the arms of Mr. Mipps, rushed sobbing to her father. 'Papa! Oh, Papa!' she cried. The Squire put his arms about her and made a clumsy attempt to calm her. His awkward pettings and the embarrassment that most Englishmen feel at a show of hysteria were charming and endearing. But all his efforts were

to no avail, as Maria let out the full force of pent-up self-pity.
Determined that others should share the horrors she had been
through, she plunged into lurid descriptions of how terrified she
had been, of how Jean, her husband, had left her in Paris all
alone in their great house, of how all those ugly people came
and frightened her, and then how Cicely came and she couldn't
understand why she looked ugly too. She had sung and shouted
and behaved in a horrid manner, and that dreadful man who
had kept ordering them about—of how he had been half naked
with a picture on his arm—a ghastly picture of a
shark—tattooed, like sailors have, and how they had never seen
his face because he wore a hideous mask, but that the crowd
seemed to know him and like him too, because they did what he
said and didn't touch them, and everywhere he went they
shouted, 'The Scarecrow! Vive L'pouvantail!' Seeing that she was
indeed holding the attention of her audience, she determined to
vent some of her bewildered anger upon her sister, telling of how
Cicely had actually appeared to enjoy it, and that the Scarecrow
had paid more attention to her, because he had left them and
made a special journey to get her riding-habit back, when she
said she would look funny going back to England disguised as
a French peasant. But she, poor Maria, had nothing but what
she stood up in. She had lost everything. Husband, house, and
all her pretty clothes. This made her cry so much that she could
speak no more.

The Squire was quite desperate, with repeated, 'There,
there. No one's going to hurt you. Your father's here.' He
implored Cicely in God's name to tell him what had happened,
and what did she mean by all this wild talk.

Major Faunce, who up to now had kept silent, now came
forward with a somewhat sinister question: 'Yes, indeed. What
does she mean? I shall be glad to hear an explanation.' The
Squire, who had forgotten all about the Major in this confusion,
did not catch the tone of suspicion in the soldier's voice, so he
introduced his daughters, and looked appealingly at Cicely to
help him out, which she did with, 'Pray, sir, forgive our
unladylike arrival at this evening party.' Then, turning to her
father, she said in a whisper loud enough for Major Faunce to
hear, 'Papa, pay no attention to Maria—I told you she was
hysterical, poor pet.' Then once again, but this time looking

round the room, she changed the subject. 'But where is your host? Where is our beloved Doctor Syn?'

The Major was quick with his reply. 'He was called out to visit a sick woman. But I am afraid this is not an evening party, Miss Cicely. I am here on business. The only invitation we have had tonight is from the scoundrel whom your sister has just been talking about. In the King's name, I must ask you to tell me more about this French Scarecrow.' The Squire indignantly retorted to this: 'Nonsense, Major Faunce. I'll not have my daughters questioned at this hour, and after all they have gone through.' Then added as if he had just thought of it: 'Now, Cicely, child, tell your father all about it.' Cicely went over to her father, and upon seeing that the dear soul was wearing the expression of a bewildered bloodhound, kissed him and asked to be forgiven for having caused him so much anxiety. But she explained: 'You recollect how anxious we all were about Maria. I did not tell you I had planned to go and help her, for I knew you would not let me go. Oh, 'twas easy enough to get there. Bribes and a fishing-smack. And 'twas easy enough to get to Paris. All I had to do was to make myself the complete sansculotte and shout and scream with the mob. It was nothing. I know the language.

Thanks to you, Papa. And as you know, I had friends there, though now heaven knows what has happened to some of them. As to the man Maria talks about, well, there were so many wild characters I fear she must be confused.

Indeed, poor goose, she scarcely recognized me. There she was, cowering all alone in that great house. Hadn't been out for days, all the servants fled.' This awakened in Maria fresh memories of the departed glory of her married life, and she let out a howl of anguish. 'All right, Maria my lamb, 'tis over now,' said Cicely, who continued to talk with her father. 'It is a terrible thing they are doing, Papa. We were forced to witness ghastly scenes. And all the time the mob was getting nearer to Maria's home. We would have been in more danger had we stayed.'

All this was too much for the Squire. He just did not begin to understand what Cicely had been doing. Any more than he had understood why Maria had gone and married a Frenchman. All he could stammer out was: 'It's deuced confusin'. Two girls—alone. Someone must have helped you. Was it this French

Scarecrow?' Major Faunce cut in with: 'Sounds more like our English Scarecrow to me. There's his signature on the barrels.' Cicely replied to this with spirit that since he had not been in France, how could he know anything about it? 'Everyone in Paris these days looks like a scarecrow. They've all gone mad—wild. Scarecrow! L'pouvantail! they all shout. But it might mean anyone. They might have meant me, for a looked scarecrow enough.'

'They did not mean you, Miss Cicely!' The voice came from the dark shadows by the front door. Harsh, impersonal, yet with a hint of humour, as it continued: 'Your revolutionary clothes suited you admirably.' All had turned suddenly upon the sound, and there was no mistaking who it was. There he stood, masked and mysterious, the dreaded Scarecrow himself—with two thousand guineas for his capture. No one could move, for he held two heavy pistols in his hands, and bowing said: 'L'pouvantail, at your service.' This movement caused Major Faunce's hand to fly to his belt, but the harsh voice rapped out: 'Don't move! I have you covered, gentlemen.' And thereupon, seeing Mr. Mipps, who indeed appeared to be terrified, he ordered him to disarm the red-coats. 'A wise precaution,' laughed the Scarecrow, 'since I see the Major's fingers twitching to be at his belt. It would be foolish to disobey, and we don't want to rob the Revenue man of the little surprise I have prepared for him. I must ask you, gentlemen, to oblige me by stepping into those barrels.' Mr. Mipps had rapidly removed both swords and pistols from the soldiers, and at the moment resembled a miniature arsenal.

The Scarecrow spoke to him, ordering: 'Here, you, little man. Assist the gallant red-coats into those convenient casks.' A brave man, the Major's first instinct was to refuse, but the Scarecrow went on inexorably: 'Come, come, Major, if the ladies can use these to travel across the Channel, surely you will not mind a little trip along the sea-wall.

Why, I envy you the experience of seeing Mr. Hyde's face when he opens them. I dislike being kept waiting, Major. Make haste!' There was nothing for it. The reluctant soldiers had to squeeze themselves into the barrels as best they could. Mr. Mipps having put down all the weapons save one, almost seemed to be enjoying prodding the Major in with his own sword, as with oaths and protests they disappeared, as Mr.

Mipps, putting on the specially constructed lids, encouraged them to stay snug and have a nice trip.

The Scarecrow went swiftly to the door and opened it, calling three times the eerie cry of the curlew, and from the shadows came four masked and hooded figures. Upon swift orders from the Scarecrow they went to the barrels, waiting whilst he changed the wording on each, so that the chalked message now ran:

To Nick Hyde, Rev. Man, With Comps. From Scarecrow.

Then, lifting the barrels, they carried them to a covered cart that waited on the sea-wall. When all was ready to move, the Nightriders mounted their wild steeds and escorted the strange cargo swiftly and silently along the straight coast track to Sandgate.

Chapter 12. In which Cicely Forgets Her Gloves and Doctor
Syn Forgets to

Remember Maria sat sulking—a forlorn heap—on the settle
by the fire. She was tired and dispirited, with a head that
throbbed from her cramped voyage. She was no longer the
centre of interest and she resented it.

Here she was, home and safe after her terrible experiences,
only to find that the ghastly creature had followed them here.
She couldn't understand it. And what was more, Papa seemed
to be amused, for there he was at the window laughing and
watching the Scarecrow giving his dreadful orders. Maria felt
that he should be paying more attention to his miserable
daughter. As for Cicely—there she was looking as fresh as
though she had just left her own bedroom at the Court House to
go a-riding. Sitting astride the long, low firestool, in the most
unladylike manner, she too seemed to be thoroughly enjoying it,
looking up to the window and laughing. Maria could not laugh
when she thought of that poor Major, and was annoyed because
she would have liked to have seen more of him. He was really
quite attractive; she wished she had not looked so dreadful. This
thought plunged her into tears again, and it was then that the
Scarecrow returned, closing the door, and sweeping them with
a low bow.

'I must apologize, ladies, for my somewhat crude sense of
humour,' he said, 'but I fear I could not resist playing the eel to
those elephants. You need your papers, of course, Sir Antony.'

The Squire looked surprised. Now where had he heard
those words before? He tried to remember, but his mental efforts
were interrupted by the Scarecrow saying: 'May I express my
gratitude, Miss Cicely, for your admirable attempt to keep my
identity a secret?' Cicely got up from the stool and went over to
him boldly. Maria thought she went too close, and turned her
head away disgusted.

'It was the least I could do, sir,' said Cicely in a warm tone.
'And I might have succeeded had not this goose here blabbed
all.' She turned and entreated: 'Papa, Maria, have you no word

to say?' Maria buried her head in a cushion. 'I don't want to speak to him.

Papa, tell him to go away.' And then, hoping for sympathy: 'Oh, my poor head! 'Twas terrible, the discomfort.' This did not produce the desired effect upon Cicely, who, with a show of spirit at her sister's ill manners, said with some impatience: 'Fiddlesticks, Maria. The discomfort of a few hours is better than losing your head. Lud, miss, pretty though it is, 'tis sometimes foolish enough.' The Squire, agreeing with Cicely that Maria should at least thank the gentleman, said that although he could not yet understand what had happened or what had not happened, he was naturally indebted to the Scarecrow for what he had done, but, damme, he was placed in such an awkward position.

As Magistrate he ought to arrest him, at which the Scarecrow, bowing low, asked him if he would care to try.

Sir Antony, knowing that he had not a chance of doing so, blustered to hide his confusion and said that it would be a poor sort of gratitude. 'And you, sir, know that, or you would not risk being here. But what I want to know is'—and Sir Antony came to the point—'law-breaker as you are, what made you do it?'

'Call it a whim if you like, sir,' answered the strange creature, and he turned slightly towards Cicely, 'though I am more pleased to call it my admiration for high courage. You have a daughter, Sir Antony, you could be proud to call son. Ask me how I knew of her brave venture? I have spies everywhere. Oh, call me what you will—rogue, scoundrel, rascal—aye, Sir Antony, even 'smuggler', but I have ever been in love with the gallant spirit of the Marsh.' The Squire was beginning to understand. Cicely had done a brave thing. Indeed, she had done a generous thing too, for Maria had never been overkind to her. He warmed to his daughter, and he wished after all she had come and told him what she was going to do, though he knew in his heart of hearts that, being the clumsy fool he was, he would not have been able to help her. He warmed, too, towards this curious mystery of a man before him. He wished to ask him a lot of things, but all that came out was stammered in the usual tongue-tied fashion, that as Lord of the Level he appreciated his sentiments and admired his debt, and damme, admired his ingenuity, but it must have failed him lamentably this time if all he could think of was to send his daughters home to him in barrels. 'Why the devil did you have to do that, sir?' The Scarecrow laughingly explained, 'Because, my dear sir, and I fear you know this is true, the one thing that always crosses the Channel safely is my contraband.' Cicely went to her father and, putting her arm through his, told him not to worry about how they had travelled, since the important thing was that they were safe, and they had been in great danger. She pointed out to him that though it had been easy to get there for her, it was a different matter when they had tried to leave, because Maria was escaping and she was an aristo.

'Oh, I know what you are thinking, Papa,' she said. 'Damme, sir, they would not dare to touch a Cobtree.' Here she did such a perfect imitation of Sir Antony himself that even he had to laugh. But she went on seriously, explaining that they would most certainly have dared, that being a Cobtree only heightened the danger since she was an English aristocrat. Being that, of course, the teasing girl had refused point blank to disguise herself as she did in dirty rags, insisting on wearing her latest gown. Indeed they had been followed several times, and on one occasion had been recognized by a dangerous friend of Maria's treacherous husband. They would have been denounced had it not been for their good friend here. This gentleman had seen to everything. Each time they were in difficulties he appeared. Their papers—the horses—the right word at the Barriers. Oh, she realized now that she could not have done it alone. Going to the Scarecrow, Cicely held out her hands. 'How best can I thank you, sir?' she asked. 'It seems by imploring you to leave; each moment you remain is but adding to your danger.'

At last Sir Antony realized just how much this man had done for his daughters and the danger into which he had placed himself, and he said impulsively: 'Ay, Cicely, you're right. The place is littered with Dragoons, and I warrant that confounded Revenue man will not be in a pretty mood when he's received your present. As my daughter says—the best way to thank you is to ask you to go. So go, sir, and good luck to you, and mind you don't get caught or I shall lose my thousand guineas.' Then pulling himself together—remembering that after all he was the Chief Magistrate, he added:

'Though, mind you, tomorrow I shall have to put out another Proclamation for your arrest.' The Scarecrow thanked him for his warning and said he would study the new Proclamation carefully—for his own neck told him that he had no wish to see Sir Antony lose his thousand guineas.

'As to my leaving upon the minute—that I cannot, for I must stay here until the Vicar returns. I have to pay him my tithes. Tonight it will be a considerable sum, since my latest cargo was such a valuable one.' The last remark was directed to Cicely.

Then, addressing the Squire, he suggested that the ladies must be in need of rest and it would be as well if he escorted them home.

Cicely had been watching him for some time, and with a curious little smile she asked: 'Could I not stay? Above all things I should like to see a meeting between the Scarecrow and our Doctor Syn.' 'I'm afraid I must disappoint you, Miss Cicely,' he replied, 'for this is business. Tithes are a tenth of what one is worth, so if you are good at reckoning you might too easily calculate my estimation of your value.' The Squire, pleased to get back on familiar ground, said that tithes were tithes and all honest men should pay 'em; then realizing that he had said the wrong thing, coughed loudly and prepared to take his leave, waking Maria who was asleep upon the settle.

Bowing with a 'Your servant, sir,' he led the sleepy Maria to the door while Cicely, lingering behind, said with a look of amusement which failed to hide the alert expression in her eyes: 'I am almost certainly going to ask our dear old Doctor Syn to stop preaching his horrid sermons against you.' Then, turning swiftly, she followed the others and he was left alone.

Cicely crossed the bridge that led from the front door on to the seawall. She saw that her father was taking the short cut down the steps and across the Glebe Field. In her present mood she had no mind for more questionings. Nor, indeed, to be whined at by Maria. So she made no haste to catch them up. Standing for a while in the moonlight, she felt almost sad to be at home again though her instinct told her that she should feel differently, because what had made her happy in France was also here in Dymchurch. Her discovery filled her with an exultation she hardly understood. Turning, with her back to the sea, she faced the dark, familiar outline of the Vicarage, standing clear before the ragged silhouette of the rookery, while, brooding over all, the Beacon Knoll of Aldington. This shadowed sky-line seemed to come to life and claim her, as though at this moment it saw her for the first time, and beckoned to her.

And then she knew that she could find the answer to the riddle that it set, just as she knew that now she must follow where that answer led. So, challenging the shadows, she flung her gauntlet gloves down into the Vicarage garden. Then going swiftly down the sea-wall she raced across the Glebe and overtook the others.

'So here you are, Miss,' said the Squire. 'Maria wanted to get home, and I knew if you could find your way to France and back you'd be abel to make the Court House from the Vicarage.'

'I'm sorry, Papa,' answered Cicely. ''Tis such a lovely night, and it's so good to be home. I was on the sea-wall.' It was when they were going through the Lych Gate that Cicely stopped. 'Oh Lud, I do declare I must have lost my gloves. Now where did I drop them? I'll run back and look, for they were such a lovely pair. I may have left them in the Vicarage. So you two dears go on. Do not wait for me.' And so saying, she sped back again.

While Cicely was crossing the Glebe field for the second time, Mr.

Mipps in his capacity of Parish Clerk was crossing the hall of the Vicarage with an enormous tome, marked Dymchurch Tithes. 'The Tithe Book, sir, for your settlement with the Vicar.' He spoke apparently into thin air for the room seemed to be empty. As he walked he elongated himself as if trying to make himself taller.

'You seem to have acquired a stiff neck, Mr. Mipps.' The voice came from behind the lectern. ''Tis not the Marsh ague, I hope? Or has your blushing ear been getting you into trouble again?' Mister Mipps was all indignant, and snapped: ''Tain't nothin' to do with my inflamed ear, and I hain't hacquired a stiff neck neither. I'm hendeavouring to hacquire a few hinches, halludin' to me as if I was a dwarf.

'Little man.' In front of others, too.' He put the book down on the side of the lectern nearest to him with a slam, and in his own phraseology he 'beanstalked' acros the room to get ink and quill.

Mr. Mipps was so busy with his lack of inches that he did not notice that the front door had opened quietly and around it peeped the face of Cicely.

The voice from behind the lectern continued: 'You ability for acquiring knowledge of current affairs, Mr. Mipps, would make me respect you were you a giant.' This was too much for Mr. Mipps and he retorted quickly:

'And your ability for making yourself laugh may get us all in a trouble, and I weren't at no key'ole when I 'eard that. Miss Cicely called her a goose, but I can think of a adjective; in front of them Dragoons too. Now look 'ere, Cap'n, if you persists in rollin' up your sleeve, we're sunk.' It was then that Cicely decided to knock upon the door, causing Mr.

Mipps to turn round as if he had been shot. Upon seeing her he relaxed, and when she beckoned to him he went quickly towards her.

'Mr. Mipps,' she whispered, 'has Mr. Scarecrow gone?' He was delighted to see her. He grinned. 'Yes, miss,' he nodded assuredly. But was this the right answer? He hadn't looked behind the lectern. Was it Doctor Syn or the Scarecrow? He decided on a middle course. 'I don't know, miss.' Oh, better be definite. 'No, miss.' Oh dear, he was still doubtful. 'Yes, miss.' Oh, better not to have heard at all. 'What, miss? What did you say, miss?' 'I said I'd lost my gloves, Mr. Mipps.' What a relief, perhaps he hadn't heard right after all. 'Oh, your gloves, miss,' he said with complete understanding. 'Did you, miss? I've not seen them, miss.' He began to look round hopefully. 'Where did you drop 'em, miss?' 'I didn't, Mr. Mipps.' 'Oh, you didn't!' He was completely at sea.

'No,' she went on. 'I said I'd come to see Mr. Scarecrow.' Thinking that his weather ear had run mad, or that Miss Cicely was confused after her journey, he determined to brazen it out. 'There now, did you, miss? I didn't hear you, miss.' An impersonal voice came from behind the lectern. 'You seem to be in trouble, Mr. Mipps. Is someone asking for me?'

'Yessir,' he gasped. 'That is—er—no, sir.' At his wits' end he finished in a desperate rush—almost in tears: 'It's Miss Cicely, sir, she's come to see Mr. Scarecrow, sir.' From behind the lectern appeared the benign face of Doctor Syn. 'Why, Cicely child,' he said with some surprise, 'how glad I am to see you back. Mr. Mipps has been telling me of your extraordinary adventures.' Mr. Mipps, determined not to be brought into it again, and thinking his own adventures quite extraordinary enough, hurried back, for Horace, who at least couldn't answer back, for Horace, who had been his friend and confidant for many years, was a large black spider that lived in the beam from which Mr. Mipps slung his hammock, waking him each morning by sliding down from this fighting-top to the lower deck of Mr. Mipps's nose.

Upon seeing Doctor Syn, Cicely uttered a cry of disappointment. 'Why, 'tis only our dear old Doctor Syn. Then I am too late. How teasing.' Then upon seeing that the Vicar was looking somewhat hurt, she begged his pardon and told him how glad she was to see him, explaining that the reason for this late return to his house was a pair of gloves which she thought she must have dropped here. 'Though I must confess I used the missing gloves as an excuse, for I did so want to see the Scarecrow paying you his tithes.' 'Then you are too late, dear Cicely, and I am equally disappointed, for I hoped that your return here was to let me see you safe and sound.' 'Oh, but I assure you, I should have come to see you first thing in the morning,' replied Cicely, adding a little mischievously that she always knew where to find the beloved Vicar, unless, of course, he was out on some errand of mercy, which apparently he had been that night. She supposed it was that poor old Mrs. Wooley again, and vowed she would take her some hot soup in the morning, adding carelessly, 'how much did the Scarecrow pay?'

Doctor Syn looked at her with not a little curiosity. 'Why, Cicely,' he said, 'what is this sudden interest in such a complicated matter as the payment of tithes?' She glanced up at him, eyes wide with feigned innocence—and with the suspicion of a smile about the corners of her mouth, answered: 'Oh, 'tis not a sudden interest. I just wished to see if I am good at reckoning. Was it a large sum?' Doctor Syn became very vague. 'Eh, child,' he said, peering at her through his spectacles. 'Let me see: well, if I remember what I wrote in the book this time, 'twas a mere trifle.' At this she seemed to be full of concern, mixed with not a little indignation, saying that she had long suspected that his eyesight was failing, and that he could not have written aright, and she hoped that the Scarecrow wasn't cheating him, for he had told her most distinctly that tonight's cargo was a very valuable one.

'Come, let me see those glasses,' she said with pretended anxiety. 'I fear they cannot be strong enough for your poor old eyes,' as with a deal of motherly care she took them from his nose and looked through them, saying it was just what she had expected and little better than plain glass, and that she would insist upon his going to London with her father the very next time he went to visit his oculist. But for her part, were she his physician she would order him to throw away his years and not to add to them, stressing that without his glasses he might well be old Doctor Syn's younger brother. 'No, no, do not move,' she said, for Doctor Syn was trying to escape her penetrating look and the beruffled hands that firmly held his arms. But for all that, her grip tightened and she continued to gaze, frowning and fussing. 'Let me look at you more closely. Yes, 'tis true, you are pale. Perhaps 'tis exercise you need. Jogging about on that churchyard pony cannot be good for you. I must ask Papa to give you a more spirited mount, and you must learn to ride. I could teach you.' Was there a hint of a smile in Doctor Syn's unbespectacled eyes? Indeed he had no need of them. He saw as well without them as with their protective, ageing screen. He answered quietly: 'Perhaps Doctor Syn's younger brother could teach you more things than you have ever dreamt of, Miss Cicely. But I fear that I am not he, and must indeed be failing. 'Tis gracious of you to worry over a poor parson in his dotage. But let us talk of something that interests you more.' 'Why then,' she answered very quietly, 'let us talk of the Scarecrow, for he is the most interesting man I have ever met, if man he be, though I do not really think there is truth in the rumour that he is a ghost. To me, he seemed most real. Aye, and with a heart too, for I felt it beating on the ride from Paris when my horse failed. 'Tis true,' she went on earnestly, 'he appears and vanishes like a ghost, for I was swept from the saddle before I felt the horse stumble. But down it went, and I might have gone with it but for a strong arm that certainly did not belong to a spectre.' The Vicar seemed to be full of perturbed amazement at the dangers she had been through, saying what a terrifying experience it must have been. To which Cicely replied that she hadn't been frightened at all because of his superb horsemanship, but she had to admit that she had been troubled. The Vicar agreed that it must have been terrible to have been in the arms of such a desperate character.

'Oh, do not mistake me,' she protested. 'I was troubled because I knew 'twas but a few kilometres to the next village, and I would have ridden that way all night. But then, fresh horses, and he vanished again. For the most part he had spoken to me in his rough French, though for that short distance we rode in silence.' Here her voice took on a new seriousness, and she said as though experiencing it again: 'And I felt that he knew me, and in some strange way that I had known him all my life. Yes, and that we were being swept on to something more vital than escaping from the mob. Now do you understand why I am troubled?' The Vicar too seemed as if he wanted to escape. He went to the fire, saying gravely: 'It seems that this man has taken occasion to be more than a rogue.' 'Oh, but he is no ordinary adventurer.' She moved after him and knelt at his feet. 'Indeed, he is a very wonderful person. You have no idea of his efficiency—his attention to the smallest detail. His daring in running the Revenue blockade made me marvel.' She turned away from him and looked into the fire. 'So you see, Doctor Syn, having set myself a riddle, the solution of it makes me very glad.'

'And have you solved your riddle?' the Vicar asked quietly.

'Indeed, without any assistance my heart found the answer.' She turned and looked earnestly up at him. 'Dear, kind old Doctor Syn, tell me what I should do, for I am fathoms deep in love with this—pirate.' Disturbed and shaken at the word she used, he asked urgently: 'What are you saying? You cannot be serious. A man whose face you've never seen.' 'Oh, I care not what he looks like,' she cried. 'In spite of that foolish mask I should love him were he as ugly as sin.' She was laughing up at him now, and he dared not look at her, but went on protesting that it was madness.

That he had a price on his head and was hunted by Army, Navy and Revenue alike.

''Twould be madness not to love him,' she persisted gaily. 'All the King's horses and Revenue men cannot stop me.'

Steeling himself to meet that challenging look, he tried desperately to master her compelling eyes, as facing her he said: 'Then perhaps 'tis foolish of me to try.' And again, seeking vainly to convince her, asked, 'Have you stopped to consider that his madness could not be?' She answered swiftly: 'I cannot, nor do I desire to stop. My thoughts are his, and if he should command, my life.' She knelt up straight, which brought her closer to him, and putting one hand upon his arm which rested on the corner of the settle, she looked down at it, toying with the buttons on his coat and teasing said: 'I shall have no one else if he does not love me. I shall become—' Here she put her head on one side and thought deeply. 'Yes,' she announced, 'I shall become the spinster of the parish, and devote myself entirely to good works. Maybe I should commence with you. 'Tis true you have no one to look after you.' She looked down again at that intriguing arm.

'Why there, what did I say? Your sleeve, you have a button loose. My first good deed shall be to sew it on for you.' He gently moved the inquisitive hand and rose slowly to his feet, the look of fierce concentration on his face changing to one of calm purpose as he moved away from her. She remained on her knees, sitting back on the heels of her slim riding-boots, fearful yet expectant. Making no haste, he drew off his coat and let it fall. Then deliberately rolling up the right sleeve of his frilled shirt, he moved close to her and gently placed his forearm over the shoulder of the kneeling girl, as though forcing her to look at the tattooed mark upon it.

She did not turn her head, but with a caressing movement clasped the incriminating arm to her, and in a small voice asked for needle and thread with which to sew on the offending button. His deep voice was husky as he said, 'Child, you know that this can never be.'

'I have always known that it must be,' she answered, continuing casually, ''Twill only be a moment if you have a good spool of black.' 'But, Cicely, do you realize what this mark is?' ''Tis but the picture of a man walking the plank with a shark beneath. I saw it first in Paris upon the arm of a most notorious character,' and continued just as casually, ''Twas foolish of me to leave my thimble behind.' He fought desperately, reasoning with her against himself, that the tattoo upon his arm was the mark of the pirate Clegg, who should have hung in chains on Execution Dock; that it was the mark of a hunted law-breaker, the mark of a man who ruled the Marsh by fear and with his cunning. But again to this she answered simply:

"'Tis also the mark of that saintly man the Vicar of Dymchurch, revered by all that know him, and dearly loved by Cicely Cobtree, spinster of the parish, who must remember to carry her chatelaine of pins and thread.'

Though knowing he had already lost, he made a last attempt to save her from what he knew must be inevitable should he allow himself such happiness, so, without mercy, he accused his threefold personality—pirate, smuggler, parson—of being an unholy trinity—and of all the three that saintly parson was but the worst of hypocrites, mouthing his smug sermons and hiding black deeds behind the pillars of the Church. Then turning to her he demanded passionately, 'How can you love a coward?' She rose to her feet and stood before him, and fiercely she challenged with a passion equal to his own: 'Coward in one thing only: you will not say what I await to hear.' His despair was triumphant as he laughed back at her glorious audacity.

'Then not even you shall call me a coward,' he cried, and she was in his arms.

After a little while she sought the answer to another riddle. 'And how much did the Scarecrow pay?'

'Eh, child?' For a moment, and to tease her, he became again the kindly Vicar, then holding her from him at arms' length he said: 'All the wealth that was Clegg's when he sailed the Caribbean would not suffice to pay those tithes. Does that satisfy you?' She did not answer, but stood content and gazing at him. 'No?' But still she did not speak, so he went on: 'Would you have me sail up London River and loot the Crown Jewels to lay at your feet?' 'Why, Captain Clegg, should I then be richer than I am?' she asked.

'There is now but one thing that I desire.' He, in his turn, stood silent, looking at her, as she pleaded with a feigned sincerity: 'Dear, kind old Doctor Syn, pray stop preaching your horrid sermons against my beloved Scarecrow.' He laughed again and drew her swiftly to him. For Christopher Syn had remembered to forget the pirate's slogan—no petticoats aboard.

And so it was that the next morning Doctor Syn, happening to perceive from his study window a last remaining rose upon his favourite tree, went out to pick it, and there upon the frosty ground beneath this lovely challenge to the winter was a pair of gauntlet gloves.

Chapter 13. In which Mr. Mipps Discovers an Old Friend and Doctor Syn

Discovers a Secret Doctor Syn smiled and promised Cicely that although he could not stop preaching against this rascal, he would at least modify his righteous rage, adding in a more serious tone that perhaps in the near future it might not be necessary to preach upon that vein at all, since already it was evident that the Scarecrow was showing signs of repentance, and that he, as shepherd of the flock, hoped that he might be able to lead one more stray lamb into the fold. So for the third time that evening Cicely crossed the Glebe field, but this time in company with Doctor Syn. Upon reaching the Court House, she was loth to part with him so soon, and entreated him to come in, urging that having found him she never wanted to let him go, and she also knew by the look in Papa's eye that he too was in need of moral support.

To this Doctor Syn replied that the house would sure to be in great commotion over their sudden return, and that her mother and Aunt Agatha would want to welcome their stray lambs home, in true feminine manner.

Cicely answered, smiling somewhat ruefully, that in truth she knew wwell what that meant: a deal of fussings, scoldings, twitterings and floods of tears, so that she, in trying to be a dutiful daughter, would be hard put to it to squeeze out one, so happy was she, and since by his presence their enjoyment at a thorough good cry at the family reunion would have to be somewhat modified, pray, would he not come in and help her out? But he was still firm and taking her in his arms kissed her tenderly good night, vowing that he would visit them the next morning. As a final farewell Cicely whispered:

"Tis very sad that poor old Doctor Syn is in his dotage. I do hope the dear old gentleman will not be jealous of his younger brother, for in truth I am fathoms deep in love with that—unholy trinity.' And she was gone, laughing back at him as she ran lightly across the flagstoned hall. Stopping at the steps, she turned, jerking her head in the direction of the drawing-room upstairs, whence came a babble of excited voices and a sound that meant only one thing—Maria was thoroughly enjoying herself again. With a gesture of comical despair, and an expression which said, 'There now, what did I tell you?' she allowed her happiness to express itself in the most curious, charming manner. Delicately lifting the skirt of her riding-habit, as if about to sweep him a curtsey, she suddenly executed a quaint, high-spirited little jig. Then, with a further gesture of humourous resignation, she waved to him and stumped off up the stairs.

He had watched her, enchanted, and stood for a while after she had gone, smiling at the thought of her lovely youthful grace, and he made a vow that he would sacrifice all rather than hurt a hair of her head.

Closing the front door, he looked up to the stars, stretching himself as though to reach and thank them, and breathed a vast deep sigh.

Then he strode off down the village street. So light was his step, so high his head and heart, that had any man seen him they might well have thought, 'Here must be the younger brother of the man we know,' and, indeed, he was not following Doctor Syn's usual habit of returning to the Vicarage before setting out upon one of his nightly expeditions. He certainly was not in the mood, this night, for the joggings of his churchyard pony. He laughed alooud when thinking again of her audacious offer to teach him to ride, and a great longing seized him to let the world know who he was and the things that he could do. And thus exalted, he left the village and strode out across the Marsh.

Some twenty minutes later he reached the loneliest spot—a small dilapidated cottage that the Marsh-folk shunned, for in their seafaring, superstitious minds they feared the old woman who lived there, believing her to be a witch and in the Devil's pay. In the eyes of these simple folk Doctor Syn became the more respected because he did not fear to visit her. But then the Vicar was such a very holy man.

Upon this night he was not the only one who had the courage to enter Mother Handaway's abode, for three others were there before him.

The fact that it was avoided by all God-fearing folk, and by reason of its lonely situation, cut off by intersecting dykes whose dilapidated bridges were unsafe, gave this poor hovel a value to anyone who wished to work in secret.

For many years it had served the Scarecrow well, for in a dry dyke close to the house was a well-built, underground stable, dating, some said, from the days of the Roman occupation. Its roof was the natural pasture soil and its only door was hidden beneath a stack of drying bullrushes. The inside was commodious and dry, owing to the excellent drainage system of the builders in those ancient times.

With these advantages, therefore, it was an admirable hiding-place for the Scarecrow's wild, black horse, Gehenna, and used as well by another gentleman whose way of business demanded secrecy. Gentleman James sheltered there when a hue-and-cry was at its height, or when the Scarecrow wished him to ride as deputy. In this way the Authorities had been fooled many times, for having seen the Scarecrow in one part of the Marsh, dumbfounded Dragoons or Preventive men, discussing their experiences the next day, would discover that this fearsome creature had also appeared some miles away at that particular time, and the rumour had grown that the Scarecrow was in truth a demon. So it appeared almost natural for this terrifying, unearthly horseman to disappear in the vicinity of this haunted spot. The smugglers took full advantage of the old woman's fearsome reputation, and saw that it was enhanced by weird shriekings in the night and oily smoke rising from the chimney-stack, thus giving encouragement to many a gruesome tale about the old woman's secret practices. The old hag's appearance was enough to quell the stoutest heart. Sharp curved nose and pointed chin guarded her one-toothed, mumbling mouth. Her evil eyes were beady and protected by straggly brows that matched the grey beard upon her chin. Her hair hung in long rats' tails, and her gnarled fingers made her hands look like claws. Half crazed, she too believed herself the witch of popular belief, for had she not conjured up the Devil in the likeness of that holy man, the Vicar of Dymchurch? And did not the Devil pay her more golden guineas than a poor parson could ever afford?p

Upon this night she sat in a corner by the fire surrounded by her clawing cats, huddled and mumbling to herself, while round a table, seated on barrels, talking and drinking, were three men.

Heaped into a pile in front of Jimmie Bone was a various assortment of the kind of trinkets that delight a feminine heart. It waas the Highwayman's habit to keep in reserve a goodly selection of such baubles, and he took great care always to have some about him as a reward for services rendered.

Though as a rule these gifts were bestowed carelessly enough, upon this occasion Mr. Bone did not seem able to make up his mind. He scratched his head, took up a ring, only to put it back in favour of a brooch or bracelet, and then thumping the table which made the whole heap jump, he cried out in his perplexity: 'S'death, I cannot tell which one would suit her best.' The other two looked up, surprised from their earnest conversation.

'Why, what troubles you, Jimmie?' asked Mr. Mipps. 'Can't you find one to your likin'? Seems to me that a wench should be well-pleased with any of 'em. Who's it for? That new one at the Red Lion in Hythe, I'll be bound.

Now bein' a sandy-'aired, I should suggest a garnet, or isn't it 'er? If you describes 'er we might be able to assist. Pedro 'ere will give you first-rate information. 'Ad to leave Spain, he did; too many se±oritas wanted to call him Papa, didn't they, me old flirt-man?' 'No, no, my excellent Mipps,' protested Pedro, in laboured English.

'The senoritas wish me to call on their Papa.' 'Means the same thing in the end, don't it, you old Spanish bullfight? Anyway,' he went on to Jimmie Bone, 'what he don't know about what they want ain't worth tellin' to your auntie. So come, give us a look at her riggin' and we'll tell you 'ow to deck her figure'ead.'

The little Spanish sea-captain tugged excitedly at his beard, his black eyes dancing at the thought of hearing a description from Se±or Bone of the girl who was lucky enough to please him. His weatherbeaten little face, tanned to old leather and having indeed the same texture, wrinkled into a mesh of smiling expectancy. He turned his grizzled head this way and that, which made the golden rings in his ears flash in the light. He spoke with the knowledge of an expert: 'I know, I know, before you start, I know. She is like the peach against the wall ready for the—'ow you say?—ah, the pluckings.' Mr. Bone had other ideas on the subject, though he seemed as unable to describe the lady as he had been to select her present. After much humming and ha-ing and entreating them not to laugh at him, he confessed that although the lady in question was sparkling, witty and full of charm, he didn't know what colour her hair was as she wore the most enormous white wig, and that she stood no higher than the tip of his horse's nose, had a face like a bright little robin, was unmarried and well-nigh eighty.

'Well, blow me down and knock me up!' cried Mipps. 'If that ain't Miss Agatha Gordon at Squire's, I'll keel-haul myself.' 'That's the party,' cried Mr. Bone. 'As nice a little old lady as ever I robbed. But I've give back her jewels and I want to apologize with a keepsake.' Captain Pedro was too bewildered to speak. He could not understand how it was that so fine a caballero as this highwayman should be hearttroubled by an old lady of eighty. Like all foreigners, he knew, of course, that all Englishmen are mad, but he had not imagined anyone being as strange as this. He was hoping to hear more upon the matter when the door opened and Doctor Syn stood looking at them.

The effect on Mother Handaway was remarkable. She stretched out her scraggy arms straight before her with finger turned up and palms towards her master as though to ward off any curse he might think to hurl at her. By her averted frightened eyes, and lips that muttered invocations, the three men at the table knew that the old hag was in the grip of fear, waiting to hear whether the inscrutable black-clothed figure was angy with her.

He did not keep her long in this awful suspense. Though he had walked the Marsh, his soul had still been singing with the stars, and he could not find it in his heart to enjoy the power he exercised over this misguided creature, so in a quiet calm voice he said: 'You have done well, old mother, and shall be well repaid. Go to the stables, and light the lanterns there.' After uttering a wild cry of joy, she fell forward in ecstasy of genuflexions, and when she heard another kindly order—'Go. There, there.

All's well'—she chuckled in delight and, followed by the cats about her, hobbled past him through the door.

Quickly Doctor Syn closed the door behind her and with a smile of real affection lighting up his eyes went over to the table from which the three men had risen.

"'Tis good to see you, Pedro,' and he took the Spanish captain's hands in both of his. 'You managed the last business so well and with such care for the valuable cargo in those barrels—oh yes, I have heard how gently they were handled—that I am reluctant to send you back again so soon to France.

Mipps will have told you that there are two prisoners to be taken to our harbour in the Somme, and there is no one who can slip through the blockade like our Pedro ù' The gratified Pedro interrupted with an emphatic: 'Ah no, my Captain, there is you. There were moments when the good Greyhound slid before the wind and first the French and then the English battleships let drive at her that Pedro thought, 'What will the Captain do now? Will he tack here or there? Hold his fire or answer them?' Ah yes—your Pedro needed you. But your luck held with me—and home we got.' 'Would that I could have been with you, Pedro,' said Doctor Syn. 'The call of the sea remains as strong as ever. You did well, my friend. Was the cargo—troublesome? I got your message.' 'Ah—the bookmarks. 'Tis good, our system of the post at the bookshop. I would I wrote such good letters as our young boy Jacques. I speak—he write, and he deliver it.' Thumping himself on the chest, he spat out in disgust: 'Bah—Pedro! Unlettered, ignorant Spanish pig. Bah!' 'You have a good deal of courage which makes up for your lack of letters, my good little Pedro.'

'Just as my weather ear makes up for me lack of inches, eh?' said Mr.

Mipps meaningly. Then, seeing that the others had not understood, except, of course, the Vicar, Mipps explained: 'Another of the Captain's little jokes.

Gentleman James is lucky. Can't be called a dwarf. Though I wouldn't mind so much being a little man and someone was to put me in a barrel—full one, mind you, not empty. And that reminds me, talkin' of barrels. Had a message from Vulture. Them coopered Dragoons got to Sandgate lovely. Says he popped them other two you didn't want to ride over the Marsh with into barrels as well. Oh, and he found two more lurkin' about he didn't like, to which he did ditto, just to make up the nice round half-dozen for Mr. Hyde.

Left 'em in a row on the doorstep. I'd like to give my weather eye a treat when he opens 'em. You're askin for trouble with Mr. Hyde. He'll be Mr.

Seek now.'

At which they laughed heartily. 'Ah,' cried Pedro. 'I do not think his cargo please him as mine please me. At least, the half of it. That miss—a brave one. Rough or smooth—all same to her. When all was well and as you told me, Captain, I let them out between the decks. The tall one—she clapped me on the back and say, 'Good Pedro. Why did you not let me out before? I heard the guns, I could have helped you man them.' But the little one'—the thought made Pedro hold up his hands and flap them in disgust.

'She scream at me as though it were my fault. She say, 'You let me out. You stop the boat and let me off.' Had it not been for orders, Pedro might well have say, 'Go then, miss. The water, it is deep and wet, but if you wish, 'op it.' Alles. Pouf!' The noise conveyed what he meant. That he was extremely glad to be rid of her.

Doctor Syn looked at his fob watch, and said it was some ten minutes short of midnight and time to be saddling up.

'You will ride with Mipps to the beach, Pedro,' he said, 'and the luggers will take you off during the run, and put you aboard the Greyhound.

She's off Dungeness, is she not? Mipps, saddle Gehenna now, while I have word with James here.' Mipps nodded, and with an 'Aye-aye, sir,' took Pedro by the arm and the two little men went off together, their back views very similar.

'Well, Jimmie, what news?' asked Doctor Syn as they went to the fire and sat down in the chimney-seat.

'If it's personal news you mean, then James ain't got much to tell you, for them bloody red-robins—beg pardon, Vicar—them nice Bow Street Runners, is remarkably quiet. Expectin' them to jump any time now, so if you don't hear from me you'll know I'm taking my vacation at Slippery's this time. The false run went off according to plan. 'British Grenadiers', eh? I made the Dragoons dance to a different tune. 'Over the Border Away, Away.' I took 'em across the Kent Ditch and got 'em lost in Sussex. 'Well and truly lost', you said, and well and truly lost they are. We turned the signposts, so if they do happen to get out they'll go trotting back into Sussex again.' The two men laughed heartily at this. Then Jimmie Bone slapped hand to knee and exclaimed: 'Zounds—talking of finding and losing—no news I said, and here I am with some in my pocket.' And he drew out the wallet he had taken in Quarry Hill from Captain Foulkes.

'There's something here that I think you ought to have,' he said. 'You see, I've had a good deal of experience with gentlemen's wallets, and this one sort of puzzled me. 'Here,' says I, 'is a good one. Hand made. Beautiful stitching. Gold initial and made of Russian leather.' There it was in my hand, empty—although it didn't feel empty. A nice exciting crackling of paper.

'James,' I said, 'you may have stumbled on this gentleman's emergency note,' so I turns it over and has a good look, and there at the top was a different stitching. So, Gentleman James being curious, I ripped out the stitching and inside here was this.' He drew from behind the outer leather a thin folded paper, covered with writing, which he handed over to Doctor Syn.

'You can read the language—I can't. But I can read a name, even in French. And that's why I thought you'd better have it.' Doctor Syn turned to the name, and gave a long low whistle of astonishment. Then quickly reading the letter through he looked up at the highwayman, and his voice was grave. ''Tis good that you have such a sensitive touch, Jimmie. Here's a stupendous piece of news indeed, though for a time I've had an inkling that something was afoot. I'll deal with it, James.

As you have gathered, it is a letter written by none other than Robespierre himself to a Monsieur Barsard. For the present I must urge you to keep even that knowledge to yourself. All I can tell you other than this is that he proposes ù'

Upon that instant the nearby hooting of an owl was heard, and the door opened. Doctor Syn quickly replaced the letter in the wallet, which he put in his pocket, as a figure entered the room. Masked and hooded, it was terrible to behold. One might have expected its voice to be sepulchral. Instead came, surprisingly enough, the plaintive, muffled voice of Mr. Mipps. 'Oh, me mask. Don't fit,' he complained. 'Give Pedro mine. This didn't fit him neither, but it'll give me cruel headache, sure as coffin nails. Owls is on. 'Ear 'em? Ain't you ready? 'Orses are. Why, blow me down! Ain't you chose your present yet? Ain't you been lingy? Better be quiddy.' Mr. Bone made a rush for the table and quickly sorted out some half a dozen trinkets, and turning, begged Doctor Syn to give him his advice, telling him that he meant to make a personal apology to Miss Gordon with one of them, and which did he think suitable?p

With a nod of approval for his gentlemanly thought, Doctor Syn began to make his choice from the articles when Mr. Mipps, who was at the table inspecting some of the others, cried, 'Knock me up solid—'ere's the very thing and you've been and gone and missed it!' He held out for them to see a brooch, a dog's head carved out of crystal, painted, and set in gold looking remarkably life-like.

'Why, yes,' cried Doctor Syn, "tis indeed the very thing. For though it is not a poodle, it is at least a white dog and bears a faint resemblance to Mister Pitt.' 'Poodle,' repeated Mipps. 'Is that what you calls 'em? A old-fangled name for a new-fangled dog. Looks more like one of them clipped yew hedges to me.' Mr. Bone, admitting he had been dense, besought Doctor Syn to give it to her when convenient, to which Doctor Syn replied he would do so the very first thing in the morning, with her own as well. Then, as Jimmie Bone had already been out once that night and ridden hard, he bade him go to rest, adding that he would be informed of the next run, which probably, he said, would not be for a week.

The warning cries of the owl becme more insistent as Doctor Syn leapt into the dry dyke and through the secret door.

Three minutes later three wild mounted figures dashed from the stable, topped the dyke and galloped seawards, whence came the twinkle of innumerable lights as the 'flashers' sent their message round the Marsh.

Thus did Pedro say good-bye to his master upon the beach at Littlestone, where a lugger, divested of its cargo, signalled him to board.

The diminutive Spanish captain, mounted now upon the shoulders of an enormous fisherman waiting to carry him out waist deep to the departing vessel, was almost as tall as the gaunt figure astride Gehenna.

In this curious position the two men clasped hands and the Scarecrow whispered: 'When you reach the Somme and hand your prisoners over to Duloge, bid him from me to watch for a certain Monsieur Barsard. And now, farewell, my little Pedro.' Standing at the edge of the sea, horse and man motionless, one dark shadow looking bronze against the merging silver of the sea and sky, Doctor Syn watched the lugger till it was almost out of sight, and wondered if his good friend Duloge would meet with one Barsard.

Chapter 14. Concerning a Late-blooming Rose and an Early Visitor

Doctor Syn sat at his desk in the library, in a silver vase before him one late-blooming rose, its red velvet petals already opening to the heat of the room, though he had picked it but half an hour before in the frosty garden beneath his window. Beside it on the table lay a pair of gauntlet riding-gloves. He looked at them and smiled as he noted that they had taken on the shape of her slim, determined hands. The fingers slightly curved as though still mastering some unruly horse, and at the sight he felt a mighty pull at the reins of his own heart. He raised his head and, looking through the curved panes of the bow window, saw behind the sharp etching of the rookery trees the many spiralled stacks of the Court House chimneys. He smiled again, imagining the bustle inside that house, surely continuing from the night before. He wondered how she'd slept, or whether, like himself, she'd been wakeful to the dawn, and then remembered, somewhat wistfully, that her youthful health would undoubtedly have claimed the sleep which he had wooed in vain.

But in spite of his night's activities and the fact that he had not slept, he felt alive and exhilarated, deliberately stamping from his mind any dark thoughts that might have lingered there. It was with the suspicion of a sigh, therefore, that he forced himself to return to another urgent matter. Taking from his pocket the wallet which Mr. Bone had given him the night before, he fell to an examination of its contents.

There seemed to be some points in Robespierre's threatening letter to this Barsard that puzzled him, for he read it carefully two or three times, referring to this line or that, his eyes tightening with concentration, and his intelligent face set into lines of perplexed determination. Then like a barrister preparing his brief he wrote upon a slip of paper the questions he had asked himself during his perusal of the letter, and against each question worked out problematical answers. His writing, scholarly and small as print, easy enough to read in the ordinary course of events, assumed a different form, and his fine pen, which usually travelled rapidly, moved carefully, each letter separate, so that upon finishing a phrase it looked like a row of curious numbers or hieroglyphics. Doctor Syn was in fact writing in ancient Greek.

Having come to a satisfactory conclusion, he replaced the letter in the wallet and, putting it in his pocket, rose and went to a distant bookshelf. Here he selected a calf-bound tome, and, taking it to his desk, opened it at random, made a mental note of the page, placed his Greek notes within, and closed it, carrying the volume to its original place upon the shelf.

He then drew from his pocket a notebook which he used for jotting down parochial items—such as notes on sermons—a text here, a phrase there, so that no one upon opening it would have been surprised to see an extra jotting—Willet on the Romans, page 123.

He was standing by the fire filling his churchwarden pipe with sweet Virginia tobacco when there came a respectful privilege-to-work-there knock upon the door, and upon his pleasant 'Come in', Mrs. Honeyballs's smiling countenance appeared round the door; her rosy face, still shining from the morning soap, peeped out from underneath a large mob cap, while her ample figure, confined within a quantity of starch, bobbed dutifully, as she asked in her usual lilt: 'How are you this morning, sir? Hope I'm not intrudin'. Mr. Mipps has told me you breakfast at the Court House. Oh dear. Here am I forgettin'. Left him on the doorstep. Such a swagger gentleman. Standing on the doorstep. Shall I ask him in, sir? Didn't hear his name, sir. Met you in the coach, sir.' Doctor Syn did not seem to be surprised at this early visitor, though amused at the manner in which Mrs. Honeyballs announced him. With a kindly smile he said: 'Thank you, Mrs. Honeyballs. Will you ask Captain Foulkes to step in?' She bobbed and went out again, unable to suppress her own opinion, which was, 'What an hour for callin'

' Drawing briskly at his pipe, the Vicar stood waiting, an inscrutable smile upon his face.

Captain Foulkes entered the library, and, advancing to the fire, bowed and said: 'I trust, reverend sir, you will forgive my intrusion at this hour, but the weather being fine and the sea air most invigorating, I thought an early rise and a gallop before breakfast would benefit my health and blow away the plaguey cobwebs of London.' His manner this morning was very different. The arrogance gone, it was almost conciliatory, though his clothes belied the statement of an early rise.

Indeed, they did not have the air of a man who had recently completed a fashionable toilet and ridden but a few miles. Instead they bore signs of hard riding, and his eyes, slightly bloodshot, had the look of one who had for hours been staring into darkness. The Doctor, noting this, told himself here was no morning canter for the health. More like an all-night gallop for his purse. He had come to find the Scarecrow and was obviously not wasting any time.

But the Captain continued with his dubious apologies. 'The tide being low, and the sands hard, I had a good gallop, and on enquiry from a fisherman I found I was at Dymchurch, opposite your house, and bethought me of your invitation.'

'Why, Captain Foulkes, of course. You're very welcome. Pray do not excuse yourself, for I too have been up for some considerable time.' The Captain may have given him a doubtful look, but Doctor Syn did not appear to notice and continued: 'Ah yes—the coach. You had a most unfortunate experience. Dear me. That highwayman. So barbaric to want to rob a fellow creature of his boots. But take comfort in the thought, sir, perhaps they pinch him. Oh, I see you have procured another pair.' Indeed the Captain was wearing some very smart though extraordinarily muddy Hessians. 'Then it cannot be my carpet-slippers you have come to borrow,' continued the Vicar.

'Now let me see, what was it you wanted? A weapon. Yes. Yes. He took your sword as well. Well, you shall have the choice of my armoury,' and pointed towards the only corner of the library that was unoccupied by bookshelves.

Captain Foulkes, following his gesture, was surprised to see the finest collection of Toledo steel that he had ever set eyes on in all his swordsman's career, and wondered how they came to be in the possession of this country parson. But Syn went on, explaining: 'As I told you, in my youth I was considered not without promise in the art. I have not always been,' and here he laughed playfully, 'the fusty old parson you see before you now, for I must tell you, sir, that in my travels I have preached the

Word in many far-flung places—from the Chinese Islands to the Red Indians in the Americas.

Charming people—much more civilized than we are. I was no Quaker, sir, and thought it best to have good steel about me. So I made my little collection—more or less as a hobby, of course. Now take your choice.' The Captain appeared to be overwhelmed with such generosity, and told the Vicar that although he remembered his kind offer, and would be delighted to avail himself of it, he had in truth only come that morning to pay his respects and offer his apologies, for he knew he had behaved somewhat churlishly in the coach, as indeed he had also done at Crockford's.

Doctor Syn made light of this, saying that the London air always made him too a trifle testy, for the noise and bustle, to say nothing of the late hours, were apt to fray the nerves, but that now, he hoped, the Captain was feeling more invigorated after his little rest-cure in their humble corner of the world.

'For,' he continued, 'did you not say that you were visiting the coast for your health? No, no, of course, you had another reason. How foolish—my poor old brain. It all comes back to me—your wager. You were coming down to rid us of our Scarecrow. Is that not so, sir? Yes, of course, that's why you need the weapon. That was the only reason for your visit, was it not?' The Captain appeared to be relieved at this question, for indeed he had been wondering how to broach the subject, and having selected a sword to his liking (Doctor Syn noting with amusement that he had chosen the finest in his collection), he went on to say that in truth there was something else—that he had come to the Vicar for advice and assistance. Doctor Syn replied that it was a curious coincidence, for but yesterday morning another member of Crockford's ahd called for the same purpose, and he understood that the young gentleman had been an acquaintance of Captain Foulkes. 'Now what was his name?' he said. 'Dear me, my memory. Oh yes, Lord Cullingford.

Quite a charming boy—if a trifle misguided, but I rather think I succeeded in bringing another stray lamb into the fold. It appeared that the poor youth was somewhat in debt, and,' he continued confidentially, as though they, as older men, knew the ways of the wicked world, 'I lent him some few hundred guineas from parochial funds. Oh, I have no fear of not getting it back, for he seemed to me the soul of honour, and told me he fully intended quitting his extravagant life to join the Colours. I had succeeded, you see, in persuading him that to try to catch this rascally Scarecrow single-handed was in my mind only asking for trouble, since the Army, the Navy, and the Revenue alike have never succeeded in catching him, and that the chance he had of winning the two thousand guineas reward was remote indeed. He then admitted that in the Captain's case it was a different matter, as of course he had heard that Captain Foulkes was such a brilliant swordsman, if indeed he was lucky enough to meet the Scarecrow, and he wondered, having also heard of the Captain's offer to meet the Scarecrow in open duel, whether his challenge could be accepted, adding wistfully that there was a fight he would like to see.' Foulkes was not a little annoyed when he heard that Lord Cullingford had stolen this march upon him, and then had turned 'so mighty pious', and he vowed that he would attend to the young puppy at his convenience, though at the moment his own affairs were too pressing to worry further upon the subject, and the Vicar had somewhat mollified him by his flattery. So he admitted that though he had come to Doctor Syn for advice about the Scarecrow, that also was not the only reason. Then, flattering in his turn, he said that he had heard Doctor Syn was such a good man that even the miscreants of his parish were not afraid to approach him for guidance, and that in truth they even paid him their tithes. So he wondered if it would be possible for him to convey a message to that confounded highwayman who had put him to such inconvenience. 'For,' he went on, 'not only did he take my sword and boots, but he deprived me of something on which I set great sentimental value, in short, my wallet, given to me by a dear friend. If he would return it I am willing to pay a large reward, as well as allowing him to keep such money as he found inside it, without complaint to the Authorities or personally seeking redress.' To this the Vicar replied that it was a very grave matter and he could not promise Captain Foulkes an assured satisfaction, for he never knew when these naughty rogues were going to 'bob up next', though as a rule they were punctilious in paying their tithes. Then, looking somewhat apologetic, he said: 'I fear I very stupidly refused to take my tithes from Mr. Bone due for his latest misdemeanour, because of his gentlemanly gesture in returning to me all the valuables which you saw him take from Miss Agatha Gordon. He told me himself that he had never been privileged to rob such an aristocratic, charming old Scots lassie, and asked me to give them back with his apology.

Why, he even sent her a little personal gift, in lieu of her forgiveness. Quaint fellow,' he chuckled, 'romantically inclined, though I suspect 'tis the first time Gentleman James has played the gallant to a lady of her years. But there, I fear all this must be very annoying for you, having lost something of such great sentimental value. Your dear friend—passed on, no doubt?' Then seeing that the Captain's expression was blank, went on: 'No? Oh, and a wallet too. Most irritating. All one's private papers. So intimate. I feel for you most strongly and will certainly do my best.'

Once again the Captain had that curious feeling that he was being laughed at, and felt the same qualms of doubt concerning the Vicar's sincerity. But stifling these feelings as he still hoped to make use of the Vicar, he thanked him and, summoning up an uneasy laugh, he suggested: 'I merely thought, sir, that if this highwayman is so prompt to pay his tithes, the same thing may apply to this Scarecrow, and were you to be so—'fortunate', shall we say?—as to meet him, I would be exceedingly grateful if you would convey a message to him too.' Doctor Syn once again became the Shepherd of his Flock, as without the hint of a double meaning he assured his visitor that, though he would not betray the confidences of a black sheep any more than he would of a white, at least he would do his best. 'You see, sir,' he went on, 'I do not feel so uneasy about you as I did about poor young Cullingford, so if I am successful in arranging this meeting, perhaps you will do me the honour of allowing me to be your 'second'.' The Captain looked a little surprised at this last remark, but before he had time to reply the Vicar continued. 'It is none of my business, I know,' he said with deference, 'but I must say I am a little perplexed, for apart from what I am sure will be an exhilarating fight, I am at a loss to know your motive in calling him out, for a gentleman of your means can surely not be in need of such a paltry sum. A personal matter, no doubt? Some slur upon your character? I quite understand. Pray forgive me for my impertinence.' The Vicar appeared to be so understanding and so genuinely concerned about the matter that Foulkes, all suspicions swept away, was encouraged to go still further, and told the Vicar, very confidentially, that his challenge to the Scarecrow was in reality a blind; that he had no wish to kill him but to meet him, as he was entrusted with a very special proposition from a certain gentleman called Barsard. Adding that he felt sure the Scarecrow would not refuse his offer as it would be very lucrative, and came from a man who had unlimited power. 'Indeed,' the Captain now seemed to be playing his trump card, 'he will not dare refuse when he learns from me certain information gleaned from the distant Caribbean Seas.' If these words meant anything to Doctor Syn, he did not show it.

Indeed he appeared not to understand, and his bewildered expression drew the Captain still further, as with a condescending smile he said: 'I see my meaning has escaped you, sir, for your way of living and your holy mission during your travels would not have brought you into contact with the uncivilized tyrants of the Caribbean Sea, and one in particular, Clegg, the famous pirate.'

The Vicar appeared to be most amazed, as he asked, 'But what have the mortal remains of Captain Clegg, which in truth lie buried in our churchyard, to do with what you have just been telling me about?' 'Because,' replied the Captain triumphantly, 'through certain knowledge of this Clegg's activities, and what I have since learned about the Scarecrow, I would stake my last card that they are one and the same. You look astounded, sir, but I had no difficulty in convincing a gentleman I met last night. A very disgruntled gentleman, who had just been put to great indignity and shame by the Scarecrow and his gang, and when I had expounded my theory to this officer of the Dragoons he told me that his brother many years ago had had the same suspicions, but nothing came of it.

Nothing may come of this, if the rogue does what I ask him.' The Captain appeared to have every confidence of success, so Doctor Syn did not protest, but anyone seeing his look of bland astonishment would never have guessed what was really in his mind. But the Captain may have felt something of this, for he rose and sought to take his leave, not without some astonishment that the parson made no effort to detain him or question him further. So, again thanking him for the loan of the sword, he was about to take it up when he noticed on the table where it lay a book. Absentmindedly he turned the leaves as though he was engrossed in his own thoughts. Then closing it with a snap he remarked that it was a very fine translation of the |niad. Doctor Syn's left eyebrow rose as he said, 'Ah, amongst your other accomplishments, I see you are a scholar. I was indeed fortunate to come by so good a copy. Since you are interested, pray borrow it. I will remove my bookmarks. I have an unfortunate habit of making little notes and leaving them all over the place.'

The Captain accepted the book graciously enough and took his leave, riding back to Hythe with his trophies: a useful sword that he wanted and a French translation of a classic for which he had no use.

The family was already at breakfast when Doctor Syn reached the Court House. The meal was very nearly over, but as he was considered one of them only the briefest apology was necessary to Lady Caroline, who insisted on serving him herself. In fact, this morning she seemed very bright and attentive to everyone, in contrast to her usual querulous self. To Sir Antony she behaved with the utmost affection, fussing round him with many a 'There, my love', and 'A little more, my pet'. She anticipated his every want, which called forth from the Squire when her back was turned at the hot-plate a mighty wink directed towards Doctor Syn, whose obvious meaning was that his yesterday's rebellion had brought her to heel. The Squire was in excellent humour but for one thing: that those confounded smugglers had had the audacity to use his horses again, and that now when he had got the chance of a good day's sport there wasn't an animal fit to ride, with the exception of Cicely's mare, Stardust, whose stall had been marked with a chalked cross, and she was going to ride herself—selfish girl! Even this was said in jest, for today the Squire could not bring himself to be cross with anyone. Since Doctor Syn's arrival Cicely had appeared to be intent upon her cup of chocolate, so busily stirring that it was in danger of making all who watched it dizzy, and not daring to look up she had stared at it herself, but knew it was not only that which made her head and heart both spin. Upon her father's remark, however, about Stardust she glanced up. Doctor Syn was looking at her with a faint twinkle in his eyes, and she returned it boldly, one delicate eyebrow raised. It was lucky that at that moment all the Cobtree family were engrossed upon their breakfast, for the look in Cicely's eye would not have deceived anyone. It said, triumphantly, 'So it was you. Thank you.' Then, as it softened, just, 'I love you.' One person at the table, however, was not so busy with her breakfast, nor was she deceived. Aunt Agatha had caught that interchanging glance and knew what it meant. She was delighted, and intended to find out more, wishing that that naughty highwayman had not taken all her jewellery as she would have liked to present Cicely with the diamonds there and then for being intelligent enough to find out what she already had suspected. That behind those great spectacles and air of slow, scholarly charm was an everyouthful spirit of romance, a great heart, and a quick brain—in fact a man.

Aunt Agatha had not been married, but she had an unfailing instinct in these matters. So giving Mister Pitt an extra lump of sugar as a mark of approval that he too had had sagacity in licking the said gentleman's nose, she purred in anticipation as she promised her own romantic soul much future pleasure in the unravelling of this exciting secret.

After breakfast, however, she had a deal of flutterings on her own account, for upon leaving the morning-room through an ante-chamber, her small white hand through Cicely's arm, Doctor Syn stopped for a moment to collect some things which he had left upon a chair. He turned to her and with a low bow and an enchanting smile said: 'A tribute to what every woman should possess, and which you, Miss Agatha, possess in abundance—wit, charm and courage.' Then, handing her a bundle tied in a silk handkerchief, he said: 'This with the compliments of Gentleman James to his wee Scots lassie, and this, madame, with mine own regard, hoping I have found a true Scots friend.' The old lady took the crimson rose and her fingers trembled slightly, her wise old eyes were almost over-bright as, sweeping him the most graceful Court curtsey, she answered softly: 'I have heard, sir, that all good Marsh men pay their Scotts and so maintain the ancient Wall, but in truth, sir, you have paid such tribute to an ancient Scot that she will ever try to maintain the friendship that you ask.' Here, curiously enough, she held out her hands to the two of them.

Cicely watched this touching scene and her heart glowed. She applauded his gesture in thus giving the rose where another girl might have been petty, wanting it for herself; and she was amply rewarded, for, taking from his pocket a single glove, he handed it to her and said: 'And beneath the tree from which I plucked my solitary symbol of admiration for your aunt I found'—and here his smile was not devoid of mischief—'this solitary glove. I fear you have lost its fellow.' And so it was that in one morning Doctor Syn had bestowed several trophies, loaning the first to a man he did not like and bestowing the others upon two women that he loved. Aunt Agatha had the jewels which she wanted and a rose she had not expected, and Cicely but one glove for which she had no use, yet hoping that the other lay against his heart she thrilled and valued it the more.

Chapter 15. Doctor Syn Receives an Invitation, and Sends One

If Mr. Bone had experiended difficulty in selecting a suitable gift for a lady, Aunt Agatha appeared to be having equal trouble in the choice of one for the opposite sex. Not that her experience was letting her down, but she could not find anything suitable for a gentleman of his profession amongst all this assortment of feminine fripperies. The jewels so lately returned were spread about over the bed, and she turned over and sorted, and then turned over again the objects she had picked out. Cicely sat perched at the foot, leaning back against the spiral post, giving her opinion every now and then.

Proudly pinned at Aunt Agatha's bosom, fastening her fichu, was the gold brooch set with the crystal head of a dog, whose eyes, peeping out from the frills and flounces, were every bit as bright as those of Mister Pitt, who was watching the proceedings from beneath the bedspread.

'No, child,' the old lady laughed, 'not the gold true-lover's knot—nor the pearl locket with my hair in it, for it might surprise him somewhat to know that I was once a blonde, since he has only seen me in this hairdresser's contraption. Oh, Lud, had we but something appertaining to his naughty trade—a tiny pair of gold horse-pistols, a mask with sapphires for the eyes—though,' she added roguishly, 'I warrant they would not shine as brightly as his do. But there, we have not even a silver spur, and cannot send him a bracelet made of elephant's hair, since his activities on horseback on Quarry Hill. Steep as it is, 'tis not comparable to Hannibal's elephantine ride across the Alps.' Cicely jumped from the bed, exclaiming, 'Why, Lud, madame, what a ninny I am! Sitting here watching you rack your brains while I believe I have the very thing. I'll fetch it for you straight,' and off she went to her own room, returning in a few minutes with something in her hand. 'There,' she said, 'will not this suit your naughty beau, ma'am? At least it tallies with some of his equipment,' and she held out for Aunt Agatha's inspection a golden riding-crop set in the form of a pin, its handle encrusted with diamonds and its thong looped in a true lover's knot. 'Pray take it, ma'am. 'Tis one I bought myself, after I had first cleared the broad dyke without a splash.' Aunt Agatha was delighted. 'I vow, child, and you are quite to my satisfaction,' she cried. ''Tis, as you say, the very thing, though I observe you are insisting upon my sending a true lover's knot to the gentleman, you wicked miss. And since I am sending him something that belonged to you, I shall give you something that he returned to me,' picking from the bed a large velvet case which she handed to the girl. Cicely opened it and saw winking up at her a magnificent set of diamond ornaments—necklace, ear-rings and stars for her hair, and being too excited to speak, could only gaze while the old lady continued: 'Do you not thank me, child? They were to be yours anyway. But now you can wear them at my birthday party. I told your Mamma that she was to excel herself since it will be my eightieth anniversary, and I think I deserve it for staying the course. I intend to write some of the invitations myself, this afternoon. Now let me see'—and she looked up at Cicely with a twinkle. 'Is there not some special gentleman you would like me to ask? A beau from Hythe, or a pretty Dragoon from the garrison at Dover?' Cicely twinkled back at her, but did not speak. 'No? Well, there are but two gentlemen that I care about in the vicinity. That dear old Doctor Syn and that sinful young horseman, and I vow I shall invite them both.' One hour later Miss Gordon's French maid, who by now had become reconciled to this land below the sea, partly because it was in sight of her beloved France but chiefly because of the flattering attentions of a young groom, went tripping down the village street, Mister Pitt at her heels and two large envelopes in her hand.

As usual, after a certain tune had been played and whistled, no one seemed to be about. Indeed she passed but two people, the first of which, a large woman who in passing her muttered audibly, 'Goodness, there's that foreigner! What is Dymchurch coming to?'—the second, none other than Mr. Mipps, who was locking up his coffin shop, who exclaimed, 'Why, if it ain't that there yew-hedged poodle!' Sweeping his battered three-cornered hat with a flourish, he bowed to the enchanted Lisette, who felt that 'Marsh' after all was not so dull, since here was that nice little man whose master had told her not to worry about the Scarecrow. After a deal of excruciating French from Mipps, and much twitterings from Lisette, she gave him the two letters which he promised to deliver—'toot sweet', and hurried back to the stables in hopes of half an hour's flirtation with her groom.

Mr. Mipps found Doctor Syn was in his library, studying a large map of the Continent. The sight of his old Captain measuring mileage with dividers caused the Sexton to ask hopefully: 'What yer doin'? Looks like you're planning to set sail again. Not thinkin' of 'oistin' canvas, are you, sir?' The reply was not what he had expected, having playfully asked the question so many times, and received curt 'Nos' or 'Remember to forget, Mr.

Mipps'. This time, however, the calm, 'Yes, Mr. Mipps—tonight', made him execute a few well-chosen steps from his intricate hornpipe, until the Vicar's shattering, 'Alone, Mr. Mipps, and not what you're thinking,' brought him back to earth again, and with a long face he listened to the Vicar's plans. He brightened, however, as the scheme unfolded and he saw fun ahead, and by the time Doctor Syn had finished he was himself again—full of admiration for his master's daring idea, as, finishing the hornpipe from where he left off, he took the proffered glass of brandy and drank success to this new enterprise.

'That's the best one I've heard yet,' he said. 'Wish I was a-goin' with you.

Now then, what's me orders?' 'To begin with, Mr. Mipps, what ships lie in Rye harbour, ready to sail?' Mr. Mipps not only had them at his finger-tips but rattled them off—friendly vessels and otherwise—and the Vicar made decision on the Two Brothers. 'For,' said he, 'she's fast, well armed, and I like her owners and her crew. Get word to them that I shall be aboard before high tide tonight. Tell Jonathan Quested to be at Littlestone with his fishing-smack at dusk. He must sail me round to Rye, for I shall be staying there in my capacity as Dean to visit neighbouring parishes, and will, of course, inform Sir Antony. I shall want you to deliver some letters for me. The one addressed to Captain Foulkes which I shall date the day after tomorrow must be handed to him at the Red Lion on the same day. 'Tis an invitation he is looking for to meet the Scarecrow, though I do not doubt that he will meet more than he bargains for.' Then, turning away from Mipps and looking in the fire, he took up his pipe and said almost too casually: 'The other letter I want delivered tonight, when I have gone. 'Tis to Miss Cicely, explaining why I cannot ride with her tomorrow morning.' He looked over his shoulder and met the Sexton's quizzical gaze; grinned boyishly and said, "I am to have my first jumping lessons on a proper horse. I fear that I shall never clear the broad dyke as she can.'

'Riding lessons,' snorted Mipps. 'Serve you right if you falls off.

Jumpin' lessons. You. From a petticoat. Talkin' of petticoats, I met that French bettermy one. She gave me these,' and he took from his pocket the two large envelopes Lisette had entrusted him with. 'This for the Rev.—that's you. And this for a Mr. Bone—don't know who he is. There's somethin' in it, too.' 'Ah,' nodded Syn, not without amusement. 'Our Jimmie has made a conquest indeed. I rather think she has returned his compliment. Perhaps this will explain,' and he opened his own letter, noting with pleasure the large firm hand so full of flourishes and character, and smiling as he read the contents.

November 14th, 1793.
The Court House, Dymchurch.
My Dear Friend, As I have every intention of becoming eighty upon the 19th of this month, I wish to celebrate it, and have commandeered the Court House for a party, which would not be complete without you. Indeed I shall be desolated if you fail, for I fear my only other beau will not be able to attend (I'd give my wig to see our Tony's face if he did). I have writ him an invitation and returned his compliment with a token, so would be mightily glad if you, with your knowledge of black sheep, would see to its delivery. Cicely seemed so chagrined at the loss of her glove that although she carries it with her all the time, I had to give her some diamonds to make up for it. I shall insist that she wears them at my rout at the risk of losing my last remaining beau, so pray do not disappoint us.
Yours affectionately, AGATHA GORDON.

P.S.—On second thought I have also writ an invitation to the Scarecrow, which I hope you will also be good enough to see comes to his hand, i.e. black sheep. For knowing that poor Caroline's choice of gentlemen leaves much to be desired, and that I shall have an especial bunch of 'party' cronies for my amusement if I am not careful, so am leaving nothing to chance. I am going to be eighty but I am equally determined to enjoy myself.

A.G.

Doctor Syn appreciated the letter, knowing what the old lady meant by her innuendoes. He smiled when he thought that the old lady had noticed what the Squire and Lady Caroline had missed and would never dream could happen. So, telling Mr. Mipps to see that Jimmie Bone's letter was delivered safe at Slippery Sam's, with some added instructions that made the little Sexton howl with delight, he went to his desk and penned a grateful acceptance to Miss Gordon, saying that although he was going away for a few days on a decanal tour, not even the Archbishop of Canterbury would keep him from her party.

He left Cicely's letter to the last, although it was the shortest, reading thus:

Cicely, I am going on a visit with my younger brother. Pray do not worry, for I shall be back in time to compare your eyes with Miss Agatha's diamonds. It may interest you to know that I am not jealous of my brother—I have an idea that I am younger than he is.

CHRISTOPHER.

P.S.—Pray inform your father that I am gone across the Kent Ditch.

'This his fault. He should never have made me the Dean of Peculiars.

Mr. Nicholas Hyde had spent the morning in the town of Rye, mixing business with pleasure in its many taverns. He had learnt, after some expense laid profitably out in strong ale, that the shepherds and cowmen were in league with the smugglers and were used for passing messages swiftly. This special code, invented by the Scarecrow himself, evolved a complicated manipulation of livestock—the position in a certain field of a particular animal meaning some keyword. Some three hours later Mr. Hyde, in his capacity of Revenue Officer, put this valuable information to the test.

Standing on the bridge across the Kent Ditch, which commanded a good view of both counties—Kent and Sussex—it certainly seemed that something was afoot; for what he saw was not the ordinary shepherding of flocks.

In a field close at hand he noticed that seven sheep were separated and put into the next field—a little further on a white horse was moved from one side of a field to another—while two black cows and a goat in kid were put into that same field. Turning, he saw the same thing happening about a quarter of a mile away. Then on again, and on, and so the message flew, till on the Harbour Quay at Rye the captain of the Two Brothers gave orders that his crew and vessel must be ready to sail on the next full tide.

So that in the language of the smuggler shepherds:

At seven sheep punctually a white horse stepped aboard the Two Black Cows, which sailed at the next goat-in-kid.

Chapter 16. Citizen L'pouvantail not at your Service

Paris—and dusk already falling on another day of bloody entertainment for the mob. This was the Reign of Terror, reaching its peak but a month before, when the head of the beautiful Queen, the hated Autrichienne, had rolled into the basket. That was a feast indeed, and appetite whetted by the blood of royalty became voracious for any food that bore the faintest resemblance to the once powerful class they loathed and used to fear. And so the knife fell day after day, filling the baskets beneath that ghastly symbol of their age. Still their hunger was not satisfied, though the supply grew with the demand, for as the number of highly born showed signs of dwindling, these human vampires fastened themselves on any who bore traces of gentility, denouncing friends and enemies alike. A powdered wig, a jewelled snuff-box or dainty heel beneath a silken gown, any of these enough excuse for Madame Guillotine.

'A bas les aristos! A la lampe! Vive le Republique! A bas la tyrannie!' Yet enflaming the populace still further and committing more atrocious crimes of treachery himself was, strangely enough, a man of outward refinement. In the sadistic release of their pent-up fury, the newly founded citizens did not realize that these pale, proud, foolish aristos who, smiling, disdained the knife, had never been so tyrannous as this one man—Maximilien Marie Isidore Robespierre. All-powerful, Robespierre alone could still affect the powdered hair and exquisite clothes he condemned and was abolishing. This ruthless tiger preserved the dress and demeanour of respectability. Reckless, yet devoid of passion, greedy of blood, yet his private morals irreproachable. Politically courageous, though physically an arrant coward. Such was the tyrant of the day. He stood, this evening, at a window overlooking the Place de la Revolution as the final tumbrils jolted quickly to unload their offerings to Madame Guillotine before the dark. Rumbling and creaking they crossed the Pont au Change, along the Rue St. HonorT into the Square before him. A dripping November fog hung over the Seine, but could not damp the enthusiasm of the crowd, as from windows, parapets, roofs and leafless trees they watched this free amusement. As in turn each well-dressed actor made his first appearance on this grisly stage, the hush of anticipation changed to wild applause when he took his final curtain in the grim comedy of La Guillotine, the most popular actress in Paris.

Suddenly there was a disturbance from the back of the crowd: a latecomer elbowing his way through the screaming red-capped women who shouted greetings and tried to detain him. 'Vive L'pouvantail!' they cried, but he pressed on, reaching the other side of the Place, from whose houses hung the tricolour banners of new France.

He passed beneath the window from which Robespierre looked, dived down a side street and knocked at the postern door.

He was admitted immediately, for he was expected, and conducted to an upper room, where a man stood waiting for him. Robespierre turned from the window, greeting him with, 'Welcome, Citizen L'pouvantail,' then, with a wave of his hand towards the window asked, 'And how does this organization compare with yours? I see your popularity here almost rivals mine, which sets me wondering what my reception will be in England when our system of LibertT and EgalitT spreads to your country. But of that later.' Motioning his visitor to seat himself, they went to the long table upon which stood wine and glass amongst a mass of papers, documents and maps.

Robespierre filled a glass which he handed to his guest and then poured a little for himself which he diluted with water. The Scarecrow's mind worked quickly. Behind his inscrutable mask he smiled cynically. Here was a man guilty of spilling the blood of thousands of his countrymen yet afraid to taste the full-bodied wine of the country he had plundered. He waited to see if the man himself would prove as weak as the wine he drank, knowing full well he could afford to wait because of his own strength. Having thus summed up his character, a vain and mediocre man, he found it tallied with the outward show.

Robespierre, though not a dandy, was dressed fastidiously. A well-cut velvet coat of claret colour, white knee-breeches, stockings to match, all these the finest silk, while the large cravat and exquisite lace at his wrists proclaimed the salon and the boudoir—but not the bloody scaffold. Rising from a studious forehead, his hair was brushed back neatly and well powdered. His face, though capable of striking terror to his unfortunate victims, seemed to the Scarecrow to be the face of a clown with its tip-tilted nose and protuberant eyes.

Robespierre, scrutinizing in his turn, making little of what was before him, apart from fantastic clothes, and irritated that he could not see his opponent's eyes and brow and so gauge the character of this man with whom he hoped to have dealings, politely requested him, since he was in the presence of a friend, to lay aside his mask.

To this the Scarecrow shook his head. 'Your pardon, citizen,' he said, 'that I cannot do, for 'tis my bargain with Gehenna that when I wear these clothes and ride with the black devil, it is not meet that any man should look upon the blasted face of Sin. Believe me, such an evil sight would be distasteful to a gentleman of obvious refinement like yourself. No man unmasking me could look and live to tell what he had seen.'

'Then keep your mask, citizen, for I am not experimenting. I have no inclination to be thus blasted into hell before my time. But come, let us to business. Barsard has worked swiftly, I see. Your request last night for an interview was sooner than I expected. He told you of my plan? Well, what do you think of it?' 'Since I do not know your Barsard, citizen, he could hardly have told me of your plan.' 'Then why are you here?' Robespierre sprang to his feet and put out his hand to seize a bell upon the table. But the Scarecrow's hand was already there, as with a note of irony he said, 'Do not fear, citizen. I beg you not to be alarmed, although perhaps it is excusable. This meeting, I assure you, is entirely my idea. I also have a plan. It is a strange coincidence, this—each having a plan and thinking of the other. Now which shall be unfolded first—yours or mine?'

Robespierre had been plainly agitated on hearing that this man knew nothing of his agent. Then why was he here if Barsard had not sent him? Was it assassination? Since July the thirteenth, when Marat had been struck down, he had been haunted by the dread of sudden death. Had he not stood with Danton and Desmoulins hoping to see on Charlotte Corday's face what fanaticism looked like, so that he might know it when he met it? Was it even now behind that mask? Was this the reason for the mask? Was it even now upon him? And so he remained standing, his own face now resembling a death's head mask, from which his eyes alone showed life. But the Scarecrow spoke again. 'I beg you, citizen, compose yourself. I assure you I have no designs upon your life.' Then, as the cheering of the mob outside grew louder, he waved his hand in the direction whence it came and added: 'You and I, citizen, have no need to resort to those methods, for I am here on your account as well as on mine own. But who is this Barsard? It seems I am indebted to him for this meeting.' The Revolution leader seemed to be reassured and sat down once more in the gilt chair which seemed so out of place in this great empty room. He did not speak, but poured himself another glass of wine, this time without the water.

The Scarecrow, watching his reactions, was amused. It was so exactly what he had expected, and to satisfy the other's curiosity and put himself in a stronger position, he assumed the air of a man who is about to put his cards on the table.

'Since I have the idea that your plan may be similar to mine own, I will unfold mine first,' he said. 'I am not so modest as to assume that you have never heard of me on both sides of La Manche. You must know then that my organization is vast and unassailable. The fleet I have built up is well-manned and easily man£uvred. In fact the only thing that crosses the Channel safely is my contraband. I have lived, as you know, for the people, and my love for my countrymen is England is as great as yours for the people of France. Therefore I come to place myself by your side. Together we can do much.' Robespierre was amazed. His great eyes protruded still further, as, thumping the table, he said excitedly: 'But, citizen, that is my plan! 'Tis almost as though you have come straight from Barsard. I told you of my hopes that LibertT and EgalitT would spread. Together we could make it spread to England. Keep running the blockade; you shall have every assistance on my side. Keep sailing with your contraband, but give me constant passage for my agents, who can spread our ideas of freedom in your land.' He leant over the table eagerly and, taking up a dossier, he showed the Scarecrow the names of six of his best agents, who already had their orders.

They would, he said, throw the country into confusion, and if more were sent every time there was a run of contraband, very soon they would achieve their object. He had already perfected a plan to overthrow the Government, the monarchy and that sacrT English Pitt. With the unfolding of his plan his face too became the face of a fanatic, so infatuated with his own inspiration that he did not notice that his visitor had laughed. For indeed the Scarecrow could not suppress it as he had a sudden vision of another Mister Pitt, and of what Miss Agatha would have to say to that.

But Robespierre, now intoxicated by his own conceit, gave full rein to his imagination, and painted such a fabulous picture of a united republic with himself as head that the Scarecrow marvelled at the man's audacity.

Robespierre went on: 'Your ships are fast, my men are ready, our tide is at the flood, so let us take it. Without your help this plan collapses. When can you sail?'

'Immediately!' The Scarecrow's prompt decision pleased the madman, little thinking that the masked smuggler had already formed a plan as mad as his. Robespierre showed promptness too. To augment the dossier in the Scarecrow's hand, he found six others, each proving what a hold he had upon these trusted agents. Damning evidence, indeed, were it to be produced against a spy by England now at war. On that score, however, Robespierre had no qualms. Agents were well paid. If they were caught they knew the consequences, and took them. What he had already learned about this citizen L'pouvantail assured him that such a man with everything to lose would never range himself upon the side of a Government that had put so high a price upon his capture. No, the English Crown would pardon any of the Scarecrow's men who turned King's Evidence, but for its very dignity could not be tolerant towards the man himself. His defiance of the Law had been too flagrant. This was one English rogue that Robespierre knew he could trust, and as he listened to the rascal's chuckling over the descriptions of the spies, the arch-schemer was satisfied that this agents were in safe hands.

Details were then arranged. Three of the men would meet him at the Somme. The other three would ride with him from Paris, and, much to the Scarecrow's satisfaction, Robespierre penned a letter empowering the Citizen L'pouvantail to commandeer whatever form of transport he required. For him all Barriers were to be open without examination, no one was permitted to unmask him. In short, this citizen rode on the Republic's business and was neither to be hampered nor asked inquisitive questions. Robespierre's signature sufficed.

"Tis well to know the background of the lives of people you work with,' remarked the Scarecrow as he placed the documents in his breast pocket. 'There is but one thing more, I think. How do I get in contact with this Barsard, since he is already over there? In case of a mistake which might prove fatal to our schemes, I must ask you for his dossier too, for whatever credentials he may offer, I shall feel safer if I can put questions to him—dates, places, any fact that he must answer in detail, so that I can know he is your man.' Robespierre nodded and went to a cabinet, as he answered: 'I rejoice to see that my Lieutenant-General in England is so thorough.' He selected a paper and handed it to the Scarecrow, adding: 'There, citizen, read this with the others at your convenience. You will find there a most original career—a character that you would hardly credit in fiction. He is a man I should not choose to be an enemy.' The last drop of the Knife for that day sounded outside the window, and a howl of enthusiasm mixed with disappointment that the curtain had fallen. The Scarecrow jerked his head in the direction. 'The Citizen Robespierre has a quick answer to any enemy. I think you need not trouble yourself on any such score. I will now leave you this promise—that you shall hear of quick results upon this matter'—and he touched the outside of his breast pocket in which the papers were concealed. 'And what you hear will make you say, 'That Citizen L'pouvantail accomplishes all that he sets out to do'.' Then, after drinking a toast to the success of this same citizen, Robespierre graciously accompanied his mysterious guest as far as the postern gate.

Having me the three who were to ride with him from Paris at a little tavern off the Rue St. HonorT, and in which a good dinner was served, the Scarecrow ordered the others to mount and await him, for he had a little private business of his own to attend to with the proprietor, who for many years had been one of the Cognac procurers for the contraband supplies. This merry rogue, after receiving his next order, whispered: 'Two of those

Robespierre agents are but dull dogs, citizen, bred in the Paris sewers until they saw there was a profit in being able to speak the English tongue. Oh, they're useful enough, if throats are to be cut, but their intellects are not enlightening. The other is a different proposition. He was once a favourite at Versailles. Amusing. He will make you laugh.' 'Robespierre has told me of him,' chuckled the Scarecrow. 'A pleasantspoken rascal. I think you're right. No doubt his history will make me laugh.' It was this Citizen Decoutier whom the Scarecrow chose to ride beside him, while separating the others to prevent them talking, one ahead to rouse the Barrier guards and one behind. Decoutier certainly was amusing in a grim fashion, but his humorous anecdotes, in which he figured as the central figure, proved him to be a most depraved and despicable character. Indeed the Demon Rider of Romney Marsh could not have been accompanied by three worse fiends had he been the very Devil himself, and when they reached the rendezvous on the banks of the Somme the other three proved every bit as evil. This, as it happened, did not distress the Scarecrow. He was glad of it. It made his plan the easier to carry out. Though when he met his own Lieutenant, the engaging giant Dulonge who organized the fleet of luggers from the secret harbour on his own territory, the Scarecrow confessed that it was good to drink good brandy with another rascal who could lay claim to an honest humanity.

The Scarecrow found that the Revolution had not changed this old friend of his one whit. Like Robespierre and Decoutier, he did not fear to show he was something of a dandy, but in his case no one could criticize, for his huge frame carried an arm that could kill an ox, and such strength could never be concealed beneath lace ruffles.

To him the Scarecrow unfolded Robespierre's plans and his own. He agreed on every point. They went together to the quay and made arrangements with the captain of the Two Brothers to take the six aboard and feed them, Dulonge vowing he would not spoil his own appetite by sitting down with such villainous characters. 'For,' he cried, 'they all look as though they would rather eat their own grandmothers than my good saddle of lamb.' The two friends sat down alone, and over their meal served in his spacious ancestral dining-hall they planned their future policy and how to pass quicker news of the movements of the ships of war so active now in the Channel. Certain of one thing, however, that so long as Robespierre's interests were served their lugger fleet need have no fear from the French Navy.

After this meal they both went to the prison building on the quay, where Pedro welcomed Doctor Syn. Here were housed all those traitors who at some time or other had tried to betray the Scarecrow. 'I think friend Barsard will not lodge here,' said Dulonge, 'for you will deal with him, and if he comes my way I'll silence him.'

The Two Brothers was ready for sea, and the Scarecrow, after a farewell to Dulonge and Pedro, went aboard, and the voyage began. At the mouth of the river a shot was fired across their bow by a French frigate, and at the Scarecrow's order the captain hove to and allowed an officer to come aboard. 'No one may leave home waters,' said this officer. 'The British fleet is out and our ships will give battle.' 'Cast your eye on this, my little citizen,' replied the Scarecrow, showing him his passport from Robespierre. 'The arm of La Guillotine can even stretch to sea, as any of your officers will find who hinders the Two Brothers. Tell your captain to put to sea and keep the English from us.' The officer apologized profusely. He hoped indeed he had not detained the Citizen Captain, who sailed in the Republic's interest, and he was rowed back to his frigate, where he did not scruple to frighten his captain with what the strange L'pouvantail had said about La Guillotine.

This incident showed the Scarecrow that so long as Robespierre was all-powerful he had a letter of safety from the French. His only fear of serious interception was therefore from the British. In spite of his secret plan he realized that the presence of French spies aboard would look black for the captain of the Two Brothers and worse since the other passenger (himself) was a notorious malefactor wanted by the Crown. So on this voyage the Scarecrow decided not to be a passenger. He took the tiller. He took command, and in the dark hours before the dawn, no lanterns showing, he ran the gauntlet of a British line of men-o'-war. But these giants were watching for bigger fish to tackle than this swift clipper, that appeared and vanished like a ghost. It was the old Clegg that navigated the Two Brothers to Dungeness. It was here that the six Frenchmen huddled on the deck, close together for warmth, were badly frightened, for the Two Brothers was hailed in the darkness by a voice proclaiming the authority of the Sandgate Revenue cutter. 'Name your vessel,' cried the officer. 'The Twin Sisters, fishing,' sang back Doctor Syn. 'We'll come aboard, and see your catch,' called out the officer. The Scarecrow had crept forward to the for'ard gun. There was a loud report, a flash of flame, and then the splintering fall of wood. He had unstepped their mast.

Over went the tiller, and the Two Brothers shot out again before the wind, tacked back and then, instead of landing to the west of the long nose of shingle, she crept into the Bay. The three hoots of the owl were heard and answered by the scrape of stones. The Frenchmen did not understand this, but the Scarecrow did. Twelve men, under the command of one called Hellspite, were hurrying across the pebbles with back-stays on their feet. The Two Flat boards of wood attached to the shoes for crossing the miles of pebbles.

Brothers was heading for the land end of the Ness where the old Marsh town of New Romney nestled. Here the horses were ready, and six stalwart fishermen in masks carried the Frenchmen to the shore. They neither asked nor knew what men these were, except that they were landlubbers who feared to wade in the dark. Ashore all they saw in the swinging lantern light were six more Scarecrow's men, just like themselves—hooded and masked.

'Is all prepared?' the Scarecrow had called across the few yards of shallow water from the deck of the Two Brothers.

'Aye—aye. Hellspite here and horses ready,' came the answer.

In a few minutes all were transferred from deck to saddle and then, following the Citizen L'pouvantail, who had proved his loyalty to Robespierre by firing at a British ship of war, the grisly-looking cavalcade set off along the sea-wall road. Passing Littlestone they turned into the Marsh, and in and out the intersecting dykes they galloped. As they rode, the Scarecrow turned his charger alongside that of Hellspite.

Leaning down in the saddle, no one but Hellspite heard the whisper:

'What of the Beadle?' It was the voice of the Sexton of Dymchurch that answered: 'It was too easy. I was drinkin' with him. But he was out before I 'ad a chance. 'E ain't got no 'ead for liquor, that there Beadle.' 'And the keys?' 'I got 'em. 'Angin' on me belt. Did you fare well across there?' 'Aye, Mipps—I'll have a tale to tell you. At dawn we'll crack a bottle.' And the Scarecrow reined back and for a time rode with the Frenchman Decoutier.

They did not ride into the village of Dymchurch, but skirted it, keeping to the Marsh fields that lay behind the Church. Here they dismounted and, tying their horses to a sheepfold fencing, the Scarecrow whispered to the Frenchmen to walk in silence as they were near the end of their journey. He told them that he was taking them to his underground headquarters where there would be good food and drink, as well as security. As the way was difficult, he ordered each Frenchman to be supported on either side by his own men, and then they crossed a bridge and stumbled into the blacker darkness of the Rookery and at last down outside steps, where a door was silently unlocked by the little figure they had heard named Hellspite. 'Prenez—garde—silence,' warned the Citizen L'pouvantail.

A minute later the Frenchmen heard a door close behind them, and Hellspite lit a lantern from his 'flasher' and told the Nightriders who had led them to remove their charges' masks.

The lantern light showed them a bare room with a groined roof, the only furniture a long table clamped to the floor between the flagstones and two clamped benches. One window higher up in th grey stone wall was shuttered from the outside and barred within.

Decoutier produced a pack of cards and sat down at the table, saying he would play for any stakes till supper should be served, or was it breakfast, he asked—adding that he hoped the fare would be better than the room. ''Tis like a room in the Bastille,' he said.

The Scarecrow had meanwhile ordered the Nightriders to take away the spare masks and cloaks and to bring food. Hellspite slipped after them to hurry things along, while the Scarecrow produced a large bottle of cognac.

'You shall be host for the moment, Citizen Decoutier. Drink yourself, then see your fellows have some, and do not spare it, for I assure you there is a cellar full to hand.' He thumped the wall behind him and whispered: 'And there is such a kitchen on the other side this wall. Fit for a King's Magistrate, I vow. You'll have food presently and then perhaps you'll let me share the dice with you. We must be silent, but that's no bar to merriment, I hope.' He tiptoed to the door, listening cautiously. 'Ah,' thought Decoutier.

'He is a careful one, this guide of ours. No wonder Robespierre trusts him.' The door shut—and then it happened—the awful creeping cold of doubt—followed by the ghastly grip of fear. For all around that table had heard the creaking of a lock shot home.

Chapter 17. A Surprise for Seven Gentlemen

Mr. Mipp was feeling very well that morning. He had had the sort of night he revelled in. Drink, tobacco and the story of his master's adventure had carried him back to the good old days. He had laughed till his sides ached, he had drunk himself sober, and smoked so many pipefuls that the room resembled a Channel fog by the time they opened the casement to let in the dawn. Indeed, the cosy library of the Vicarage might have been Clegg's cabine in the Imogene. There was also the added anticipation of seeing the village astounded once more at this latest escapade of the Scarecrow. It so happened that the morning was as foggy outside as it had been in the library; a thick blanket of mist enveloped the Marsh. This called forth the remark from Mr. Mipps that he didn't know they had smoked so much. Then hurrying along with the Vicar as they went towards the church, this same fog occasioned a slight accident.

Opposite the churchyard wall, not being able to see farther than the tip of his pointed nose, Mr. Mipps inadvertently tripped over something. Like Mrs. Honeyballs, he knew exactly where he was and exactly what he was doing, but he derived great satisfaction in making his planned performances convincing.

In the most aggrieved, innocent tones he was able to muster, he pretended that he had hurt himself, as he hopped delightedly round the Vicar on one leg. 'Ow, me poor leg! Why, blow me down if I 'aven't gone and tripped over the stocks. Ought to know where they was by now, oughtn't I? And knock me up solid, if there ain't some naughty person in them.' He peered closer. 'Why, goodness gracious me, Vicar—it's the Beadle!' The Vicar appeared to be astounded. 'The Beadle, Mr. Mipps?' 'Now whoever could 'ave put him there?' said Mipps to the fog. 'Oh, what a wicked man! He smells of drink.' At that moment the Beadle opened his eyes and groaned, and between sneezes and moans managed to tell them that he did not know who had put him there, or what had happened to him since he had left the Ship Inn the night before. He protested bitterly and demanded to be released. His head was splitting and he was going to complain to Mrs. Waggetts about her beer.

How to get him out was now the question.

'Well, you're the Beadle, ain't you? Where's the key?' asked Mr.

Mipps. 'You ought to know if no one else does.' He knew perfectly well that the key was in the Beadle's pocket, where he had put it the night before, but he suggested that the Beadle should look through his own pockets. The Beadle argued that he always carried official keys at his belt, and since he 'wasn't no acrobat' Mr. Mipps had better help him, and sure enough the key was found. Upon being released, the portly Beadle was so stiff and dizzy that Mr. Mipps felt obliged to assist him to the Court House Lodge—telling the Vicar that he wouldn't be a minute and handing him the keys of the church.

Twenty minutes later Mr. Mipps opened the vestry door and grinned at the Vicar. Then he came in and closed it carefully behind him. 'All accordin' to plan, sir,' he said delightedly. 'Started off lovely. The Beadle feelin' a bit guilty like, said he'd better go and see what had 'appened in his absence, though as the cells had been all empty, he wasn't expectin' no trouble. Well, down he goes, and he certainly found what he didn't expect, a whole room full of it. He reads them papers with the Scarecrow's signature what was pinned on the door, and then there weren't no stoppin' him. He dursn't look in even, though I 'ad a good peep. There they was, all six, sleepin' like babes, with ever such a surprised look on their faces and that there laudabum-brandy bottle empty beside 'em. I done what you said, told the Beadle not to breathe a word to none, but to report it quick and Bristol fashion to the Squire. But he's too scared to gossip, sir.' 'That's as well, Mipps,' nodded the Vicar, 'since we do not wish it to reach the ears of Barsard until we are ready for him.' At that moment there was a rap upon the vestry door, and a muffled excited whisper: 'Christopher. I say, Christopher. Are you there?' Mr. Mipps's wink to the Vicar plainly said, 'And now we're off.' The door opened and round it peered the bewildered face of the Squire.

'Good morning, Tony,' said Doctor Syn. 'You're up betimes.' 'So are you,' replied the Squire. 'Beadle told me. Didn't know you were back. Thank Heaven you are.' 'I have but now arrived from

Rye,' explained the Vicar. 'I came by boat; but there, what news I have can wait. I did not think to see you till the birthday festivities tonight.' 'Festivities!' snorted the Squire, closing the vestry door and coming to the table at which the Vicar sat. He leant over and said excitedly: 'It won't be only birthday festivities we'll be havin' when this news reaches London. I say, Christopher—the most astoundin' thing's happened. I don't know what to make of it.' From his appearance the last remark was obvious for he was in turn both angry and delighted. Dressed in his hunting clothes, he complained that the Scarecrow had spoilt yet another good day's sport. 'Though, mind you,' he said, 'I'm deucedly grateful to the fellow.' 'I don't quite follow you, Tony,' said Doctor Syn. 'I should have thought the fog would be the cause of stopping your amusement.' 'Oh, that'll clear,' said Tony. 'But what the Scarecrow's done will want a lot of clearing up. In fact, damme, I don't know how to begin. I suppose I ought to send a messenger hotfoot to Mr. Pitt.' The Vicar purposely misunderstood. 'Why, whatever has Miss Agatha's poodle been up to now?' 'No, no, I don't mean that toe-bitin' little brute. I mean Mr. Pitt. The Mr. Pitt. The Minister of War.' Then, seeing that Mipps was tactfully about to withdraw, he added:

'No, my good Mipps. Stay here. I think perhaps that you can help us, and you ain't the gossipin' sort—' At which Mr. Mipps pulled his forelock and thought that it was better to be inside in the warm, even though the vestry had got a nice big key'ole.

The Squire came straight to the point. 'Now lookee, Christopher. As far as I can see, I've got six French spies in my Court House. And damme—I don't know what to do with 'em.' 'Well, Tony,' and the Vicar shook his head, 'I've heard of red snakes and pink elephants early in the morning, but French spies is perhaps the latest fashion ù' 'No—no, I'm perfectly sober—sober as a judge this morning.' The Vicar smiled. 'The comparison is questionable, Tony,' he said.

'Oh, don't you Caroline me,' snapped the Squire. 'I'm too worried—I tell you, Christopher, I have six of Robespierre's picked men, and they're a present from the Scarecrow.'

'Good gracious me, Tony. Being in the Vestry I am persuaded you are not pulling my leg. Yet I cannot credit it. Six?

In the Court House? Present from the Scarecrow? How on earth could they have got there?' 'Oh, don't ask me—ask the Beadle.' (Really, Christopher was being confoundedly stupid this morning. He had hoped for good advice, and here he was making idiotic suggestions about coloured animals. Pink elephants, indeed! He wished the Beadle had seen pink poodles—or been bitten by a white one. What with using his own stocks for a night out and then his excuses about the strength of Mrs. Waggetts' liquor— The Squire couldn't think of anything bad enough for him, seeing that he was perfectly sober himself that morning and had therefore no fellow-feeling for a thick head.

Apart from all this the Beadle's terror of the Scarecrow irritated him beyond bearing, since the great fat oaf should represent his own strong arm of the law instead of shaking like a jelly. Now, damme, Christopher was taking the attitude that the whole thing was a parcel of lies!) 'But how do you know that they are French?' asked the Vicar. 'And how do you know that they are spies? You say the Scarecrow sent them to you?' 'How do I know?' repeated the Squire. 'Because I can read,' and taking from his pocket a number of papers, he slammed them down triumphantly on the vestry table. 'There you are—read for yourself. They were fastened to the door of the Common Cell. Damn' fool Beadle wouldn't take them down. Had to do it myself. My French ain't good, as you know, but what I can't speak in their God-forsaken jabber I can just manage to read, and if this don't prove them six to be as dirty a lot of scoundrels as the man who put his signature to it—that 'Robespeer'—then my name ain't Antony Cobtree. Come, man, read 'em yourself. You're the scholar here and I want your advice. Don't you realize, Christopher, that this is a hanging business—not down here, outside my windows, thank God—but at the Tower of London—and it's our Scarecrow who's done it. Damme, I always said the fellow had some good in him. This'll make him more popular. Lud, Christopher, I don't know what to do.' Doctor Syn at last appeared to understand the importance of the situation. 'I do admit,' he said, 'that you are faced with a devilish tricky business. Do you think that this will gain the Scarecrow's pardon? For much as I disapprove of him, you're right in saying that he's struck a blow for England. But they could hardly pardon him unless he pledged his word to cease his illegal trade.' 'I know what I'd do here,' cried Tony. 'I'd use my authority and pardon him out of hand, then call him as chief witness for the Crown. But what those tom fool London judges will do is a very different matter. Now I ask you, Christopher, what in Heaven's name is the best course for me to take?' This was the opportunity that Doctor Syn wanted. He told the Squire that in his opinion the whole thing should be kept quiet, and that he, as Chief Magistrate of Romney Marsh, should go to Mr. Pitt and tell him everything.

'You realize, Tony, that the Scarecrow has done you a service which will reflect much honour on you?' This the Squire did realize, and agreeing that the matter should be handled for the moment in great secrecy, asked how he could account to the village for the six prisoners in the cells. Doctor Syn's advice was that he should instruct the Beadle to keep silent on the true facts, and to put about the rumour that they were smugglers caught on the Marsh who were now awaiting legal proceedings. He turned to Mr. Mipps and said with a smile:

'Although I know it is against your principles to tell untruths, yet since the Squire has been so gracious to allow you to hear this staggering news, I feel sure you will see that the village hears only what they should. You understand?' 'Oh, yessir,' replied the Sexton promptly. 'I don't like falsehoods, but I don't mind foxications. Sussex smugglers, you says—Sussex smugglers it is, until such time as the Squire says 'tisn't and tells 'em what they really is.' The Squire thanked Mipps for an honest man, but failed to notice the look of complete understanding that passed between the honest gentleman in question and his master.

It was further decided that Major Faunce of the Dragoons should be taken into their confidence, and Mipps was despatched to require his presence immediately with four of his best men in the official rooms of the Court House. So within the hour under military escort and preceded by a slightly confused Beadle, the Chief Magistrate, the Vicar and the Sexton descended to the cells.

On the flagstones in the passage Mips pointed to a pile of weapons—some dozen pistols, three or four cutlasses, and one sword and sheath that that seen better days which Doctor Syn recognized as the dandy's, lay in a pile by the Common Cell door.

Major Faunce admitted grudgingly that the Scarecrow certainly was thorough, for the prisoners had evidently been disarmed, and that it was as audacious a bit of work as ever he had seen. The sight of these weapons, and the presence of the Dragoons, lent the Beadle sufficient courage to unlock the door. He was still uncertain as to whether he would be punished for his unwitting help in the Scarecrow's latest exploit. So in order to regain a little self-confidence, he made a deal of official pother in selecting the right key from the vast Government collection at his waist. He directed most of it to Mr.

Mipps, his parochial rival, in order to make up for his lack of dignity earlier on.

The great key clanked and turned in the lock, and the heavy door swung open. This noise struck some chord in the fuddled minds of the six prostate men, and slowly six pairs of drugged eyes opened, shut, and opened again. Truth dawned on their stupefied brains. Here was no symbol of the Reign of Terror—Citizen L'pouvantail, Champion of the Republique and friend of Robespierre, but the calm impersonal strength of English faces, and behind them what was unmistakably the scarlet of military. Standing out from this awe-inspiring group was the tall, spare, black-robed figure of a priest. To them the meaning was clear, the surprise—unpleasant. Six pairs of eyes closed desperately in the vain hope that this was but a dream.

Chapter 18. Aunt Agatha Scares the Scarecrow

Miss Gordon was in a pleasurable flutter, as she sat at her dressingtable and surveyed herself in her large mirror. What she saw pleased her, and she gave her reflection a smile. She was looking her best. In fact, this was one of her well days. No young girl dressing for her first party could have taken more pains than she did that evening. She was eighty—was proud of it—didn't feel it—and had no regrets, except—well—but that was a very long time ago, though how vividly she remembered that other birthday party—not hers—but his. It was the last time that she saw him, for he went to join the Prince in those wild days of the '45'. She hadn't been young then, so her love wasn't just a girlish dream. It was mature and full of promise. Though it was denied her by a Hanoverian bullet, she had remained true to that promise and it had given her courage to face the lonely years.

She looked back down those years and found that they had not been so lonely after all. She had wanted to give herself to one person, but since this was not to be she had given of herself to many and her reward was great. She had attracted to herself interesting people from all walks of life, and she never lost the love of youth, and therefore kept alive an unfailing instinct for romance. She had sensed this intangible something a few days ago, and felt that very soon both conspirators would seek her out. She was ready for it, and she had a vast knowledge of humanity from which to draw.

Tonight, therefore, she was as excited as if it had been her own romance, and when a gentle tap upon her door broke her reverie, she cringled with anticipation.

Upon her gay invitation, Cicely swept in like a golden cloud, and both ladies regarded each other with approval, exclaiming simultaneously, 'Lud, how pretty you look.' At which both burst out laughing at having made the same ordinary remark.

'For,' said Cicely, 'it is the wrong word—you look magnificent,' which in truth the old lady did.

Her ruffled gown of white and silver brocade, and her high white wig turned her into a Royal figure. Cicely saw that she was wearing her Gordon sash in honour of the occasion, and very little jewellery save for her rings and the dog's-head brooch.

The old lady stepped back and looked with head on one side at her niece—Cicely had taken trouble for someone and it had been worth it. The gold of the full dress showed off the warmth of her skin and reflected against the gold lights in her hair. 'And I vow you look magnificent too, child,' she smiled back at the radiant girl, noting with satisfaction the eager expectancy in her firm young body and the tender expression in her eyes. Here were the signs she had looked for, and she wondered just how much was going on inside that proud little head, with its sweep of auburn hair and clustered curls.

Cicely smiled back at her and held out the velvet case she carried, saying that she had come in to be shown how to wear the jewels to the best advantage, and would Aunt Agatha put them on for her. She knelt down and the old lady clasped the diamonds round her neck and pinned the stars in her hair. But when it came to ear-rings and brooch Cicely laughingly demurred, with 'Lud, I dare not wear more, for already Maria is like to scratch my eyes out seeing she's only wearing Mamma's second best garnets.' 'You need no jewels to set you off,' cried the old lady. 'And I wonder what gentleman will agree with me on that score. Well nigh all of them, I expect.' She decided now to tease Cicely. 'Why there—I knew I had a bit of news. The dear Vicar has returned from Sussex. But of course you will have heard of that already.' 'Why yes, indeed, ma'am.' Cicely knew full well what the old Pet was after and determined to surprise her. 'After our tedious feminine day in Hythe, I was in need of moral support, so I begged Mamma to stop the carriage and let me out, saying that I must walk or run mad. Both foolish creatures told me the wind and spray would play havoc with my hair, and that I should look a fright. But curl or no, I should have run mad had I not seen him before tonight.' She looked boldly at the old lady and laughed. 'There, ma'am. Now I've said it. Am I not a forward hussy? I saw him at the Vicarage and kissed him too. Oh, tell me what to do, for I shall never love another. And I dare not tell the family, for they do not know him as he really is.' Cicely had not surprised Aunt Agatha one

wit—but she pretended to misunderstand. Which indeed was all
in the fun of the game.

'Your Papa should know him. They were at school together.'
'Oh, Aunt Agatha, can you imagine dear Papa really knowing
anyone? But I suppose 'tis not considered the proper thing to
marry one's father's college friend.' 'Fiddlesticks, my love. Pay no
attention to what is or what is not considered the thing. You can
marry Methuselah if you're in love with him.

Doctor Syn may try to make himself out as old as
Methuselah, but he has not succeeded in convincing us, and
you are in love with him, aren't you, my pet?'

Both Cicely and Aunt Agatha knew the answer to that
question, but before it could be told there was a knock upon the
door and Lisette entered with a message from Lady Caroline to
say the dinner guests were all assembled and waiting in the
Great Hall for the guest of honour, and Miss Cicely.

The two ladies looked at one another with guilty
amusement; then they sped hand in hand along the Gallery
towards the head of the stairs. More like two sisters than great-
aunt and niece, they laughed gaily as they peeped over the
bannisters before descending.

'I vow we've timed our entrance to a nicety,' whispered Aunt
Agatha.

'Yes, they're all assembled. I see Maria is doing her best
with the Major, garnets or no. Yes—I admit she's looking well
tonight, though I never did care for pink myself. And look at
Doctor Syn. Why, nobody could accuse him of being Methuselah
now. He looks for all the world like a racehorse waiting to be off.
How elegant he is tonight. I never noticed his broad shoulders
before. It is because we're looking down on him no doubt, 'tis
tiresome having always to look up. I wish I were as tall as you,
child. 'Tis quite delicious keeping them in this suspense.' The
old lady chuckled.

Indeed Doctor Syn was in such suspense that he had quite
forgotten to be the parson, and the fact that the old lady was
looking down at him did not entirely account for this new vision
of his shoulders. For subconsciously he had braced himself to
meet this new disturbing element. Standing by the great fire
listening with but half an ear to Lady Caroline's prattle, he
caught sight of himself in a long mirror hanging on the opposite

wall, and for the first time in many years he almost hated his protective cloth. He wished that he could dress to suit his mood, and his mood being dangerous he would have been better clothed in all Clegg's daring insolence. He longed to know what these good people would do should he be thus suddenly transformed and appear before them in his scarlet velvet—but above all he wanted her to see him in his swaggering glory, instead of this creeping, churchyard black. He almost cursed himself for his cowardice in not declaring who he was. Then suddenly his mood changed again, and flamboyance leaving him, he felt very small and humble, with but one desire, to run away and hide, lest he should disappoint her after all. Yet this was the man who had but two days before laughed in the face of the Terror and struck cold fear to Robespierre's heart. And here he stood, all three of him, afraid of one young girl.

Above the chatter round him he became aware of voices and laughter high up in the gallery. He glanced in that direction and then laughed as well, for there they were and he knew what they were doing—peering from the fighting-tops before setting their sails for the attack—like the two naughty pirates that they were. He was no longer afraid, and as they came down the stairs demurely holding each other's hand, his heart melted. The glorious contrast that they made—the white and silver of the fine old lady and the young girl's golden warmth against the background of the tapestries—held him enthralled.

Half-way down the stairs Aunt Agatha whispered to Cicely behind her fan: 'Doctor Syn is looking so handsome now that I vow I shall steal some of your dances with him, for my other two beaux will never attend. Perhaps it is as well, for I never told your dear Mamma that I'd invited them and one could hardly expected poor Tony to approve.' Cicely whispered back: 'Then you are the only other woman who shall dance with him tonight. Even so, ma'am, I am not sure that I shall trust you.' She gave her aunt's hand a squeeze as they reached the foot of the stairs. The old lady returned it like the arch conspirator she was and then was claimed by the company.

Since this was merely an informal dinner before the main body of the guests arrived, the small dining-room was used, and since it was a family gathering with the exception of his old friend Sir Henry Pembury and Major Faunce, the customary ceremony was dispensed with.

Cicely, sitting between Major Faunce and Sir Henry, wished that the Major would pay more attention to Maria and that old Sir Henry would not tell her so many anecdotes of his young days. Across the table through the branches of the silver candelabra she could see Christopher, neatly dodging her mother's domestic barbs and concentrating his attention on Aunt Agatha, which lady directed across the table to her favourite niece a wink worthy of Mr. Mipps himself.

With the dismissal of the servants after each course the conversation became easy and natural, and unhampered by necessary caution, since the chief topic was the strange happenings in the cells that morning. Sir Antony was in fine fettle, cock-a-hoop taht he was to ride to London the next morning to visit Mr. Pitt. He became so naughtily pompous that one might have thought he had done the whole thing single-handed. He even so far forgot himself as to round on Doctor Syn and to expound to him the very theory which he himself had laid down that morning. The Vicar could not help laughing when Sir Antony, booming his arguments across the table to Sir Henry, ended up with: 'Much as I disapprove of him I think I'm right in saying that he has struck here a blow for England.' Having delivered this piece of borrowed oratory, he infuriated Lady Caroline still further by monopolizing the conversation and the wine, giving vivid descriptions the while of what he would or would not say to Mr. Pitt. In point of fact he knew quite well that when he eventually did see Mr. Pitt he would as usual be completely tongue-tied, so he took this glorious opportunity of airing the views he knew he would forget. He pardoned the Scarecrow a dozen times and then condemned him again, until Sir Henry, also a Justice of the Peace, cried out: 'But you can't condemn the rascal, Tony. Don't you see the Crown must have him for a witness, and ex necessitate rei, if you follow me?' 'Of course—of course,' put in Tony, who didn't at all. 'Then he must and will be pardoned.' Here, much to everyone's astonishment and Aunt Agatha's delight, the quiet voice of Cicely broke in upon the gentlemen. 'Has it occurred to any of us that he may not want a pardon? For my part I do not think he does. Nor do I think he will come forward.' But Major Faunce was inclined to agree with Cicely. 'Though,' he said, 'I have a theory that my brother shares with me, that the Scarecrow is none other than the famous Captain Clegg, believed by some to have been hanged at Rye, and buried in the churchyard here.'

Cicely knew that she dared not move lest she betray herself. Nor did she trust herself to look at Christopher, but sat, her heart contracted in the grip of deadly fear, while Faunce beside her went on doggedly: 'If this is true then it will be worth his while to stand as witness, for then his pardon would be doubled. But can they do it? Can they pardon a high-seas pirate?' Sir Antony was emphatic on this point. 'The Crown can pardon anyone it pleases—but they've got to prove he was Clegg and how would you set about that?' The calculating voice of the soldier answered. 'Because, me dear sir, the mark of Clegg is on his arm, an old tattoo mark. A picture on his right forearm of a man walking the plank with a shark beneath.' Here Maria broke in excitedly: 'But that was the picture on the arm of the man who rescued us from Paris and ù'

There was a sudden sharp splintering of crash and Cicely's glass shattered against the candelabra, spilling its red wine over the table. She was profuse in her apologies, but she had achieved her object, for by the time all was quiet again after the dabbings and the moppings-up, people were wondering what they had been talking about, and started afresh. All but Faunce, who sat silent and stubborn beside her.

Cicely was pale, but the set of her chin was determined and she now looked round as though challenging anyone to reopen the subject. Two people alone noted this and loved her the more. Aunt Agatha and Christopher Syn.

But Maria would not be put off, and turning to her sister, continued: 'You seem to forget what I saw in Hythe this morning, Cicely. I don't think the Scarecrow is as wonderful as all that, since there is one spy he has not caught.' Now everyone was all attention to Maria she glanced triumphantly at her sister and went on: 'I know he is a spy and a very dangerous one, since it was he who forced my poor Jean to do all those terrible things, and then betrayed him. And then you know what happened.' Here she became tearful and was about to tell Major Faunce how her young foolish husband had been denounced and guillotined when Doctor Syn, as though to change the painful subject, spoke to her across the table. 'Dear me, I wish I had known you were going into Hythe, Maria, dear child. I would have asked you to do a little errand for me. To call in at Mr. Joyce the saddler for a pair of blinkers that I ordered for my churchyard pony. I fear she is getting beyond my control—she actually unseated me the other day—having caught sight of the Beadle.' Cicely alone noticed the gleam in his eye and hurriedly looked away for fear of laughing outright. The Squire was about to say that he quite agreed with the pony—but the Vicar continued, 'But there, I beg your pardon. You were telling us something interesting. What you saw in Hythe, was it not?'

Maria was delighted that the Vicar had for once deigned to notice her, and broke off, without so much as asking the Major's pardon, to answer him:

'Oh, dear Doctor Syn, did I not tell you? 'Twas while Mamma and Cicely were in the Bonnet Shop, and I was alone in the carriage, that I saw Monsieur Barsard. I know it was he. But I did not wish him to see me, so I hid and then I watched him through the window after he had passed. So I am quite sure it was the brute. But I don't really see why you should all be so pleased with the Scarecrow since he has failed to catch the leader of Robespierre's spies.' It was at that moment that Lady Caroline, thinking that her daughters had taken too much license in the conversation, and seeing a restive look in Sir Antony's eye, which meant one thing only—port—rose to her feet, and the other ladies followed suit and accompanied her to the drawing-room.

Aunt Agatha's eagle eye had not missed any of Cicely's reactions, and she felt strangely protective towards her now she knew what the girl was faced with. She applauded the deliberate action that Cicely had taken in silencing Maria, and vowed she would not rest until she had probed this disquieting problem further. For what at first had seemed to her the Overture to an ordinary though charming Romance, now took on an almost menacing air and her fey Scots instinct told her that something vital was unfolding before her very eyes.

So she waited opportunity to draw Cicely aside, and taking both her hands in a surprisingly firm grip told her to be of stout heart, and that she was with them whatever might befall. Her Highland home was at their disposal, and, if they had to take the journey hurriedly, why, then, Gretna Green could be taken on the way. From the strong fingers of the little old lady into Cicely's hands, then through her very veins, there seemed to flow some of the virile fighting spirit of the Gordons, for her chin went up and her eyes lost the haunted look that had clouded them during that period at dinner. She smiled very sweetly, then leant over and kissed her little great-aunt.

Lady Caroline bustled back, and through the open door came the strains of an orchestra tuning up. She begged Cicely to hasten to the ballroom as the guests were already arriving in droves and that she could not see to it all by herself, Maria had vanished and that tiresome gentleman, your dear Papa, was not yet out of the dining-room. From the noise issuing from that room she strongly suspected that he had opened another bin. She would stay and rest awhile with Aunt Agatha, for she knew she was dangerously near a 'fit of the flutters'.

So for the next hour Cicely, abandoned by the rest of the Cobtrees, played the hostess, launched the party, received and introduced so many people and danced with so many others that she had no time to think of herself.

It was during one of those duty dances that she had the leisure to glance around her, for it was a minuet, and her partner was as slow as the music. For some time she had been conscious of eyes upon her and searched the throng for a sign of him.

When she reached the top of the hall she found him looking down at her from the gallery, which had been thrown open to the villagers and was thronged with eager, shining faces. She was so relieved to see him and to find that he was not dancing with anyone else that her heart missed a beat and, missing a step, she had to do an undignified little hop to right herself. When she looked up again he had vanished. Her heart sank again, yet when the music finished she made her way to the door, and there he was, standing in the midst of a crowd. He saw her—indeed he had been waiting for her—and excusing himself he made his way towards her. 'Why, Cicely, child,' he said in his best parochial manner, 'you must not overtire yourself. You have been dancing for the best part of an hour. I know you will find it hard to tear yourself away from all these young men, but I prescribe a rest and a glass of punch.' He put his hand under her arm and led her swiftly through the hall.

Not a word was spoken, but she seemed to understand, for she ran from him to return with a hooded cloak, and together they went out. In the muddy drive he stopped, picked her up and carried her in his arms through the lych-gate to the Church Tower.

Kicking open the door he stepped into the dark and then on and up the spiral steps he carried her—through the bell-chamber, and at last the battlemented roof. Here he set her down, and holding her at arm's length they neither of them spoke, but were content to gaze. And thus they stood until their spirits merged and became one with wind and stars and hung there motionless in space.

* * * * *

From some mid-distance came the hooting of an owl and in a dry dyke half a mile away a pair of merry eyes looked up in the direction of the Tower, waiting for a signal.

It came—a vivid flash—and then again, answered from far away by moving lights that joined and came towards the watcher, while the hooting of the owls grew louder, moving with the lights towards Dymchurch Tower.

* * * * *

Miss Gordon was enjoying herself. She was seated in a cosy alcove within ear's range of the music and within eye's range of all that was going on, surrounded by the Lords of the Level and young officers of Dragoons.

They were all paying her the attention that they might have shown to a young and beautiful woman. In fact, Agatha Gordon was holding a court. Her slender foot tapped, her lace fan fluttered, and her bright eyes danced this way and that. While she was allowing herself a few moments' relaxation by listening with but half an ear to a rather stodgy old gentleman, out of the corner of these same bright eyes she distinctly saw beneath a tapestry a golden brocaded dress and a pair of elegant buckled shoes with black silk hose attached go swiftly through the Hall.

She had hardly stopped smiling to herself in satisfaction when the Squire came up and asked if she had seen that minx Cicely. To which Miss Gordon replied that indeed she had not seen the best part of her niece for the best part of an hour, but that she herself would like to dance and would he lead her out. She was laughing to herself at her neatly turned yet truthful phrase when she passed Maria, who was attempting to interest Major Faunce, and she commanded them to come and join the dance since it was nigh twelve o'clock and she was going to cut her birthday cake. She did not fail to notice Maria's black look but sailed on to the ballroom on the arm of Sir Antony. By the time she had led the unwilling Squire through the complications of quadrilles 'twas but a few seconds before the hour, and all the guests assembled at one end of the room to watch the ceremony. But no sooner did the first stroke of midnight ring out than the orchestra sounded as though they had become confused, one half played one tune and and the other struck up a different though more familiar air. This finally won the day and soon the whole room had it. On the first notes some quickly hushed titters were distinctly heard coming from the gallery. Agatha Gordon laughed outright, for the tune was none other than the 'British Grenadiers'. But the turne persisted and the titters grew louder, for the villagers knew what it meant and hoped to see some fun. Then suddenly the ballroom was full of masked figures who moved swiftly in and out, driving the company before them with cocked pistols. The guests were too astonished to protest, though there were a few screams and some convenient faintings into the arms of the nearest gentlemen. Some thought it was a joke, for it was all so swift and orderly, and the surprise was complete. But hardly had they regained their breath when from the great window behind the orchestra there leapt a fearsome figure, masked and cloaked, who cried out: 'The Scarecrow at your service. And for once you need not be afraid. I have come to pay my respects to the lady whom you are honouring tonight, Miss Agatha Gordon.' If anyone else was afraid, certainly Miss Gordon was not. She revelled in it, as with great strides he reached her and swept a low bow. 'Will you do me the honour of treading a measure, ma'am?' he said. The crowd were aghast. 'Such impudence! What audacity! What will Miss Gordon do?' But this lady merely dimpled and held out her hand, for she had seen that prominently displayed upon his black cloak was a golden riding-whip with a diamond handle. He called for a minuet and the company, watching spellbound from a distance, saw her talking and laughing. To a graceful rhythm the dancers moved—the tall gaunt Scarecrow and the little silver lady.

Point down one. Point down two. Sweep, bow. Curtsey.

'I got your invitation, ma'am,' he whispered. 'And I wouldn't have taken the risk for anyone else.' Again point down one. Point down two.

'You're a naughty, wicked rogue,' she said. 'But I hoped you'd come.' Sweep. Bow. Curtsey.

'I see you are wearing my brooch, ma'am. So I hope I am forgiven.' 'I see you wear mine, sir. You certainly are.' The Scarecrow had moved nearer to the pillaried entrance, where, spying a figure dressed in black, he called out, 'Why, Doctor Syn, my greetings to an enemy. Come, sir, I'll be generous. Let me see if you can dance as well as you can preach. 'Tis my command. We'll dance a foursome.

Bring out the golden lady standing by you.' Here was entertainment indeed. The villagers hung open-mouthed over the gallery, jostling for place. What would the parson do? The parson stepped out on to the floor, and sweeping a most accomplished bow to Miss Cicely Cobtree gave her his hand and led her out.

The band struck up a merry jig, and the strangest dance that was ever seen began. All four were voted good, but the village had it that the Vicar was by far the best, while the four dancers never enjoyed themselves so much, each knowing who the other was and thoroughly appreciating the joke.

The music stopped 'midst thunders of applause, but when it seemed that the Scarecrow was about to take his leave, Miss Gordon had a sudden inspiration. In ringing tones so none could fail to hear she cried: 'Since I have granted you your wish and trod a measure, I have a request to make from you.

There is a problem to be settled. Indeed it will benefit you, sir, if I am right.

Some say the Scarecrow is none else but Captain Clegg the Pirate, and bears upon his arm a strange tattoo—the mark of Clegg. Come, sir, roll up your sleeve and end this argument for good and all.' Again the spectators held their breath, while the Scarecrow swiftly rolled his sleeve and showed his forearm—bare. Such a burst of cheering had never yet been heard in Dymchurch, while the Scarecrow, bowing over Miss Gordon's hand, whispered: 'You're the bravest, cleverest Scots lassie I have had the privilege of robbing and dancing with.' And he was gone, and with him went the Nightriders.

The cheers lasted for ten minutes, for though the Dymchurch villagers were used to exploits of the Scarecrow this was perhaps the pleasantest, most entertaining and romantic they had ever known, while even Mrs. Honeyballs was forced to admit that the Scarecrow behaved himself so nice that she wouldn't have minded dancing with him herself. But a goodly proportion of the cheering was directed towards the little old lady herself, for they all agree that she had behaved print and peart, and it was a good thing that she had so neatly cleared up that silly theory once and for all. Now everyone knew that their Scarecrow was not that pirate Clegg. The gentry for their part were just as enthusiastic, and the whole gathering was so busy with this gossip that it was not for fully twenty minutes that Miss Agatha remembered her cake. She could not think when she had enjoyed herself so much and she chuckled at the audacity of Mr. Bone, while fully appreciating who had been at the back

of all this scheming to make her birthday party pleasant, so she was very glad that she had had the sense to explode for him the theory about Clegg. Now Clegg could rest in peace unless someone was very careless. So she gave herself a mental pat on the baack and felt that for eighty she had really not done badly. Her pleasant reverie was interrupted by the Squire, who, having hung about on the fringe of the proceeding all the evening, feeling rather out of it in his own house, was not in the best of tempers.

So he asked her somewhat testily when she was going to cut that confounded white mountain of confectionary that was clutterin' up his library, though he failed to remark that he thought that same piece of white confectionary would look just as well sittin' on her head as what she'd already got on it. It only lacked a feather—and he wished he had the courage to stick one in.

Aunt Agatha agreed that what with one thing and another she'd forgotten about the cake. But as the custom was to use a special dirk for cutting it, someone must go and fetch it, since she never travelled without a good sharp pair of them. She called for Lisette, who knew where they were.

Lisette, however, was at the moment getting more fully acquainted with the English and their outlandish customs. Therefore she was blissfully unaware of her mistress's need of her. Aunt Agatha's impatience almost resembled the Squire's for she thoroughly dratted all foreigners and said she would fetch them herself, and that meanwhile her candles were to be lighted.

Tripping back along the east wing with Mister Pitt in attendance, she was humming lightly the 'British Grenadiers'. Rounding the corner into the Long Gallery she saw something extremely suspicious. In fact, she could hardly believe her eyes, for having seen the Scarecrow disappear through the window about twenty minutes before, what was he doing peering about in such a nasty way outside the best bedrooms? For one ghastly moment she thought she had been wrong about Mr. Bone, but then the figure straightened itself, and standing with its back towards her she knew by the shape of the shoulders that this was not her naughty rogue. Aunt Agatha's instinct for the cut of a man's jib was infallible, and her good Scots blood was up. Who was this upstart who dared impersonate not only one, but two of the people of whom she was extremely fond? She advanced swiftly and silently, while Mister Pitt, who for all his ribbons, bracelets, and trimmings also had within him the blood of fighters, emulated his mistress and crept forward with quivering nose. Dirk in hand Aunt Agatha struck, and in the words of the Psalmist—'in the hinder parts', putting the prowler if not to perpetual shame certainly to momentary discomfort, for the point was sharp and Aunt Agatha had a strong wrist. He let out a howl of surprise and pain which coincided with Aunt Agatha's Gaelic war-cry and command to proceed, while Mister Pitt carried out a series of worrying sorties under his own generalship. Down below in the library the candles (eighty) had been lit and the cake was ready to be borne round the ballroom by two powdered flunkies, while the orchestra had already started (what they thought) a brilliant imitation of the bagpipes.

So to the skirlings and whirlings of this music and uttering many strange cries of her own, down the stairs and into the ballroom came in triumph Miss Agatha Gordon of Beldorney and Kildrummy, preceded by her prisoner and the never flagging Mister Pitt.

Realizing that something had gone wrong and that this figure was obviously some impostor the guests pressed round to see the fun. But the villagers grew suspicious and angry and very soon the whole place rang with boos and cat-calls. The more adventurous came down from the gallery—then all followed suit. Crowding the ballroom the pressed round the pretender, and things might have gone badly for this unfortunate, had not Doctor Syn saved the situation. He spoke to his parishioners—reminding them that they were guests in Sir Antony's house—he made them smile—he made them laugh—and soon order was restored. He and Major Faunce relieved Miss Gordon of her charge and took him to the Chief Magistrate, Sir Antony. The man, more angry than frightened, for he was within his rights, was ordered to remove his mask. He proved to be none other than the new Revenue Officer from Sandgate, Mr. Nicholas Hyde, at whose discomfiture both the Squire and Major Faunce were secretly delighted. When the Squire angrily demanded what he had been doing in the Court House in such a garb, Mr.

Hyde retorted in similar tones that seeing that his job was to catch the Scarecrow he was at liberty to use any methods to do so, and as he suspected everyone and made no bones about it, Sir Antony included, he thought that by dressing as the Scarecrow he would find out who was and who was not friendly towards the rogue. That was his explanation and he stuck to it. But as Mr. Mipps so aptly remarked afterwards: 'Serve him right for prowlin'. And if he tries to sit down, he'll soon find out who his friends are in these parts, and it don't always do to set a sprat to catch a mackerel.'

Chapter 19. November Lightning on Toledo Steel

Mr. Mipps's chin dropped as his head fell forward. His pigtail shot up and he awoke with an agonized cry, and a disgruntled 'Aye, aye, sir'. His hand went to the back of his neck and rubbed away the pain. He yawned and then with some difficulty opened his eyes, while fishing with the lanyard wound round his neck for the enormous timepiece attached to the end of it. This silver turnip seemed to possess an independence of its own, for its master never knew into which pocket or beneath what garment it had come to anchor. He was not surprised, therefore, when after several tugs on the lanyard, it dislodged itself from beneath his ribs, and made a chilly passage up his chest. He studied it carefully, and yawned again. Five minutes to go before rousing the Captain, for Mr. Mipps was doing the middle watch.

Sitting cross-legged on a high-backed chair in the library, he had endeavoured to keep awake. But being tired through lack of sleep the night before, and not being a man to leave a thing to chance, he had evolved a plan for keeping himself on the alert. By an intricate contraption of nautical loops and knots, he had lashed his tarred queue to the back of the chair so that if he dozed off and sagged forward, he got a rude awakening with a sharp pain in his jiggergaff. This had just worked according to plan, and as he had no further need of its spiteful co-operation, he leant back, hooked his finger through a loop, pulled, and was free. He then uncrossed his legs with difficulty, got up and kicked the logs into a blaze. Shaking himself and taking a swig at the brandybottle completed his operation of waking up. This done, he mentally weighed anchore, and cramming on canvas, set to work lighting the candles and generally getting things ship-shape. Usually when doing these things, he would accompany his movements humming his own particular ditty—the Song of the Undertakers, composed by himself, which accounted for the gloom of the subject and the liveliness of the tune. On this occasion, however, he was not in the mood—which meant that he was worried.

Mr. Mipps was an optimist. He had a cheerful disposition. In fact, there were but two things that had the power to upset him—the insolence of Officialdom, for whose bungling he had a supreme contempt, and the fortunes of his beloved master. After so many years of faithful service, sharing storm and calm alike, he knew Christopher Syn so well that he could tell in a second the state of his mind by every expression, every gesture, and each inflection in his voice. He had already realized that his idol had two sides to his character—the dreamer and the man of action, and while he respected the first he preferred the latter because he understood it. Lately, however, Mipps had been baffled by a cerain sort of vagueness in his manner, and yet on thinking it over he realized that this casual preoccupation was accompanied or closely followed by reckless high spirits.

It might have been that this new restlessness had made the Vicar feverish, but this was no case for Doctor Pepper, for no one knew better than Mipps that there was nothing wrong with his physical health, and this gave rise to the nasty suspicion that he was mentally sick—in fact, that he was in love. He was genuinely worried, for on the only two occasions when there had been anything wrong, his master had been spiritually hurt—the cause in both cases being a woman. The first—his young wife's infidelity, which turned him pirate and sent him raging round the world to seek revenge, and the second—the death of Miss Charlotte, which had sent him temporarily insane. Not that Mr. Mipps disliked women or did not want Doctor Syn to find happiness with one, but he had a feeling at the back of his mind that it would be wrong, because as far as Doctor Syn was concerned, women had spelt 'Disaster', and it was for this reason alone that Mr. Mipps had always remembered Clegg's slogan: 'No petticoats aboard'. But here was Clegg himself forgetting to remember his own orders.

This seemed almost fatal to Mipps, because in his twisted little soul he felt that it would be only through a petticoat that Syn could come to grief, and his curious sailor's instinct corroborated this idea. Yet with these disquieting thoughts filling his mind he, too, had forgotten something, which was that, within the next hour, his master had other dangers to face.

A low rumble as from distant guns reminded him of this, and alert once more he hurried to the window, anxious about the weather. It was pitch dark, sea and land black—the sky a menacing copper. Another low dull grumble from the heavens. The whole night was filled with foreboding as if it were attuned to the Sexton's thoughts. But with an effort he changed them and coming out of the deep waters, he went briskly to the fireplace, picked up the kettle for the shaving-water, and went up the stairs to wake the Vicar. And as he climbed aloft, he sang defiantly the Undertaker's Song.

On leaving the Red Lion Inn at Hythe about this time, Captain Foulkes was in high spirits. He had had an excellent supper, and then whiled away the few hours preparatory to starting out with a pair of bright eyes and several bottles of wine. Doctor Syn's letter was in his pocket, telling him that he had managed to arrange his desired meeting with the Scarecrow and asking him to present himself at the Vicarage at 4:30 on the morning of the 20th, as the place of assignation was but a few hundred yards from his house. He was full of confidence that the Scarecrow would see eye to eye with Barsard and he intended to get a written agreement authorizing them to use the smugglers'

fleet. He laughed out loud when he thought upon his next step, which was to carry out his original plan and to win the wager. When all was said and done—one could always find a use for two thousand guineas—if only to buy back the smiles of that sulky Harriet. He was still safe as regards the time limit, by leaving the coast at daybreak and riding post-horses he could be in London that night, with a day to his credit. As to the proof of his winning the wager, it was all too easy. Since, as the old parson seemed to enjoy London and to frequent the gaming houses, he would be only too glad to come up the next day by coach to be his guest for a day or so. Indeed, since Doctor Syn had expressed his wish to act as second, and had confessed his passion for watching sword-play, why then let him do so. He'd see the best fight he'd ever seen and was unwittingly playing into the Captain's hands. He laughed again when he thought of the stir he would cause in London by taking the parson with him into Crockford's and making him tell Sir Harry Lambton and the rest what he had seen. He did not deceive himself that they would believe his story without this proof, but damme, they would have to take Doctor Syn's word by reason of his cloth, and was he not a friend of the Prince Regent? While the lights of the 'Red Lion' were still glowing behind him these intoxicating thoughts seemed only to need this five-mile ride before materializing. But as he rode on, and the way curved in and out the dykes, not only had the shining windows disappeared but with every yard the way grew darker. He was glad that the ostler had advised him to carry the stable lantern, which he now held in his right hand, swinging it this way and that, peering into the darkness to enable him to distinguish road from dyke. This demanded all his concentration, for not only did his way become increasingly difficult but his visions of success became equally obscured, and in their place unwelcome thoughts took shape. Then his horse shied, and the Captain, cursing, thought he saw a scoffing luminous face that grinned at him from the further side of a broad dyke. He looked again, but it had gone, and other shadows took its place. Then he became aware that there was movement on the Marsh around him. He spurred the frightened animal on, but whether he went fast or slow he heard the sound of horses' hoofs behind him. And then he lost his way, and followed a light that seemed to dance ahead of him. It led him past the dark lump of some small hovel from whose chimney there oozed red, oily smoke, then on, and over a bridge that sagged into the water as he crossed, while behind him from the evil spot he had just left came unearthly screams and mocking laughter. Somehow he found the road again and at last came into that long stretch that runs beneath the sea-wall. It was then he heard a distant angry rumble of thunder and as he looked at the ominous sky a great white undulating mass leaped up before him and with a cold embrace it crashed about him and disappeared. He was wet through, but spurring hard the next wave fell behind him. It did not take him long now to reach the Vicarage, for he remembered exactly where it was. He tethered his horse at the gate and rang the bell, and as he waited for admittance, he realized that he was late, cold, and extremely uncomfortable in mind and body.

Doctor Syn was waiting for him and deplored the state of his clothes.

He begged him to come and dry himself by the library fire, while Mipps saw to the horse. After a warming glass of grog in this pleasant atmosphere, the Captain recovered something of his spirits. He asked Doctor Syn what arrangements had been made, whether the rendezvous would be a private one, or if the Scarecrow would have his followers with him. He explained that though it took a lot to frighten himi, he had had a most uncanny ride, and that he would welcome Doctor Syn's presence at the meeting, because being a holy man it would counteract the evil of this devil-ridden place.

He used this flattering argument to get the Vicar on his side, because he realized that should he be seen killing the Scarecrow after he had struck a bargain, he must show some very strong motive, and determined to use the excuse that he was ridding the community not only of the Scarecrow but Clegg as well. So he brought the conversation round to this by asking Doctor Syn if he had met a certain Major Faunce—though he did not expect the reply that he received.

'Major Faunce—oh dear me, yes!' said the Vicar. 'I was but dining in his company last night—a charming man—I knew his brother very well.

They both strongly adhere to your interesting theory that the Scarecrow is in truth the pirate Clegg. I listened to him most carefully—and I knew that he was right.' Doctor Syn seemed quite pleased that he had discovered this incriminating fact about his sworn enemy—but what he said next staggered the Captain, for it almost appeared that he had read his thoughts.

'Well, sir,' he remarked blandly, 'since as you doubtless know there is one way of proving this common identity, the tattoo upon Clegg's arm—why do you not take this occasion to provoke him—dare him to show it to you and then—'—he made a vague gesture. 'Oh, I know you told me you only desired a meeting,' he continued, 'but really, sir, think what a benefactor you would be in ridding the community of such a tyrant—I must confess I am heartily sick of having to use his identity to keep my parishioners in their proper places. My sermons—you know.' Captain Foulkes was amazed. 'S'death,' he thought, 'the parson's positively bloodthirsty.' He warmed towards this curious creature and began to appreciate why that damned rogue Prinny cultivated him, for an unscrupulous cleric can be plaguey useful in more ways than one. His chief worry had vanished, for he was now sure of co-operation and he became again the confidant swaggerer.

'Come, then,' he cried, 'one more drink, a toast to a death that shall be nameless—and let me couple it with long life to Doctor Syn.'

With a charming smile the Vicar raised his glass. 'I find you so persuasive, sir—I repeat: "To a death that shall be nameless and'—he chuckled—'long life to Doctor Syn." They put down their empty glasses.

The Captain regarded Syn appraisingly. 'I had a mind,' he said casually, 'to go unarmed—but since you too are so persuasive, I think it would be best for our own safety to carry swords. I take it that if the occasion should arise, you are still willing to be my second?' The Vicar seemed to be childishly delighted and accepted this great honour. 'I will most certainly go as your second,' he replied. 'But you have so imbued me with the fire to destroy a villain that I could wish the pleasure were mine.' Here Bully Foulkes so far forgot the respect due to this wolf in sheep's clothing that he clapped him on the back saying that he was glad to meet such a sly dog.

Curiously enough the parson, also laughing gaily, replied in French:

'L'eau qui dort est pire que celle qui court. A good proverb, sir, and one I flatter myself I have always lived up to. For indeed a calm exterior is more to be feared than a Bombastes Furioso ù' Then seeing that the Captain's laughter had somewhat abated, he said: 'We must not let our sense of humour blunt our purpose, for our swords are as sharp as our sense of duty.' The Vicar's servant also appeared to have a sense of duty, for upon that instant there was a respectful tap upon the door, and bidden to come in he stood humbly pulling forelock, though only his master saw the excited quivering of his jigger-gaff.

'Beg pardon, sir, for interruptin', but you asked me to remind you at odd moments about Mrs. Wooley's complaint.' 'Oh, dear me, yes,' replied the Vicar. 'I had indeed forgotten. I shall start almost at once. Thank you, my good man.' He turned to the Captain and said with what might have been a wink: 'A poor old woman is in need of comfort. You understand.' The Captain understood. 'Zounds,' he thought, 'the fellow's a marvel.

He has the wit to keep it up in front of his servant.' 'Well, sir,' went on the servant, 'if you're a-goin' out in all this dark, I'd best come with you with a lantern.' The parson shook his head. They would take the pitch-torches, he said, and bade his servant go to rest. But the servant persisted, 'I never rest when you're out. Are you sure you'll be all right? There's a storm comin' up. I knows it by them curlews.' The Vicar did not appear to have heard this last remark, for with a silken handkerchief he bent down and flicked one buckled shoe. 'Dear me,' he said. 'Too bad. Mud.'

The Captain was amused to see that the servant's face was a study in injured innocence, and that as they left him he was shaking his head and reproving himself with 'Tch, tch, Mud. What a pity. Mud.' As they crossed the bridge on to the sea-wall, a vivid flash of lightning lit up the sea which, as the thunder rolled away, made the darkness denser.

Each with a flaming pitch-torch held high, they made their way, casting fantastic shadows on the narrow, grassy track, one side a sheer stone drop, curving away below into the sea, which now lashed angrily against it. The track widened about a look-out hut and here the parson stopped. 'This is the spot,' he whispered, and stuck the handle of his torch into the wind-drift sand. 'Do you wait here in this shelter, for I am pledged to go alone and tell the Scarecrow that all is well and this is not a trap.' The Captain nodded his assent and slipped between the hut and the wall's edge, whilst Doctor Syn vanished into the darkness of the other side.

What Captain Foulkes now felt was perhaps the culmination of all that he had experienced in his mind since that night at Crockford's when he had first met this Doctor Syn. Since that meeting it seemed that he was no longer in command of his own destiny and that he was caught in the toils of some vast spider's web, only subconsciously aware that this black figure was the centre of a patterned weaving, knowing every quiver of it and had almost hypnotized him. So he waited, struggling in his mind, like a stinging wasp, for the right moment to escape the outer fringes by force.

He stood above the sea, watching the fire-play of November lightning round the giant groups of brooding cloud that hovered till some signal should let drive the full fury of their prophetic wrath. Then suddenly, as if they had received a sign, the clouds began to move, and a voice behind him, harsh and imperious, rang out: 'The Scarecrow waits for no man, Captain Foulkes.'

Foulkes turned and saw what had been described to him a hundred times, though face to face, a hundred times more terrifying, as in this weird setting of the lofty wall, hanging between the clouds and sea, the pitch-torch flickered its unholy light up the gaunt figure to the horrors of its grim, carved face. Even as he watched, It spoke to him again: 'L'pouvantail—at your service, Monsieur Barsard.' The Captain stood silent, his mind too paralyzed to adjust itself to what this strange creature had just said. Then he was asked a question. 'What is your business with me, citizen, Spy?' He had no answer. Forcing his frozen intellect to explain how this man knew his secret, he remembered the missing wallet—the highwayman—could he be—? He had heard rumours— But before he had time to reply, as though in answer to his thoughts, the Scarecrow, with a contemptuous gesture, threw something towards him. It landed at his feet—a flat, dark object—his wallet.

He bent eagerly to pick it up, and thumbed it furtively. The paper was still there. Yet this man must have read it; else how could he have known? Again the Scarecrow answered for him: 'Yes, I had it from the highwayman. He has sensitive fingers, but cannot read French, though a name is a name to all men, and he is my friend. Doctor Syn told him that you wished it back. The paper is still there, though you will have no further use for it. I do not work through intermediaries. You thought to put a proposition to me, but I did not like your method of approach. To hide a black project behind a bragging wager to kill a wanted man is unworthy of a brilliant swordsman.

'So the proposal that you thought to make has been attended to, for I do not accept terms—I make them. And I made them to Citizen Robespierre.

For though the paper enlightened me abotu a certain Monsieur Barsard, my organization is so complete that I already knew of the scheme he wished to put to me. I went to the head of your organization and he told me what fantastic plans he had. It was simple, because I had already decided to play my part in them.' Dimly the Captain grasped one thing. It sounded as though this giant smuggler was on their side, and yet he told himself he must be careful. He had made the mistake of approaching him as Foulkes instead of Barsard. But though Barsard's plans had come to naught, Foulkes still had a card to play, and this he would make sure of. But where was the parson? Why had he not returned? He looked about him, peering into the darkness, anxiously.

Once more he got a reply to his unspoken question.

'The parson will be with you, Captain, soon. I will bring him back when we are ready, but we still have a few points to clear up.' Assurance of the parson's return and what it meant to him restored a little of the Captain's confidence and he said with some spirit: 'Since Citizen L'pouvantail has taken the business out of the hands of Citizen Barsard, I am at a loss to know what other points are left.' 'There is the vital point of making England revolutionary, and it would interest me to know why Captain Foulkes, a leader of the London dandies, should interest himself in this. Was it perhaps that unfortunate affair that sent you out of the country all those years ago? But after all, that's no affair of mine. One man's reason is as good as another's, and Robespierre too has a reason. He supplied me with six of his best agents. All good spies and desperate characters. I had their full dossiers. Then as I had to make decisions quickly, he generously provided me with yet another—a most enlightening document, taking one from England and a military scandal in 1774 to the Americas—the Caribbean Sea—then back to France—to England and the fashionable clubs with a reputation as a swordsman, and in frequent crossings of the Channel, a reputation as a secret political agent and a denouncer of fostered friends. So, Captain Foulkes, seeing that you and I know so much about this Monsieur Barsard, it will not be difficult for us to keep all seven spies of Robespierre in their place, and if you and I are to work and fight together, I realize that with all that to your credit, I must offer you an equal guarantee.' The Captain's spirits soared. If this guarantee was a document similar to his own dossier, why, then he would have no need of the parson's testimony. But the Captain's hopes of obtaining such damning evidence were dashed, for the Scarecrow quickly thrust up his right sleeve, and picking up the blazing torch held it over his outstretched arm upon which was clearly visible in the red glow the tattoo mark of the pirate Clegg.

'Here's proof enough to kill a man,' he cried.

Yet again Foulkes had the uncanny feeling that this man could see into his mind, and wishing to be rid of the whole thing and cursing inwardly that now he had to wait for the parson, he tried desperately to plan his next move.

So he prevaricated with: 'I accept your guarantee, Captain Clegg, for not only is it proof enough to kill a man but proof of many killed. It will be a great day for the Republic when Citizen L'pouvantail, alias Captain Clegg, is working for them. When do we start? The six others—when will they arrive? Is Decoutier bringing them over?' 'No, Decoutier is here. He came with me. I brought all six.' The Captain was astounded. Here was a leader who did not waste time.

'You brought them?' he cried. 'Then we have started already. Where are they?' 'Here in Dymchurch.' What happened then was as quick as the lightning which now flashed continually about them, for the Scarecrow's mask and cloak were tossed aside and there in the vivid stabs of light was Doctor Syn, smiling dangerously. 'Six spies are in the Court House cells and the seventh is before me. Draw, Captain Traitor, and fight to lose your wager.' His voice flashed in tune to his movement, swift and thrusting as the steel he held.

For a second Foulkes stood aghast—dumbfounded.

Then about them the storm broke, and with the unleashing of the elements the dark cloud burst in his brain, setting free in clear vision the unaccountable facts of his subconscious foreboding. As easily as the Scarecrow's cloak was tossed aside to reveal the parson, so did the curtain in his mind disintegrate into one lucid thought—the spider's web—his destiny. There, at the centre of his weaving in all this tumult of wind and waves, was the black figure smiling at the insect on the fringe of it, who waited, tense and taut, for the first move. Then, as he crouched, watching, the sword of his opponent came to life, flashing blue fire as the lightning ripped along the steel. The wasp struck. With a great cry he slit his blade from the scabbard and leapt forward to the attack. Syn was ready, steel met steel, and for a frenzied five seconds hissed and rasped, as the darts of lightning caressed both blades, spurting from point to point.

A double thrust from Foulkes was parried by Syn. He laughed above the wind wildly and with satisfaction as Foulkes leapt back. Here was a swordsman who could make a fight. Now the lightning seemed to be coming from his eyes. He waited, alert—poised for the next move. It came slowly, blades pressing and sliding in a husky whisper. Still Syn did not attack, holding a stiff defence, and the eyes of the two men burnt to each other's brains, trying to read the command before it reached the blade. Foulkes thought he knew Syn's plan. To wear him down and thus keep fresh himself.

He did not fear that strategy. A younger man than Syn, he knew, could outdistance him in playing a long game, counting on well-trained strength and breathing power. If Syn would not attack, why then he would, showing what speed could be. He leapt and thrust, seeking some weakness in the guard that faced him, but meeting that same baffling calm now so familiar to him. He rushed in now like a lithe bull, hoping to break down the defence by weight.

Syn leapt aside with riposte, but if Foulkes thought he was wearying him, he found that he was wrong, for suddenly Syn was at him in attack and Foulkes was driven back before this amazing speed. Then for some minutes the blades clanged and sputtered and the sword-thrusts moved and lunged in broken rhythm as the shooting steel licked in and out, and the torches held high in hand with curved left arms, wreathed smoke about the fighters' heads. And up and down and round upon that flat sea-wall, they traced their wild manœuvring in the close-cropped grass—fighting now by torchlight, now by lightning-flash, sometimes almost in darkness. The attack stopped as suddenly as it began, and Foulkes was once more met with Syn's immovable security.

Angered, he attacked as furiously, but this time Syn began to give him ground, and Foulkes thought: 'Ah, he is the older man. He will not stay the course.' And so it seemed, for the retreat went on, with Foulkes unflagging—driving. Once only did his opponent seem to stop, for some few seconds, but then the retreat continued, and Syn knew that his opponent had not noticed what he did, for in those precious seconds, knowing the ground, Syn's left foot, behind him, felt and found what he had sought, and measuring it mentally aby stepping back, let the retreat go on. Foulkes, thinking this the beginning of the end, pressed on with confidence, hoping with every thrust to break the guard and draw first blood. Slowly Syn backed and backed. And Foulkes, not daring to disengage his eye from Syn's was puzzled by the change of texture on the ground. They had fought in grass, but now they fought on wood. The wind here had more power, as though they were exposed on some high place. He longed to look about him, and cried, with clenched teeth and staccato voice, 'Where are you driving me, you devil!' A calm voice answered him. 'It seems that you drive me. But have a care. Fight straight. We have a bare four feet. A sheer drop either side.' It was then that Foulkes heard above the wind the rushing torrent of dyke water meeting sea, and he realized with sickening horror that they were fighting on top of the Sluice Gates. He remembered them, and thought of the black malevolent ooze so far below. He knew he had been trapped, and rage, blacker than the mud, filled him. Watching Syn's eyes he suddenly flung his burning torch straight at his face. Syn saw it coming like a meteor. No room to step aside, his mind and sword were simultaneous. His blade flew up and with the flat he struck the flying missile, sending it hurtling overhead to fall in an arc of fire sizzling in the sea. He felt a sudden numbness in his hand as Foulkes's thrust caught his upturned arm. By the look in Foulkes's eyes he knew that he had fouled to make him drop his sword, and was waiting then to pounce and murder. But Syn leapt first, and with a throttled cry Foulkes dropped his sword with Syn's blade through his neck, and clawing the air fell backwards into space, a long black fall and then—a blacker death.

From the great height of the Sluice Gates Syn looked down, holding his torch far out, its flickerings reflected in a million times in the creviced liquid below. No darker shadow on the shining surface of the fermenting kiln; but where he looked giant bubbles rose and sank, as the undulating mud rolled back to place.

Then high and shrill above the whining of the wind and borne aloft on unseen wings, the curlew cried three times.

Chapter 20. A Brand New Box of Soldiers

Thomas was late. 'Boots', who should have called him, was late. In fact, everyone was late. But as the Squire was still asleep, nobody had as yet been blamed. Thomas, expecting his ears to turn crimson any moment now and knowing that there is always a calm before the storm, tiptoed past the somnolent bulk of the Squire in the middle of the four-poster bed and opened the shutters. He made a deal of noise and coughed discreetly. The Squire groaned and slept on. Thomas, grateful for this short respite, busied himself about his master's room, retrieving various garments that had somehow got themselves into the most extraordinary places. At last all were accounted for except the wig and one buckled shoe, so being accustomed to this eccentricity, he looked in the most unlikely places. The wig revealed itself, perched rakishly upon the candle sconce which lit the Squire's most unfavourite portrait of his great-aunt Tiddy. The shoe was nowhere to be seen, though it came to light later in the day at the end of the Long Gallery, whither Sir Antony had flung it at the retreating Mister Pitt. The Squire rolled over and humped upon his face. Thomas could not postpone the evil moment any longer, so with the remaining shoe still in his hand, he gave the lightest part of the hump a resounding thwack. This having the desired effect, he stood at a respectful distance, his ears flushing in anticipation. The hump subsided. The Squire rolled over and scratched his chest. It crackled, and woke him. He yawned and said: 'Thomas, you're late. Tell Mrs. Lovell not to put so much starch in my nightshirt.' He scratched again, let out an oath, and sat up, sucking his finger. Thomas, haveing seen something most unusual, and fearing to be blamed for it, fled. The Squire flattened his chin and looked down his nose, and saw that pinned to his own nightshirst was a folded paper.

He continued to look at it, trying hard to think what he had done last night, but as the only thing he could remember doing was betting Sir Henry that he wouldn't stick a feather in me wife's Aunt Agatha's wig, then chasin' that stinkin' poodle up the back stairs, he reserved judgement on the matter. He continued to squint and peer but couldn't read it. 'Damn fool pinned it the wrong way up,' he muttered. Then, pricking his double chin in and extra effort, he located the pin and pulled it out, wondering why he hadn't thought of it before. What he saw made him leap out of bed and go to the window for better light. But there it was, the picture of the Scarecrow, and he could read the large scrawled writing without his glasses.

Dear Squire, Here is the Seventh. For Rogue, Scoundrel, Rascal, aye, Sir Antony, even Smuggler I may be, but the Scarecrow has always ruled 'Death to a Traitor'. Here was a Traitor to England whose body may be found in the mud of the Great Sluice Gates, but whose dossier signed by Robespierre might interest Mr. Pitt, Minister of War. I wished to pay you this further service because this man denounced the Comte de LonguT, your daughter's husband. Hoping that my act will gain for you much honour and not another proclamation for me, I remain your Disobedient Servant, THE SCARECROW.

Sir Antony was delighted. He started at once composing fresh speeches to Mr. Pitt and then, wishing to rehearse them, trotted out gaily to the gallery, oblivious to the fact that his feet were bare and he was clad in nothing but a nightshirt. He called all to him, but since everyone was asleep nobody came, and a sharp yapping reminded him of bare ankles and warned him to scurry to cover.

Thomas, returning apprehensively, found him all smiles, and was chagrined to find that his ears had already responded to disaster.

Sir Antony, bursting out of his London clothes, for he had put on several inches in the wrong direction since he had last worn them, was conscious of a pressing top breeches-button, and was equally bursting with a pressing desire to impart his good news to all and sundry. But he had a lonely breakfast because everyone was late. Indeed, Cicely was the only member of the family who eventually appeared. But he was so overjoyed at having someone to talk at that he failed to notice her grave expression when, on reading the letter to herself, she saw something which he had also failed to notice. On the back of the scrawled note was something that possibly even the sender had overlooked—a dark stain, which could mean only one thing—blood. Whose? Her heart pounded. So, kissing her father fondly, she told him to behave himself in London, and to say to Mr. Pitt whatever came into his head first. But whatever he did say she was very proud of her dear Papa.

Would he please excuse her, for she had an appointment with Stardust? But once out of the house she fled across the Glebe field and by the sea-wall to the Vicarage—.

After much fussin's and fumin's and losin' of tempers—forgettin' this and that, and remembering a lot of unnecessary instructions—the Squire was launched by the remainder of his long-suffering family. With delicious thoughts of freedom ahead, London and his position fully appreciated, absence of restrictions regarding port and the naggin' that went with it, he allowed himself further mental licence—a flutter at Crockford's and perhaps ù why not?—a visit to that stunnin' charmer—what was her name?—Harriet. He settled himself comfortably in his State Coach pulled by the best cattle in Kent—with Thomas in smart livery on the boot—and was further delighted by the loyalty of his tenants, who had come to cheer their benefactor and Squire on his departure for the Court. He was under the fond impression that the village knew nothing of the French spies and had simply come to watch his grandeur. Actually there was very little that the village did not know. So tho' it bobbed and cheered as his equipage rolled off in style, it was in a very ferment of excitement this morning.

Cicely tapped on the Vicarage door and got no reply, so she went round the windows and peered in, only to be met by teasing shutters. But the library window was unshuttered and unlatched—in fact, it had an enticing chink.

She had therefore hitched her dress high up round her waist in a most unladylike fashion, showing not a little pretty lace and frills, and was in the act of balancing one foot upon the water-butt and t'other upon the sill, when a voice behind her startled her into a sitting position on the flower-bed beneath:

'Now then. This is a 'oly residence—no place for showin' yer dickycum-bobs. There now,' it went on, 'now you've gone and hurt them on them bulbs—'urt them bulbs too—'urt yourself?' She turned and saw the Sexton watching her critically with cocked head.

'Oh, Mr. Mipps,' she laughed. 'How you did surprise me. If it hadn't been for these confounded petticoats I should have been through the window before you could bark.' She got up and brushed herself, then became more serious. 'Mr. Mipps,' she said, 'is Doctor Syn all right? I have a strange feeling that he may not be very well this morning.' Immediately Mipps was on the defensive.

'Now whatever put that into your 'ead, miss—he's never ill, he ain't.' Then, seeing her glance up to the Vicar's still curtained window, found excuses. 'Oh yes, miss, it is late for him, I knows, but he was out visiting Mrs.— Mrs.—' 'Mrs. Wooley, Mr. Mipps?' put in Cicely, with raised eyebrow.

'Er—yes, miss—thank you, miss—poor Mrs. Wooley, miss.' Mipps might have gone on enlarging upon that same old body's complaint, but again she cut him short.

'I just wondered, Mr. Mipps.' She looked straight at him and he wriggled. 'For I could not sleep last night, and from my window early this morning I saw strange lights in the direction of the Sluice Gates—surely that is not the direction you would take to visit her? But there, I would not pry—so if you promise me that the Vicar is quite well, why then I will not break into the holy residence.' Mr. Mipps assured her that indeed Doctor Syn was quite well, but that the poor old gentleman was having a nice long rest after his dancings and goings-on. Then, sticking firmly to his guns, though with a suspicion of his famous wink, added, 'And it's a long ride to Mrs. Wooley's—.' Cicely smiled at him and loved him for the stubborn little watchdog that he was. So, telling him to inform the Vicar that if he cared to begin his riding lessons that afternoon she would bring round Stardust and another mount, though perhaps he was not quite ready for the broad dyke jump, and she would bring the quietest in the stable. Then she was gone, sauntering across the bridge. But she turned half-way and called to the still waiting, staring Mipps:

'Pray tell the Vicar that should he not feel well enough for his riding lesson, why then I shall visit him this evening with words of cheer—for I have my duties too as Spinster of the Parish—.' Through his window Doctor Syn, lying comfortably in his bed, had heard the passage-of-arms between his best-loved friends and loved them all the more. He had a mind to leap out from the window to the bridge and take her in his arms; but feeling as he did, relaxed and quiet—though his slight wound was painful—his heart was so full for her that all he wished to do was to lie and absorb her into his very soul. A great danger had been overcome, was past, and now he thought he could afford to wait. So there he lay and pondered on the glorious possibilities ahead, weaving yet another pattern into his ill-starred life—.

Cicley strolled back through the village. She had no mind to hurry; indeed her mind was so completely his that until she saw him she must be alone; she wanted to recapture that glorious emotion of being one detached from earth, and the spirit guiding her took her to the Tower. She neither saw nor heard the many villagers who greeted her, and her expression was so beautifully remote and yet so shining that no one dared to break it; but after she had gone they whispered delightedly that 'For sure the Squire's youngest was in love and they knew who.' Had they not seen as pretty a picture as they ever hoped to set eyes on, the very night before, when their beloved Vicar had led her out to dance in all her golden youth? So the gossips prattled, discussing every detail of the gay proceedings, from the little old lady's courage to the merry impersonation of the Shadow. Though when they fell to talking of the second appearance of their idol that night they became venomous. That prowling Mr. Hyde and seek—which name, attributed to Mr. Mipps, attached itself and stuck. So the Sandgate officer of Revenue did not have a very pleasant time in Dymchurch that day, for having decided to put a bold face on it, he stayed to watch, trying to pave his way with pots of ale. But nobody seemed thirsty. Fishermen came into the Ship Inn and greeted each other with, 'What was your catch today? Did you set a sprat to catch the Scarecrow? What did you get, mackerel?' He decided not to notice—but even the children in the street ran after him, begging him to join their games of Hyde and seek.

But indeed there was another reason for gaiety, for was it so rumoured that the Dragoons had been recalled to Dover, and that Major Faunce and his men would soon be off to France? For a while they were full of patriotic feeling towards these gallant soldiers, they also secretly rejoiced that now questionable activities would not be hampered. This did not seem to be so secret either, for was not practically the whole village in the Ship Inn celebrating their departure? Few of the 'Ship' staff in the kitchen that morning recognized a smart young officer in a new uniform who put his head in at the window and greeted them, though it did not take them long when they looked more closely. 'Why, goodness me, if it ain't that young gentleman what breakfasted with us about a week ago.' And so it was—Lord Cullingford who had been posted to that regiment, and who had lost no time in reporting to his commanding officer, Major Faunce.

Later that morning, as the Vicar sat in his comfortable library, Mr.

Honeyballs announced a visitor. He was sincerely touched and very glad to see Lord Cullingford. The boy had stood before him, straight and fresh, and Syn had laughingly remarked upon the fineness of his uniform—but knew it was not that which gave him this new spirit. He had indeed and upon that moment thanked his Maker for allowing him to have been the humble instrument for its attainment. Then the boy had handed him a packet in repayment and he knew the value of trust where trust was due.

So the mounted regiment made brave show as, with drums and fifes before them they took the Dover Road. But although they understood the cheers they received, they saw no humour in the tune they played, which every British regiment follows when going off to join the wars. But the village seemed to find it funny, for it rocked and whistled and held its sides with laughter and helped to swell that merry tune 'The Girl I Left Behind Me'.

Yet hardly had this murmur died down when through the village from the other side came marching in a brand new box of soldiers.

Chapter 21. Mr. Mipps Remembers to Forget

Mr. Mipps was highly indignant. He cursed himself for a 'dawthering old sone of a sea-dog', and then, correcting himself, said he was a 'chiddering old landlubber'. He might have known the Captain always kept his porthole open. If only he hadn't been so addle-brained, he might have wheedled Miss Cicely round to the other side of the house where a chidderer is a booky.

There would only have been Mrs. Honeyballs to overhear, the old Keg-Meg.

1 'Ridin' lesson! My baggin'-'ook,' he muttered to himself. 'If the Vicar goes on bein' funny about it, I'll tell him that 'evesdrippers never hears no good of theirselfs'.' But there it was, the Captain had overheard. And here he was on his way up to the Court House with a message: 'The Vicar will be pleased to take his ridin' lesson with Miss Cicely this afternoon at half past two.' Mipps was really worried. The Captain hadn't had no proper sleep for nights—he'd gone out and got himself pinked. Now Mipps wanted him to rest, and here he was behavin' like a flirt-man.

Mipps had reached the Court House in such a dobbin that he'd given his message to the first person he saw. It happened to be Aunt Agatha, who could hardly believe her ears, when having delivered the message he looked straight at her, through her, and past her and muttered, 'Dawtherin' old chidderer.' Miss Agatha felt quite sure he did not mean her, for he pulled his forelock most respectfully and stumped off to the churchyard. Whatever Aunt Agatha felt she most certainly gave the message, for at half past two, most precise, Cicely arrived at the Vicarage on Stardust and leading one of the Squire's most spirited horses.

Even Mr. Mipps had to admit that Doctor Syn put up a good performance, for he had approached the animal with a fine show of apprehension, patting it timidly and, after many vain attempts, climbing clumsily aboard.

'Play-actin',' Mr. Mipps called it, though as he watched them riding off together he felt so strangely moved that he had to give himself a wink and a nip to get over it.

So they had ridden through the village where the Vicar made much ado about stopping and starting Red Pepper when greeting his amazed parishioners. His foot slipped many times from the iron and he held the reins as he had seen Mr. Mipps do on Lightning, Cicely watching with very bright eyes this delightful clowning for her benefit. Then they were free of the village and out upon the lonely Marsh, setting their horses towards Lympne Hill. The storm of the night before had exhausted itself with its own fury. The hill shone birght in the pale November sun, yet when it shone on Cicely's redgold hair and russet riding-habit, it seemed she warmed the sun to summer.

They had not spoken. Indeed they had not looked at one another; but now, the last farm passed, with it went 'dear old Doctor Syn'.

He straightened in the saddle and took command of the surprised animal. Then turning to her, deliberately took his spectacles from his nose and grinned boyishly—and they were off. The horses were as well matched as they, and neck to neck they galloped deliriously. Over this dyke and that, across broad fields, scattering the sheep, and on they sped, gathering momentum towards the Broad Dyke.

A watcher, who was 'lookering' his sheep and loved good horses, watched them, fascinated, clearing this wide, deep canal together in perfect rhythm, horses and riders in unison. Then straight ahead and up the slopes they climbed towards the Roman Camp, above which frowned the perpendicular wall of old Lympne Castle. Here they dismounted and let their horses graze on the lush pasture that centuries ago had been beneath the sea, while they sat down, glowing and happy, on the harbour wall where galleys once were tied, as if each to the other had belonged since those old days, united as they had been on their ride.

There they sat with all the quietness of the past about them, looking at this vast sweep of land divided from the sea by that straight wall. This was his country—here he ruled from two extremes and she sat by him like his consort.

The sun flashing on lattice panes far below brought to her mind another flashing light, and she told him what she had seen that morning early, demanding what he did and why he risked his life—for she told him she had seen the Scarecrow's letter to her father. Gravely he asked her if she remembered the conversation at dinner the night before about the rumoured pardon of this rogue, saying that now he must do all to gain it, and since this Barsard had been an enemy of England his chance of winning it was therefore greater. She remembered, she said, but she wished to forget—and he smiled at her using his own phrase; and to all his arguments on that count she would have none, saying that she loved him as he was. She bade him be silent about his past, for all she wanted was the present—looking at him almost questioningly till he wrinkled his brows, wondering if she were finding some fault in him, though she was but marvelling at this strong, strange man who was able by sheer force of character to hide that side of himself which was his best under the cloak of age. Yet she knew that if she had her choice she would not have him otherwise—she never had, she never would. Then suddenly she began to laugh. He watched her lovely merriment and sought the answer with one raised brow. She told him how since she had been quite small she used to borrow Mr. Mipps's spy-glass to watch him sitting on this very spot. 'The glass was magic and brought you to me right across the Marsh.'

And now how proud she was that no one else had been with him up here—.

'Save one,' he said. Then, seeing her quick look of wonder, told her the story of how he had first met Mipps, his other best-loved friend, and how here he had had the luck to save his life, and then not met again, till in the Caribbean Mipps had done the same for him. Her pleasure was so great to be sitting on the very spot that she turned swiftly to him, the sun behind her, shining through her loosened hair making a fiery halo round her head—.

'Then I vow I love you both so much,' she cried, 'I would that I could do the same for you, the pair of darling pirates that you are.' He leant and kissed her hands—and her strong fingers caressing his arm betrayed him.

For he could not stop the sudden wince of pain—and in a moment she was all self-reproach and tenderness. They must go home. His arm must be properly seen to. She herself would do it. And did he know that she was dining with him tonight? Aunt Agatha had arranged it with Mamma, who agreed it would be quite proper if Agatha went too.

He did not know—he accepted with pleasure. So, mounting their horses, they rode slowly back in tender teasing vein—loath to leave this darkening spot which had embraced so much of their lives and given them this shining hour. The sun dropped down and the Marsh died to be reborn in a thousand twinkling signals—for it was only then that Romney Marsh awoke and came to life.

* * * * *

How was it that they dined alone in that lovely Adams room? Seated one at either end of the refectory table, eyes meeting across that subtle distance only served to tautenteh reins of tehir inseparable selves. The answer was 'Romance', and no one knew better that Aunt Agatha how to foster that most delicate flower. But where was Aunt Agatha then? She was certainly not dining with the two disgruntled ladies at the Court House. Yet the powdered footmen there would have staked their very wigs that she was at the Vicarage, for had they not heard her ladyship's orders? 'Miss Gordon chaperones Miss Cicely to dine with the Vicar.' Indeed one of their number had escorted them with a lantern to the gate. But not having eyes at the back of his head, he could not notice the old lady's whispered farewell to her great-niece, nor that she trotted back after him across the Glebe, but that instead of going into the Court House she had deliberately set off in another direction.

The lady in question, having served to cosset her niece's romance, had planned a little flutter on her own account, and it was towards this crowded reception that she had made her way. Seated in the place of honour of the Bar Parlour at the 'Ship', Miss Gordon was holding court.

Her admirers on this occasion were very much more to her taste than the stuffy old Lords of the Level who had been invited to amuse her the night before. Her reticule being well stuffed with Scottish gold, tankards were continually being refilled with Mrs. Waggetts' special, while her gay stories and quick retorts kept the company in Rabelaisian good humour. Yet out of all this throng of fishermen, farmers, soldiers out of the new box, and village cronies in general, the casual onlooker might have noticed that her special cavalier had a pair of merry blue eyes and a popularity equal to her own. Yet in spite of the fact that she was kept so busy and was indeed enjoying herself, from time to time, and with a glow of satisfaction, she thought on her two dear romantics at the Vicarage, and wondered how they fared.

Indeed tehy were faring very well. Mrs. Honeyballs's dinner, although they had not noticed it, had been a poem, and the present scene would have been entirely to her approval, for Cicely, having attended to the dressing of a slight wound on the Vicar's arm, that same arm and its fellow were clasped around her, as they stood by the fire in the hall, candles glowing and moonlight shining through the windows.

* * * * *

Mr. Mipps had got over his 'dobbin', for he had been extremely busy and had had no time to foster it. There was Mrs. Wooley's coffin to be attended to, and Mr. Mipps, taking a natural pride in his work, did not like to be hurried, and there had been the final details of the night's run to be seen to, and the false run to be supervised. All this accomplished, there remained his report to the Vicar. He had some special messages to remember, and was hurrying to get these off his mind before he forgot. So occupied was he with tabulating these that he was half-way across the room before he noticed that the Vicar was indeed behaving like a flirt-man. This gave him such a shock that it was not until he was half-way out again that his weather eye told him that it registered something else out of the ordinary. He was horrified, and decided that in spite of what the Vicar was doing, action was necessary. He crept back and tried to attract the Vicar's attention: signalling violently, scratching his own arm and pointing to his master's, while mouthing silent protests.

Doctor Syn looked over Cicely's shoulder and smiled at him. "Tis all right, Mr. Mipps,' he said, 'Miss Cicely knows the worst.'

Mr. Mipps's signals dwindled, and his mouth opened wide in surprise.

Cicely turned and, with the Vicar's arms still round her, smiled at him too. "Tis all right, Mr. Mipps,' she said, 'Miss Cicely knows the best.' The situation was all too much for Mr. Mipps, but through his confusion one thought flashed out clear: 'Oh, Cap'n, whatever have you done to the Vicar?' he gasped. 'Beggin' your pardon, miss. But look at you standin' about in your shirtsleeves with the curtains wide and Mr. Hyde on the prowl.' He went to the window and closed the curtains, adding reproachfully: 'It's that there shark. Might catch a cold. It don't like draughts. It ain't had so much fresh air since we done it at Saratoga.' The Vicar became more serious, though he still had something of the gay recklessness that Mipps feared, as he answered: 'Thank 'ee, Master Carpenter—you ever had a weather eye for danger. 'Twas careless of me, though tonight I care nought for all the King's horses and Revenue Men.' Mipps replied promptly, 'No, but they care several aughts for you.' This was worse than he had expected, and since it was the first time he had ever been called Master Carpenter in company, he concluded that Miss Cicely knew all. So he added reprovingly, 'Looks like you're remembering to forget.'

'If you mean be that, Mr. Mipps, that I am forgetting my old slogan, 'No petticoats aboard', you need have no fear. Miss Cicely, Heaven be praised, is no petticoat.' Suddenly, remembering the scene beneath the Vicar's window that morning, much to his annoyance, Mipps found himself blushing violently, as the picture flashed before him of Miss Cicely in her dicky-cum-bobs. He was tongue-tied and stood miserably gazing at nothing—.

But Cicely, seeing the little man's embarrassment and knowing the reason for it, threw back her head and laughed. 'Lud, I hate the things, but I'm forced to wear 'em, as in truth Mr. Mipps knows full well. Pray do not fret, Mr. Mipps, 'twas my fault for trespassing.' He looked up at her gratefully as he felt the hot flush, giving up the search for his turnip-watch. 'Come, give me your hand.' Then, with her other clasped around Syn's wounded arm, she took Mipps's horny little hand in her cool firm one and cried, 'Now we are indeed an unholy Trinity.' Her battle was won—Mipps was vanquished. He knew now why she had always been his favourite in the Cobtree family.

'Oh, Miss Cicely,' he swallowed hard, feeling an unusual lump in his throat, 'I always said that you was ship-shape. At Lloyd's and Bristol fashion. Thank you, miss, you are the only person I'd be proud to call 'Mrs.

Captain', miss.' Syn too had a huskiness in his throat as he watched with tender amusement the ease with which this girl had captured the tough little pirate—and experienced the relieved emotion of having two best-loved friends discover and like each other. He hoped the Sexton would not hold it against her, but see eye-to-eye with him in his decision to claim the pardon, and release himself from the shadow of the Scarecrow. He listened to her, saying that Mr. Mipps had paid her the nicest compliment she had ever had and thanking him for making her love Captain Clegg since childhood by telling her such wonderful stories about him.

'Oh, those,' replied Mipps. 'You wait. I 'ad to shorten sail for them; but now you knows, we can cram on all the canvas—talkin' of petticoats and that there shark—there was a girl in Saratoga ù' 'Mr. Mipps,' warned Syn, though his eyes belied his severity, 'remember to forget.' Mipps's eyes crinkled too as he nodded. 'Oh, sorry, sir, remember to forget,' repeating itlike a naughty school-child. 'I must remember to forget,' which suddenly reminded him of what he had indeed forgotten.

'Knock me up solid!' he cried. 'Remember to forget, you says, but 'ere am I forgettin' to remember. Jimmie Bone—I've just had a message—he done the false run—everythin' lovely—all accordin' to plan. He goes to the Ship Inn to meet your auntie, miss, accordin' to plan. Goes to Aldington ù 'as a look at the beacon—everythin' lovely, all ready. Then what does he do but go and feel thirsty—that there Jimmie Bone. He's up a gum tree—went into the 'Walnut Tree' to 'ave one. Slap into a covey of Bow Street Runners wot come down special. Didn't 'alf feel silly.' 'Not caught?' asked Syn sharply.

'Oh no, not as silly as that—not in the 'Walnut Tree'—lovely rabbit warren. But he can't move, not while them Runners is yappin' about outside—got word to me in the usual way—said I was to tell you he didn't 'alf feel a fool but he dursn't come out—not after that little affair of the Dover coach.' Doctor Syn broke in: 'So he won't be able to light the beacon—' He thought for a moment, serious, alert. Cicely watching him, fascinated. Then orders were rapped out. 'Slight change of plan, Mr. Mipps—instead of riding with me, you will lead the Bonnington gang from Jesson Flats to the hills. Take Vulture and Eagle, while Raven and Cormorant lead the circling of the Marsh. I will see to the beacon myself. The signal is from Double Dyke tonight. I can pick it up from this window. Have Gehenna here under the bridge.' He turned to Cicely and asked her to forgive him for attending to business; then explained that when Gehenna was used from the house he came from a hidden stable beneath the bridge, and that he only had to be called to come out by himself so that the could drop into the saddle from where he was. He laughed and told her that the next riding lesson should be hers, upon Gehenna—and then added regretfully that soon they must get ready for the run and he would take her home.

It was while he held her cloak for her that there came a peremptory knocking at the front door. Mipps went to the grille and peeped through.

Closing it again, he whispered urgently: 'It's that Revenue Man. What did I tell you—prowlin' ù' Syn raised a warning finger and Mipps waited, while Cicely, eager to prove her right in belonging to this unholy trinity, was ready with his coat before he turned to fetch it. He slipped into it and quickly put his glasses on his nose—while she, sitting demurely onthe settle, patted the place beside her and whispered, 'Spinster of the Parish—parochial affairs.' The knock was repeated, louder than before, and Syn, smiling at Cicely, sat beside her and nodded to Mipps. The door was opened and Syn called out, 'Who is it, Mr. Mipps?' 'Don't rightly know, sir,' answered Mipps innocently, then in pretended surprise: 'Why, it's Mr. Hyde!' The Revenue Man, with grave face, stepped into the room and bowed awkwardly. Doctor Syn rose and with some slight surprise welcomed him, then turning to Cicely presented him as—the new Revenue Officer from Sandgate. She was outwardly so calm that both Mipps and Syn were mentally applauding new partner, but she herself knew suddenly a quiet, cold fear that grew with every word this man uttered.

Her newly acquired intuition told her that in this thick-set, slowbrained brute was danger, resembling, as he did, some giant hound who, having caught the faintest spoor of a king stag, would bear down relentlessly until he tired his quicker-moving prey. Her feeling of thankfulness that she was now at his side turned her love into fierce animal protection, though Doctor Syn seemed to need nobody's help. She listened to him parrying with fine 'rapier' speech the sabre weight of the Revenue Man's conviction. His explanation for her presence alone and at this hour—that she was kindly doing one of his duties tonight, visiting a sick woman to free him for an errand of mercy elsewhere—called for the first heavy stroke from these convictions.

'I have another errand for you tonight, Doctor Syn,' he said flatly.

'Then I fear unless it is more urgent than mine own, I cannot give you my promised help tonight,' replied the Vicar calmly. 'Please understand that I must put my duty first.' 'I am afraid mine comes before that, seeing that it is the King's business.' The Vicar looked quite shocked as he parried with a question: 'And is not mine? Surely, Mr. Hyde, your duty cannot have blinded you to the fact that King George the Third is also Defender of the Faith?' 'No, sir, I am well aware of that.' Hyde was immovable. 'But my duty has not blinded my eyes. On the contrary, it has opened them and I have formed some very grave suspicions. I must ask you to accompany me to the Court House.' 'Suspicions?' the Vicar queried. 'Can you not tell me of them here? Surely there is no reason to go to the Court House.'

'There is every reason.' Again the flat bluntness. 'I have not been idle since my last visit to you, Parson, and I told you that suspicion was my trade. I also told you that I might even suspect you, were you as good a rider as Sir Antony.' Cicely could hardly breathe—her heart seemed stifled with fear at this almost open accusation, but the man went on with other explanations.

How he had been here and there upon the Marsh, watching and listening, how he had watched the Vicarage from the sea-wall night after night, seen lights—strange activities, movements of casks. He pointed out that it was from the Vicarage that Major Faunce had been so badly used, then finished sarcasticaolly with: 'So for your own safety, Parson, should the Scarecrow pay you a visit—for I have wind that there's a run tonight—you'd better come with me! Oh, I will not put you in the cells, sir, but I have some Dragoons there who will see to your safety—.'

It seemed to Mipps that this girl had very quickly learned what had taken him so long to acquire, for he was just about to make an innocent remark when she forestalled him: 'But surely, dear Doctor Syn, your errand of mercy is very urgent. Is not the old man near his time? It would be a dreadful thing if his light were to flicker and you not near at hand.' She looked at him with such an excellent air of the troubled village spinster that Syn, being the man he was, could at that dangerous moment think of Sheridan appraising her performance against his own. While Hyde, being the man he was, could not appreciate the full significance of this parochial scene, and watched unmoved and luckily unsuspecting as the Vicar said, benignly:

'Do not worry, dear Cicely. I shall be there in time. Come, Mr. Hyde, I will accompany you. You are quite right, for the sake of the parish I should consult my safety, and 'tis true I preached a strong sermon last Sunday against this enemy of ours. But as to these activities—I have seen nothing unusual of late—have you, Mr. Mipps?' The game was being played again and Mipps as always was ready.

Having anticipated what might happen, he had under the pretext of tidying the room got out of sight and scribbled something on a flat piece of wood that he had in his pocket. He came forward with his usual confidential innocence.

'Well, Vicar,' he said, 'while you was talking to Miss Cicely's auntie—I didn't tell you this because I thought the ladies might be nervous, sir—then being so busy what with one thing and another I forgot to remember it.' 'Well, Mr. Mipps?' the Vicar helped.

'Oh yes. Well—I 'ardly like to remember it now—there was a horrible noise, so I goes out and sees a 'ooded figger flippin' round the corner of our bridge—so I flips after it on me tip 'ooves—ever so scared, and I sees 'im put something in one of them groins—dunno what it was—didn't touch it—dursn't—so I flipped back 'ere û' Doctor Syn was very grave and told the Sexton he had been most careless not to have spoken of this before as it might be something of importance to Mr. Hyde, a message perhaps—or a clue for the smugglers' activities tonight.

Mr. Mipps was most apologetic and to prove it continued: 'Well, if you like to come with me, Mr. Hyde—I can show you where it was exact—I shan't be nervous in the company of such an upstandin' gentleman as yourself ù' The Revenue Man was uncertain. He did not want to miss anything but, slightly flattered by the little man's confidence, agreed to go if it wasn't far.

'Far,' repeated Mr. Mipps, as if Hyde had asked a silly question, 'no—near—you can't go far on tip 'ooves, least I can't—perhaps you can.' This somewhat confused statement seemed to convince Mr. Hyde, and he allowed himself to be led across the bridge and over the sea-wall by the Sexton, who kept up a continual flow of facetious conversation, so as not to give the Revenue Man time to think and to let Doctor Syn know where they were.

When the voices had died away, Cicely, in one movement, was at his side. Strangely enough, it was the first time she had ever used his name and it seemed to be torn from her. 'Christopher, that man suspects you—. Oh, my darling, and 'tis all my fault. The ride—he said he had been here and there upon the Marsh—he must have seen us—perhaps as we jumped the broad dyke—and the curtains were wide when I was bandaging your arm. What can we do?'

He took her in his arms and reassured her, smoothing the worried frown from her brow with long sensitive fingers, then, holding her face in his two hands, his eyes too commanded her to have no fear. 'We have faced worse dangers than Mr. Hyde—Mipps and I,' he said, 'and now we have you to strengthen us—but listen, he will soon return and I must make pretence of complying with his wishes. I shall not be able to speak to Mipps again, so do you make a pretext of remaining here to collect the necessaries for your invalid, and tell him to give you in a bundle all the Scarecrow's clothes. When you return home, drop them from your bedroom window and somehow I shall manage to escape—and ride—for the last time, Cicely, I promise you.' She had strength now and shook her head. 'Oh, never!' she cried triumphantly. 'The Scarecrow will always ride while Aldington Knoll stands high. But do you have a care or it will be the last of me.'

He looked at her and marvelled that she could thus take the difficult way—it seemed that she had more courage than he—yet it was only for her sake that he wished to be quit of his double life—and claim the pardon. He smiled when he thought how hard put to it he would be betwixt her and Mipps.

The warning voice of Mipps approaching along the sea-wall drew them swiftly together. Then as the sound grew nearer he put her from him, and went to his desk, unlocking a drawer. He took from it a small ivory box which he put in his pocket, and was back at the fireplace when Hyde and Mipps returned. The Revenue Man was looking black and Mipps appeared to be puzzled. Doctor Syn looked up with a smile: 'Well, did you find anything, Mr. Hyde?' he asked.

Hyde glared. 'Nothing of any value to me, a hurriedly scrawled message, looks as if it hadn't been there long for the water's been up and this is dry as a bone.' He was holding in his hand a small flat piece of wood.

Mipps took it from him and read aloud with pretended bewilderment:

''Hyde's the danger on the seek or prowl—Vulture—Eagle—Curlew or Owl.' Don't run very well, do it,' he said, 'but I dunno, feels a bit damp.

Smells a bit fishy to me, too.' 'And so it does to me, Mr. Sexton,' growled Hyde, now certain that he had been fooled. 'Of good red herring. Come, Parson, if you're ready. Will you accompany us, Miss Cobtree?' 'Thank you, Mr. Hyde, but I must collect the comforts for the poor woman I am nursing tonight—' Cicely turned to Mipps and asked him if the basket was prepared for Mrs. Wooley. Doctor Syn thanked her for her good work and timely help in this emergency.

"Tis but what you would do yourself, dear Doctor Syn.' She was again the good worker of the village: 'I have only to follow in your footsteps. With such an example, what could I do but devote my life entirely to—the Parish?' Her eyes told him that indeed he was the parish, and his hands as he patted hers with friendly benignity told her again what she already knew.

Then turning to the sullen Revenue Man, Doctor Syn said he was ready to accompany him. As they were going out of the door he remarked that the moon had gone in and that it was a dark night, so that it was a good thing that the Court House was not far and that he knew the way.

These last words of the Vicar's seemed to give Mr. Mipps a deal of comfort. He shut the door and grinned: 'You hear that, miss? He knows the way. What's the orders, miss?' 'You're to give me the Scarecrow's clothes in a bundle which I am to drop from my bedroom window. Oh, how lucky 'tis the wing that faces the official rooms,' she cried. But even as she visualized him in that strong guardroom, doubts arose. If only her father had been here he would never have allowed this outrage. But there was nothing they could do, and all her fears returned. 'Oh, Mr. Mipps,' she cried, 'how can he possibly escape?' Mipps rose to the occasion. 'Now don't you worry, Miss Cicely,' he said—and then it was strange, but he used the very words Doctor Syn had done: 'We have faced worse dangers than this Mr. Hyde—the Cap'n and I. I don't say that at the moment it don't look tricky—but you take it from me that his brain's been working since that knock on the door.' He went upstairs to the old sea-chest and started to collect the necessary clothes, talking as he rolled them into a bundle. 'He's as quick as lightning in the riggin' is the Cap'n. Remind me to tell you what he done in the Tortugas ù' but on second thought decided that the story was not suitable. 'Well, perhaps I didn't ought,' he said. 'But I can tell you the one about the slave-trader off the Chinee coast. Saved my life he did—and that weren't the only occasion.

He's done it more times than a cat's fairy godmother. He's as nippy with a marline spike as you are with your knitting-pins, Miss Cicely. So if he can't think of something to diddle that there nosy Hyde and Seek I'll knock myself up solid.' He was quite confident himself for indeed he had never known his master to fail, but he had this advantage over Cicely: years of co-operation with Clegg, while this was her first experience of the Scarecrow in danger—though Mipps himself had to admit that there was some justification for her fears; in truth she picked on the one thing which did worry him—the time.

'How can he do it in time, Mr. Mipps?' she cried. 'The Court House may be full of men. 'Tis only a step but he must come here to see the flash and get his horse—he cannot do it in the time.' Mipps would have liked to have treated her as he had done, when being quite young she had come to him with childish troubles, but now to allay the doubt that he had caught from her he had perforce to be stern.

'Now look here, miss,' he said, giving her shoulder a gentle shake. 'If you're going to be Mrs. Cap'n, you'll 'ave to learn that orders is orders. I done it these twenty years and never known him wrong. He may be ready now—bundle—window ù' He gave her the basket and told her to hurry. She thanked him and said she would, asking forgiveness for having been so foolish—and once again old Mipps was completely disarmed—he reproached himself for his sharpness and proceeded to make up for it:

'There—I know just how you feel, miss,' he comforted. 'Ease your mind and listen for the signals. Remember, three cries of the curlew—three times, that means accordin' to plan—and let's hope you don't 'ear no 'ootin' of the owl.'

He opened the door and she went out, but half-way across the bridge she turned, came swiftly back and kissed him. Then she was gone, running like a young deer across the Glebe.

The Court House was dark. She thanked Heaven that Lady Caroline and Maria were abed. She crept to her own room, and extinguishing the candles flung the curtains wide.

In the opposite wing one window was lighted up and she could see into the room. She watched, fascinated and horrified, for there at a table with three Dragoons, his face toward her, looking shadowy in the thick tobacco smoke, was Doctor Syn. While yet another shadow passed across the window—darker and more ominous, and she heard the measured tread of a sentry in the yard below.

Chapter 22. The Shadow of the Scarecrow

Mr. Mipps was poring over Doctor Syn's map of Romney Marsh, marking the distances from Jesson Flats to the hills, when a curious feeling in his jigger-staff told him that he was not alone. In a flash he realized when he had done, or rather what he had not done; for being at once both moved and worried about Miss Cicely, he had forgotten to lock the front door. Someone was behind him and he knew who that someone was. He stiffened, but gave no sign. Instead he leisurely rolled up the map and started to hum his favourite song. Determined that no prying eyes should look at the map he locked it in the cupboard beneath the lectern, and then started off round the room, tidying it casually. He passed the waiting figure twice, then suddenly pretended to notice it for the first time, and he jumped in feigned surprise.

'Goodness gracious me, it's our Mr. Hyde. Shrouds, plumes and crape—you did give me a fright, sir. What 'ave you come back for? Dropped something? You shouldn't have come back to see if I was all right. I'm used to being alone.' The Revenue Man looked at him with narrowed eyes. 'Are you, Mr. Sexton?' he sneered. 'I wanted to make quite sure of that.' 'There now,' Mipps was almost indignant. 'And I thought you was making sure that the Vicar was comfortable. You know, sir, you shouldn't have taken him off like that without his slippers and his nightcap. Poor old gentleman. He'll catch the ague dead-sure as coffin-nails. Now you stay here and I'll slip 'em round to him.' 'You'll stay where you are,' the Revenue Man growled, 'and there's no cause for anxiety about the Vicar. That 'poor old gentleman' is being well cared for by three Dragoons and at the moment is enjoying himself hugely at a game of dice.' ''Ow,' said Mr. Mipps. Then he started violently and looked at Hyde. 'I beg your pardon, sir, did you say—dice?' 'Yes, Mr. Sexton—dice.' 'Oh—dice.' Mipps answered as though he had not heard it the first time. 'Dice.' He then repeated, 'Yes, Mr. Sexton—Dice,' so many times under his breath that it turned into a sing-song chant, as he went casually to the desk. The drawer was open and empty and the words changed as he sang in delighted whispers:

'The Vicar's taken his dice-box:
The Vicar's taken his dice-box:
Yes, Mr. Sexton, Dice.'

This annoyed the Revenue Man and he asked him what the devil he was saying.

'Nothin',' said Mipps. 'Only singin' what you said.' He then told Mr. Hyde that if he had come to stay the night he'd get out one of the Vicar's nightshirts.

'You'll do nothing of the sort,' snarled Hyde. 'Stay the night, I may, in this room. I just want to make sure there'll be no run tonight.' Mipps thought that he'd have some difficulty in preventing it, since the Vicar had taken his dice-box, which had never failed them yet.

His mind went back to the Chinese coast, where they had acquired this ingenious contraption. Carved out of ivory, the shaker had a false base and ordinary dice could be used, until such a time as its owner wished to get himself out of a tight corner. Then by pushing a spring hidden in the carving and shaking it downwards violently, small glass drops fell out and exploded on the table. Though no particle of glass was left to tell the tale they emitted such an odious nauseating stench, that all who smelt it were overcome with violent retching, and became incapable of offering any resistance. The effects wore off within the hour, by which time the joker, who was careful to protect himself with the antidote, would escape to play the jest elsewhere. For, after all, when indulging in a game of dice a generous amount of strong liquor is usually consumed, so the excuse could always be 'over-indulgence.' Mipps was jubilant—the only thing now was for him to elude Mr. Hyde and warn the Vicar of his presence. So, in order to put this plan into action, he said he was going to get on with his work.

'Your work can wait,' snapped the Revenue Man.

'Oh no, it can't,' contradicted Mipps, 'not Mrs. Wooley—any time now. Makin' her a beautiful coffin—best pine—brass plate and all the trimmings—you wouldn't be wanting one, would you, sir?' Here Mipps produced a foot rule and his notebook and started fussing round him, and then as though taking a great interest in Mr. Hyde's prospective funeral asked:

'What wood would you think' (he was going to say 'best') 'ù oak?' The infuriated Revenue Man told him to leave him alone and to go and get on with his work if it was within doors.

Mipps replied that it was within the next door and that he'd bring her in and do her in here if he was lonely, and Hyde, who in spite of his own trade was not fond of coffins, told him abruptly that he did not want for company, and to get out, but remain within earshot.

'Earshot,' though Mipps. 'Ear foxication,' and he set to work in the next room to put this plan into action. By an elaborate system of knots, weights, and the clock's pendulum, he rigged up a swinging hammer that was guaranteed to knock the side of the coffin until he came back to stop it. This done he was out of the back door into the enveloping darkness, all within some quarter of an hour.

Mr. Hyde prowled round the house investigating. He then returned to the hall and looked round for a place to conceal himself, and having marked one, called for Mipps to bring him some drink. The hammering continued rhythmically, so he shouted louder—still no reply, but monotonous knocking, and he strode in bad temper whence it came. Seeing Mipps's foxication working gaily infuriated him and he smashed it quiet—returning to the hall where he saw a bottle of brandy on a table by the fire. He took a generous pull, extinguished the lights save one, then slipped behind the heavy curtains into the bow of the window, where he had a good view of both inside and out.

He had not long to wait for he heard a door open and stealthy footsteps coming towards his hiding-place. His pistol at full cock, he was tense, ready.

Suddenly the curtains were pulled aside, and what he saw made him utter an oath of satisfaction.

'I have you covered,' he said quickly. 'The Scarecrow, by all that's fortunate!' The answer came back from behind that hideous mask. 'The Revenue, by all that's damnable.' Mr. Hyde was in luck. 'So this is your headquarters,' he sneered. 'My patience has been rewarded, Mr. Scarecrow. Only the Revenue Officer from Sandgate, he won't give us much trouble, you thought. Just another dullwitted Preventive man to be hoodwinked. But now we'll see who looks the fool. A local trial at Dymchurch you'll be thinking—the jury packed with sympathizers you have bribed. Judges frightened or in favour—headed by that muddlehead the Squire, if Squire he be or muddlehead.' He laughed unpleasantly. 'Nothing so comfortable, Mr. Scarecrow, sir. I'm not taking any chances. A thousand guineas is a thousand guineas either way, alive or dead, so I'm going to shoot you out of hand.' He forced the Scarecrow away from the window at the point of his gun and the black figure backed to the far corner of the refectory table.

'Quite understandable, Mr. Hyde,' the weird form croaked, 'but you are wrong. This is much more comfortable than a crowded Court House. What more could one wish for in one's last few moments—a pleasant fire, a bottle of wine, a good friend—so you will be living up to Holy Writ. Do unto others as ye would they should do unto you.' 'Holy Writ, the parson—I suspected as much when I saw you riding better than the Squire.' The Revenue Man was intoxicated with his cleverness, but one thing puzzled him. 'How did you escape from your game of dice?' The Scarecrow chuckled. 'Well, no matter—you'll not escape me.

Sit down, Doctor Scarecrow. This is indeed a pleasant surprise. Take off your mask, Doctor Syn.' The Scarecrow raised a long slim arm and swept off the mask with an elegant gesture—and the Revenue Man stared open-mouthed in dumb surprise.

Before him, dressed in those fantastic rags, high-booted, black-gloved—her lovely, laughing face with auburn hair tumbling about it, was Cicely Cobtree. She bowed mockingly: 'At your service, Mr. Hyde,' she said.

He exploded. 'Great God, is this a jest?' She laughed at his vehemence. 'A very good one, Mr. Hyde, since it never entered your dull wits that the Scarecrow might be a woman.' 'No, it hadn't,' he thought, 'so that was it; well, she'll get no change from me.' "The Parish Spinster', eh?' he sneered. 'Devoting your life entirely to good works. God! what fools we've been.' 'The cap and bells, Mr. Hyde?' she suggested calmly.

He was now all white, cold anger at her studied flippancy.

'You'll jest with me no longer, Mistress Scarecrow—and do not think that being a woman will soften Nicholas Hyde. Do unto others, eh? I'll tell you what I'm going to do with you. I'll save you hanging with a bullet—then put back your mask and say 'shot on sight' as any loyal citizen may do. Two minutes for a prayer, that's all you'll get from me. Unless you have a last request ù' Through the window behind him she saw the tiny flashing light from distant Double Dyke.

Involuntarily she shivered, not from fear of death but of failing him.

She was numb now, trying to think what Syn would do in such a situation, but to excuse her shudder, not wishing him to think she was afraid—she told him she was cold and would like a drink.

His reply was typical. 'Beggin' for courage, eh? I thought you'd change your tune—you'll have no help from me; get to your prayer.' His whole manner gloated at her powerless femininity.

Over the Marsh, coming nearer and nearer until they seemed to be in the very room, came the long-drawn mournful warnings of the owl, as from Double Dyke the flashing became more urgent.

But now she had no need of drink nor prayer, for her own unspoken prayer had been answered, and she knew as clearly as if Syn had told her exactly what she had to do. Nonchalantly tilting back her chair, she threw up her head in superb defiance. 'I never begged from man—and I will not beg of God ù' Outraged at her cool insolence, when he had expected womanly pleading, he shouted almost in desperation: 'Woman—go decently; sit up.' 'I stand.' Her voice rang out as her chair shot forward, and the tablecloth gripped between her feet slid along the polished table-top, bringing his pistol and the bottle with it to her hand. In an instant she was on her feet, covering him with his own weapon, while in the other she grasped the bottle and gave him a toast: 'The Scarecrow's health.' Then throwing him the bottle she laughed: 'Do unto others, eh, Mr. Hyde? Here's courage, sir, until next time ù' Backing towards the door, eyes fierce in spite of her smile, she mocked.

'That Parish Spinster rides to Aldington to light the Beacon for the run.' Then out on to the bridge she dashed, calling wildly, 'Gehenna! Gehenna!' and flinging herself over the parapet almost before she heard the horse's hooves, she found herself in the saddle, and spurred him up the rise on to the sea-wall road.

The Revenue Man remembered his other pistol in its holster round his waist and cursed his fingers for their fumbling. He wrenched it free and flinging to the window, broke a pane, and thrusting the muzzle through, he levelled it at the flying figure on the great black beast, silhouetted now against the rising moon. He fired: and fired again. His only answer was a mocking curlew cry; but as he watched his speeding target he saw just one spasmodic jerk which broke the rhythm of its flowing strides. Then, as though the Marsh had watched aghast this calculated deed, it took the heroic object out of sight in close embrace, to leave no trace but thudding fleeting sound. Silence. Then a strange, unearthly cry.

Chapter 23. The Shadow of Doctor Syn

The dice-box rattled. Doctor Syn lost again. The Dragoons, hilarious with drink and the sight of so many guineas piled before them, urged him to throw again. The guard-room was filled with smoke. Another all-but-empty brandy-bottle stood on the table while from outside came the monotonous tread of the sentry, and from time to time his faint shadow passed the barred unshuttered window. The evening had been a pleasant one for the soldiers in their new billet, though when told but an hour ago that they were to guard a parson, they had cursed, thinking his presence would put a damper on proceedings; but here he was, a jovial companion who gave them drinks and had a dice-box of his own, and, though he did not seem to know very much about the game, paid up cheerfully in good spade guineas.

'Come, Parson,' cried the young officer, who was the worst of all in drink. 'Your luck is bound to change. Try one more throw. Fill the glasses again, and we'll drink to your success.' 'That's very civil of you, sir,' said Doctor Syn. ''Tis good drink and warming. But I am distressed about that poor young man outside. He must be very cold. Could he not be permitted to come in and have a drink?' The young officer, eager to seem important, by asserting his authority, gave permission, and the delighted sentry was hailed in. Glasses were filled, and the parson's health was drunk. Then, as all were quite ready to relieve their prisoner of his remaining guineas, they pressed for the resuming of the game and the Vicar's throw.

Doctor Syn agreed readily. 'Faith, gentlemen, 'tis a good thing I found occasion to bring my dice with me. They have been the means of escaping many dull hours in the past, and I would be willing to lose twice this amount to such gay companions as yourselves to escape the tedium of confinement.

But this is positively my last throw so I trust the dice will not fail. Dear me, 'tis hot in here, perhaps 'tis the excitement of the game.' He took from his pocket a large silken handkerchief, and apologetically mopped his brow, holding in his other hand the ivory shaker. Then, seeming to be full of almost childish concern as to the results of his throw, he rose, and, with a charming smile, held the box high while turning away his face, hiding it in his handkerchief, making pretence that he dare not look. He shook. And shook again. The dice rattled. One long sensitive finger felt for the eye of the carved dragon. He threw. His wrist flicked round as his arm came down. The dice shot out and flashed unusually as they bounced from the force of the throw.

Whether it was the effects of the wine or no the soldiers were never sure, but they could have sworn that at that very moment they saw a faint powdery mist arise from the table.

Suddenly they were overcome by a ghastly nausea. The room went dark before their eyes and a poisonous stench assailed their nostrils and gripped their throats. They retched violently. Their eyes ran. And through the haze of their vomiting they dimly heard the Parson say: 'Dear me. Dear me. Too bad.

Whatever is the matter? I must run and fetch Doctor Petter.' Then they knew no more.

Cicely's window was dark and he felt beneath it for the bundle. It was not there. Something had gone wrong. He knew that neither Cicely nor Mipps would fail him—yet something had gone wrong. Only one thing to do:

return to the Vicarage. A cold fear clutched at his heart as he raced across the Glebe. He saw the flashes from Double Dyke as he ran, and heard the owl's reiterated warning. 'Where is the Scarecrow?' Then out of the blackness of his shadowed house, into the rim of moonlight on the wall, leapt a great beast—Gehenna. His heart leapt with it.

Gehenna—with a rider on his back—a slim, lithe figure clean cut against the sky.

Along that lofty ridge it sped like a black arrow, and apprehension thundered in his brain, in beat with the flying hooves.

Then with a noise of smashing glass a spurt of flame darted from his window. He heard the hiss of a bullet as it passed and the percussive thud of the report. And as he watched in agonized confusion another flame. It was the second shot. He saw his black horse quiver—then plunge on, the rider with it. Which had been hit? As if in answer to this unutterable possibility his whole spirit seemed to be torn from him in one wild cry:

The Revenue Man, his pistol still smoking in his hand, stood staring across the chequered patches in the moonlight as if he hoped to see that moving figure once again. Deep in his dull soul he knew his action had outstripped his reason, and that he was damned. The whole night turned accusingly against him and each inanimate thing cried 'Murder'. No movement could he see to give him hope, only the Marsh menacing back.

Then, as if hypnotized he turned—and saw in the firelit room, a vast shadow filling it and striking terror to his very bones. It was as if the Marsh had gathered itself into one great spirit of revenge; and down the shaft of moonlight through the door came the living cause of his deadly fear. He backed and backed, in mesmerized, jerked movements, while slowly—towering towards him stalked Doctor Syn.

Then suddenly a red glow suffused the midnight sky, and the whole room came to life with flailing limbs and lightning stabs of pain. He knew no more. A few deft strokes and Syn was gone, out into the night, rushing blindly towards that blood-red signal on the Knoll.

Cicely had felt Gehenna shiver under her but calmed him with her hand. She wanted to speak to him, to tell him not to fail them now, but no sound came, and she was only conscious of a numbing ache and a great longing to lie down and sleep. So she crouched in the saddle and her arms slipped about his neck. The reins were gone. But the animal charged on—giving her courage as if he knew his master's life was on his back. Lifting his mighty head, his lips curled from his teeth in a defiant scream which told her of his intended spurt. It came like a thunderbolt, which hurled the ground behind them, as over the shining pathway of the broad dyke they met the rising ground. Then on, and up, and round the way he knew, right to the skies, the great horse carried her, stopping with hooves dug in and foaming head upon the very pinnacle of Aldington. She slid from the saddle, and the soft thick turf filled her once more with the desire to rest—but Gehenna pawed the ground and whinnied, and she dragged herself towards the beacon pile. With numb fingers she felt for the flasher in the Scarecrow's pocket, and gathered all her strength for this one last effort. The straw caught, and crackled towards the tarred heart of the beacon, as the flames bit through and up as though to lick the stars. She stood swaying, warm now, and the great horse came behind and nosed her from the flying sparks. She could not mount again to ride away, but she knelt, and then lay down, and with Gehenna as her sentinel she slept, while he called out his trumpetings for help.

Heading the cavalcade towards the hills Mipps heard Gehenna's call, and his far-seeing eyes, trained in the watery places of the world, saw the black shadow against the blazing fire, the saddle empty. The Scarecrow's rule to all who fired the beacon was 'Light and ride clear'. Tonight the Scarecrow was to light it himself. What then had happened? Had the dice-box failed? If so, who rode Gehenna? Mipps had not been able to find his master and warn him of the Revenue Man's presence in the Vicarage, and had been forced to carry out his orders as arranged, with this unaccomplished self-appointed task knocking at his mind. So full of apprehension, Mipps spurred towards the beacon with Vulture and Eagle in his wake.

Every window facing the hills on Romney Marsh reflected the significant blaze. The run was on. The luggers could creep in to land their cargo. Behind a number of these same windows lurked excitement and activity. But behind one window on the wall all was still. The room was in darkness save for the warm light of the distant beacon, which embracing the chill, pale quality of the moon, gave to it an unearthly atmosphere. This mingled light shone on the figure of a man who was bound to the banisters of the staircase. His body was limp, his head sagged forward, he might have been alive or dead.

The room was deathly quiet. At last there came the sound of horses' hooves—then footsteps crunched the shingle—then whispered conversation as cloaked figures appeared in the open doorway. Between them they carried the limp shadow of the Scarecrow and placed her gently on the settee, the cruel mask still hiding her face. Mipps spoke to the Nightriders beneath his breath.

"'Ere's a damnable night's work,' he said urgently. 'A foul bullet through the back and no one we can trust to tend it. I hoped to find the Vicar here—you must ride and scour the

Marsh and tell him wwe have desperate need of him. Ride like the lightnin', and pray God you bring him 'ere in time.'

The Nightriders vanished; they understood—their leader, or so they thought, was in danger—and they rode as for their lives. Mipps was desperate. Where was his master? He knew what this would do to him, yet now he did not know what to do himself. He stood over the settle, and now they were alone, carefully, with his trembling hands, removed the incriminating mask so that she could breathe more easily. Even as he did so she spoke in hasty whisper. 'Mr. Mipps—the Court House—why did you not send them there?' But Mipps had already seen the figure of the Revenue Man lashed to the banisters with skilful knots.

'Because I knows his work when I sees it,' he said. 'And I knows there ain't four walls can hold him when he's a mind to get out and because I knows that ù' 'Orders is orders, Mr. Mipps?' she completed.

He nodded once, then sadly shook his head.

'Oh, do not blame me for disobeying him,' she pleaded. "Twas the time—I thought he could not do it in the time—and such a simple thing for me to do.' Mipps told her there was no blame to her: she'd done a good night's work and done it brave and Bristol fashion. She thanked him and a smile played round the corners of her mouth. 'There is a penalty, is there not, for disobeying orders?' she asked, then as a twinge of pain twisted the smile from her face she whispered: 'And I must pay it ù' A voice from the shadows answered her. 'Would that I could pay it for you ù' Mipps turned on the Revenue Man, who was stirring in his bonds, and lashed out like a fighting terrier.

'Aye, so you should, you dog.' This was the Mipps well known to Clegg; lucky for Mr. Hyde he did not act without his master's orders. 'So you should, you dog,' he repeated, 'as a reward for foul play.' 'No, Mr. Mipps—not foul play.' Cicely lifted herself and spoke in a firmer voice. 'He shot on sight, as any loyal citizen may do.' She turned to the Revenue Man, and though shocked to see him in his present plight, her mind could not take in what had happened. 'I wish to thank you, Mr. Hyde,' she said gently. 'The Court House would have been so crowded. I am happy here.

A pleasant fire; some wine.' She turned to Mr. Mipps and asked him to fetch some wine and a glass for Mr. Hyde. Then seeing that so tightly bound, he could not drink, she ordered his immediate release. Mipps demurred, until she laughed: 'Scarecrow's orders, Mr. Mipps.' He did as he was bid, realizing now that she must have her way in everything, and when she asked him to tidy the room lest the Vicar should be grieved to find it in such disorder, he obeyed, and found to his amazement that Hyde was helping him.

She watched them lift the heavy cloth and place it on the highly polished table; then as she saw the Revenue Man looking at her with an expression of desperate guilt on his face, she shook her head and said gently:

'That is our secret, is it not?' The Revenue Man did not know, himself. Never in his life had he felt like this before. He answered her with a newly found sincerity: 'Whatever secrets I have learned tonight shall go no further. Your teaching shames me, Mistress Parson.' She hardly heard him, for her wandering mind was out—searching the secret places of the Marsh, and a greater fear was upon her. 'Oh, Mr.

Mipps,' she cried. 'Why does he not come? 'Tis such a little time. I would that I had known him all your twenty years. Suppose he does not come.' She was trembling now, with the desperate urgency to be near him. If that could not be, then she must somehow be enveloped by him; hear his name spoken; and so she begged Mr. Mipps to tell her some story of him, saying there must be one she had not heard. Mipps was silent: not because he did not remember one—for indeed the tablecloth had brought back to his mind a scene in Santiago, where Clegg had once again escaped to save his life. But he hesitated lest it should incriminate his master. Then as she urged him to be quick, he saw Hyde's face and knew that they were safe from him. He held the glass of brandy to her lips, telling her that if she would but drink, he would begin. She obeyed him eagerly.

'Well—I remember once—there was a time—' Mipps spoke slowly and with great effort: '—he done a very nippy dodge: that was the time he saved—' He could not go on, thinking of how he, himself, would now give anything to save her and his master from this calamity. Instead, he gulped, and the tears ran down his poor old nose. 'Oh, Miss Cicely, Mrs. Cap'n—Miss ù' She looked at him and loved him, finding excuses to save his embarrassment. She hoped he had not caught Marsh ague, he was shaking so.

She feared it was a cold, for indeed his eyes were running. His weakness gave her strength, and she fumbled for her kerchief, a tiny square which she handed to him, saying: 'Come, give me the glass and do you take my handkerchief.' She shivered: 'Is it not cold? Mr. Hyde, come nearer to the fire and let us drink a toast.' The Revenue Man hardly knew what he did or said, but he moved towards her and she heard him give a toast—a strange one, from his lips.

'The Scarecrow.' And then she saw behind him in the doorway what she had prayed to see just this once more, and her lips moved: 'Christopher.'

As in a trance the wild-looking shell of Doctor Syn, dishevelled from his frantic searchings on the Marsh, moved like a shadow and was on his knees beside her. She took his trembling hands and with what little strength she had, tried to bring him back. 'L'pouvantail, at your service.' It was a very gay whisper. She put her head on one side and smiled at him—a tiny, frowning smile. 'Forgive such a clumsy rendering of the part. Perhaps, after all, I am—but just a petticoat. And I was wrong. The Scarecrow is a ghost.

For he must always rise while Aldington stands high.' As though to prove her words, the beacon flames leapt higher and the whole room lightened up and seemed ablaze. 'You see,' she said. 'The Beacon is alight. I heard the curlew cry three times. I should have heeded Mr. Mipps, but thought you could not do it in the time. What could I do as Spinster but devote my life— All the King's horses and Revenue Men—'

He was looking at her in dumb agony, and she, caressing and stroking his arm, looked down and was the memory of a dream. She slipped her had beneath his sleeve till her fingers rested on the branded mark. 'Why, Doctor Syn,' she whispered, 'your sleeve. The button is still loose. It will only take a moment if you have a spool of black. I have forgotten my chatelaine.' She raised herself and, leaning forward, kissed him lightly on his bowed head, so close that only he could hear her sighing words: 'Dear, kind old Doctor Syn, I am so happy. My first good deed shall be—' And she was gone.

And with her went the Beacon light, for at that moment it had flared up higher than before, to flicker swiftly out. The silent room was now quite dark, save for the arrow stabs of moonlight that shot in from the window, and the shining pathway through the door.

The husky voice of Mr. Hyde broke the silence. 'I, too, was wrong. The Scarecrow is a ghost.' He moved humbly and stood behind the stricken man. He also wanted help, and strange, this parson was the man to give it. He longed to take the Vicar's hand. Instead, he turned and, passing Mipps, said quietly: 'You know where you can find me. I shall be ready if he wants me.' And then he crossed the bridge and went his way along the Dymchurch Wall.

Mipps made no attempt to hinder him. He knew the danger there had passed, and here at hand another must be reckoned with—his master's reason. There might be one way to save him. If he could make him see that here was no lost love: rather, a gallant ending to a member of the Brotherhood.

With his hand on his master's shoulder he looked down and said:

'I pays my respects to Captain Clegg's Lieutenant. God Bless her gallant spiriti. Come, Cap'n, we must carry her home.' But she was home already.

Chapter 24. The Shadow of Clegg

Mr. Mipps was frightened. In fact, he was desperate. He had thought that his master might lose his reason and run wild. That he could have understood and dealt with as he had in the old days with the raving Clegg, which terrifying though it had been, was not in any way comparable with this new phase; for here was a Doctor Syn whom Mipps had never met before. Since the night he had carried Cicely to the Court House, he had not uttered one word. For three days he had not been seen to eat or drink, and he certainly had not slept, for Mipps had watched him pacing the library at night and striding the Marsh by day. Mipps had shadowed him, hardly letting him out of his sight lest he should end his misery by some violence.

Here was no brandy-drinking demon, but rather a cold, calculating fiend; as though the man were fighting with his soul over some vital problem. Out of all this a conviction came to Mipps that he had reached the climax; for had he not put his affairs in order as if he were going away on some long journey? Mipps instinctively knew that this journey was not to foreign parts and the life they used to know.

The Sexton was not alone in his anxiety. The whole village shared it.

They had been told that Miss Cicely had met with a riding accident. But there were certain things that mystified them. The sudden departure of Mr. Hyde, who for no apparent reason had stopped prowling, Doctor Syn's neglect of parish work (he was not even at the funeral), his wild appearance, and his eternal vigil on the Marsh, never astride the fat white pony; the Squire's absence in London; and above all the fact that the Scarecrow had issued no orders, so that the vast organization which meant to so many a living was at a standstill.

There was, however, one person who did understand, and who in all her wisdom was biding her time. Miss Gordon, though profoundly shocked, feeling that she was in a way responsible for that night of tragedy, determined to keep her promise of maintaining friendship. It was in this frame of mind and upon the fourth day at noon that she encountered Mr. Mipps, a sad little figure upon the sea-wall, looking through his telescope. She noticed, however, that it was not trained upon the shipping in the Fairway, but having his back to the sea he was sweeping the hillside across the Marsh. He was looking through it intently and did not notice her approach. She asked him if he had it focussed upon the old Roman harbour steps at Lympne. He turned sharply and looked at her in some surprise, for indeed he had had it fixed upon that very spot. She begged him to adjust it to her eye.

There in that circle of the telescope, framed like a miniature, was what she had been expecting. She turned to the worried little Sexton and together they evolved a plan. Returning to the Vicarage, she swept Mrs. Honeyballs out of the way, and prepared with her own hands a tasty meal. Mipps saddled the white pony with panniers into which the food and wine were packed, and within a quarter of an hour a quaint little party set off. Miss Agatha rode the Vicar's pony, followed by Mr. Mipps on Lightning, his very aged donkey, while Mister Pitt, the poodle, frisked and trotted on ahead. Inside Miss Agatha's vast reticule swinging upon her arm was a beautiful, bound, clasped book, whose small golden key reposed in the old lady's purse.

'And so, Mr. Mipps,' she had said, 'if he can eat the meal, drink the wine and read this book, he's cured.'

* * * * *

Two hours later Mr. Mipps was again looking through his telescope upon the sea-wall. This time he was watching for a signal. At last it came; bright flashes that caught the glass and made him blink. But Mipps did not care. On the contrary—he threw his three-cornered hat into the air and executed there and then his famous hornpipe.

* * * * *

Miss Agatha was sitting in the sunshine, her plaid spread out upon the Roman pavement. She held in her hand a very small mirror and with the help of this was arranging a naughty wind-blown curl, though for quite a long time after it was arranged satisfactorily she continued to flash her mirror in the sun, making it dance here, there, and everywhere. Indeed, once she inadvertently caught the Vicar full in the face. He looked up from his book and smiled, but returned to it again while she repacked the baskets. There was very little left.

Some life had returned to Doctor Syn's face. The full French wine too had done him good, but the book upon his knees, as Aunt Agatha had predicted, was his real salvation.

He turned the pages and his face reflected what he read. At times gay—then sad—amused and tender. And, indeed, there were times when the tears fell unashamedly on to those carefully written pages.

He went back to the beginning of this endearing volume and re-read the title. Round childish handwriting.

'Cicely Cobtree—her Book. Given to me by my Great Aunt Agatha upon my fifteenth birthday, November 25, 1775. I shall keep it for my journal.

Very special thoughts and happenings.' Strange that today was another 25th of November, her birthday and that the first 'happening' should be of him. He read: 'My dear Papa's best friend, Christopher Syn, has returned from the Americas. I wish he had come home before. He tells exciting stories.' Then further on: 'Doctor Syn is now our Vicar here. I like Church now. Though I had always imagined for myself a tall fair gentleman. I know now I was wrong. I like his eyes best. Oh yes—and his voice. I am sure Charlotte is in love with him. I wish I was her age, and had fair hair.' Another page: 'A lovely day. I talked to Mr. Mipps. He's back from Sea, and he's going to be Sexton.' Over again: 'Sister Maria the Silly had a nightmare about the Scarecrow. He is supposed to be a Ghost in these parts, though Papa says not to be frightened; he is only a smuggler. I think he sounds exciting—but I still like Doctor Syn best.' More leaves turned and now the Vicar's face was grave. 'Dear Sister Charlotte was buried today.

They say it was a hunting accident, but I know different. I have not told anyone but I think it had something to do with Doctor Syn and the Scarecrow—I dreamt that she died for the Scarecrow. I wish I could have done it—but I would rather die for Doctor Syn.' Then further down that same page: 'I watched him today through Mr.

Mipps's spy-glass. He looked so lonely on the Roman Steps. I know that I could comfort him. I wish I could sit there for ever by his side.' Here the tears blurred his vision, and he turned and seemed indeed to see her by his side in the sunshine with that fiery halo round her laughing face. But she vanished and once more he sought her in the book. 'Today Mr. Mipps told me another wonderful story about the pirate Captain Clegg. How he escaped and saved Mr. Mipps by doing a trick with a tablecloth. I practised it and broke Mama's best SFvres cup. She was very cross. But I don't mind. It does work. I wish I could make up my mind which I love best—The Scarecrow, Captain Clegg or Doctor Syn. I still think Doctor Syn.' Aunt Agatha watched him as he turned to the last entry. Now the writing was fine and mature. Then he looked up towards the Knoll with an expression of peace and yet determination, and Aunt Agatha knew what was in his mind, for she too had read those last words.

'The Scarecrow will always ride while Aldington Knoll stands high,' and below: 'My riddle has been answered. I love all three.' Aunt Agatha leant over and with a firm little hand closed the book.

'She was right—you cannot quit. No more talk of confessions. If you must turn over a new leaf then let this be your guide. She too took the adventurous way. We're all of us pirates,' she said, and her eyes were very bright and very wise, 'bearing down upon each other in full sail. Flashing broadsides.

Glorious encounter. Then we part for distant seas.' He looked at her. His eyebrow quivered. Then he rose to his full height and sweeping her an elaborate bow said: 'Welcome, Pirate. You, Agatha Gordon of Beldorney and Kildrummy, are worthy of the Brotherhood.' Miss Gordon smiled up at him, well pleased. She knew that she had won this 'glorious encounter'.

* * * * *

That night the library at the Vicarage once more resembled Clegg's cabin in the good ship Imogene. Plans were being made. The room was heavy with tobacco smoke. The brandy was good. Four pairs of feet were on the table and the chairs were tilted back. Four pairs. Top boots—Gentleman James; buckled shoes—Doctor Syn; sea boots—Didymus Mipps; and a very

small pair of elegant French slippers—Agatha Gordon. Glasses were raised and Clegg's pirate song roared out from four throats:
'Here's to the feet what have walked the plank.
Yo-ho for the dead man's throttle—.'

Lightning Source UK Ltd.
Milton Keynes UK
UKOW04f1546180917
309416UK00002B/474/P